MAXWELL'S *Fall*

TIELLE ST. CLARE

An Ellora's Cave Publication

www.ellorascave.com

Maxwell's Fall

ISBN 9781419936841

Edited by Briana St. James.
Photography and cover art by Les Byerley.

Electronic book publication August 2009
Trade paperback publication 2011

MAXWELL'S FALL

ฆ๑

Prologue

ꕤ

"Ballroom full of people—designers, models, me and a few other photographers and of course, the press." Max cradled the phone to his shoulder as he stretched out on his bed. "I'd been dodging her all night. Did *not* want to deal with her. She finally catches me." Jackson—Jax to his family—grunted so Max knew he still had his attention. "You know me. I don't want to cause a scene."

He ignored the choking sound on the other end of the line and continued on with his tale. Timing was everything. "I'm trying to be polite, trying to get her to move on but damn, whatever I said, it was the wrong thing. She just snapped."

"What happened?"

"She grabs the front of her *very* expensive designer dress and yanks. Rips the thing in half. Glitter's flying everywhere. She pulls back the edges and screams 'Are my tits too small? Is that why you won't fuck me?'"

"You're kidding."

"No lie." Max answered his twin's groan, pleased to recognize the laughter in his brother's voice. Something was going on with Jax and Max didn't know what to do. Even separated by more than a thousand miles, Max was determined to take care of his brother. So he did what he always did—told stories, made Jax laugh, until he could weasel out what was wrong with his twin.

"What did you do?"

"I looked at her tits. What else was I going to do?"

"And..." Jax prompted. Max hesitated because well, truly, it hadn't been his finest moment.

"She's right. They're a bit on the small side."

"Tell me you didn't say that."

"No." Max rolled his eyes. His brother should know he had better sense than that. "I said, 'Lady, it's not your tits that are too small, it's your IQ.'"

"Max, you didn't."

He winced at the memory. "Yeah, it just kind of slipped out. But she only got in one good punch before I escaped."

"She *hit* you?"

Max could practically see his brother jolting up in his seat, ready to jump to his defense. As twins they were protective of each other. Doubly so because of the wolf's innate tendency to protect its pack mates.

"Don't worry. She hits like a girl."

Jax laughed and the sound comforted Max. Whatever was bothering Jackson wasn't so intense that he'd lost his sense of humor. That was the first thing to go when Jackson was stressed.

"Don't let our sisters hear you say that."

"God no." Max hadn't lost all sense of self-preservation. Bridget and Kiki would take him down if they heard him.

"So uh what happened to her, standing there, you know, topless?"

"Ah, it's Vegas, baby. Topless women aren't that unusual."

"Only you, Max. This kind of shit only happens to you," Jax said. The clink of ice in a glass told Max that Jackson was enjoying a drink. Probably a G&T. Max shuddered. He didn't know how Jax drank that stuff.

"I don't know why. It wasn't like I egged this girl on." Even though Jax couldn't see him, Max shrugged.

"Mom always said you just fall into trouble."

"And you rise above it." He laughed hearing their mother's voice in his head. The family joke was that Max just fell into trouble—usually involving women. His mother didn't seem to mind. She used to tell him when he fell for the right girl, he'd fall hard and the landing would be soft. He thought about Dani, his—well, he wasn't sure what she was at the moment. He was pretty sure he hadn't fallen hard for her, not the way Mom predicted, but that didn't mean they weren't good together. The sex was hot and she was beautiful. He didn't need a "mate", didn't want one.

He shook his head, clearing his thoughts and ready to make a sharp transition in topic. And get to the purpose of this phone call—what the hell was bothering Jax?

"So what's going on with you?"

"Nothing much."

The way he said it—with just a quick sigh—made the hair on the back of Max's neck stand up. His brother was keeping something from him.

"Jax." That was all he had to say—a warning that he wasn't going let this go.

Jax hesitated then said, "Max, I'm fine. Just helping out a friend on a project. It's nothing big."

A low hum of excitement ran beneath Jax's voice. That combined with the fact that Jax wouldn't tell him what was happening made Max's muscles twitch. Jax was the sane twin. The thought of him being tense and secretive made the hairs on the back of Max's neck stand up.

Max tapped his finger on his thigh. He opened his mouth, ready to ask again. He wasn't letting Jax off that easily.

"How's Dani?" Jax asked. Max shook his head. Pretty clever, switching the focus to something *Max* didn't want to discuss. His failed—or failing, more accurately—engagement.

"Uh, fine."

"Doesn't sound fine."

Damn, his brother could read him as well. "No, she's good. Really." He tried to inject a little enthusiasm into his voice.

Jackson didn't press and Max was grateful. The impulsive decision to get married had been quickly followed by the realization that things were moving a bit too fast. When Dani had suggested they "take a break", Max leapt at the chance. Still, it was embarrassing to get unengaged three weeks after it had happened. He'd talk to Jax about it at Mik's wedding, get some advice on how to tell the parents.

"When are you heading to Mik's wedding?" He looked out the window of his apartment. The lights of the Vegas Strip glittered in the distance. He'd been thinking about going out, dropping twenty bucks in a slot machine. He didn't gamble much but occasionally it was a way to kill time. Better than sitting around his place thinking.

Jax was probably doing the same thing in his house, staring at the night sky. That Jax had ended up in Alaska was still a surprise. That they'd ended up living in different states was part of Max's discontent. He liked being near his brother. But for now he needed to be here and Jax was reasonably settled up north. They got together several times a year. Often meeting up and going to visit their family.

Max listened to Jackson's groan and smiled. They obviously felt the same way about the family gathering. With Mik getting married, their mother would turn her attention on them. He could already hear the gentle nags about when he and Dani would be setting a date. "The Thursday before," Jax said.

"Cool, that's when I'll arrive as well. You bringing a date?"

"Right." Jackson laughed. "None of the women I know would exactly blend with our family. You bringing Dani?"

He sounded eager, teasing, trying not to press but Jax definitely wanted answers.

"Probably not. She's got a new show starting. Bad time for her to be gone. Listen, I'd better go."

Much longer and he'd break down and confess.

"Yeah. Have a good night."

"You too, Brother."

Max hung up and tossed the phone on the bed. It wasn't just that something was going on with Jax, something was wrong inside Max as well.

Without even noticing, he realized he'd gotten up and started pacing, doing his whole caged animal impression. He needed to see Jax. The phone worked but he needed to connect with his brother. Needed to *see* his brother. And then maybe he'd find the courage to make the face-to-face confession that he and Dani were "on a break".

He flipped open his laptop and got online. The only thing on the schedule for the next week was a bathing suit layout. Though he hated missing the opportunity of seeing models in tiny clothes, the urge to visit Jackson took precedence. He'd find someone to cover the shoot while he made a quick trip to Alaska.

Chapter One

ꟾ

When no one answered the door, Max dug into his pocket and pulled out the key ring Jax had sent him two years ago when he'd moved in. It was crazy. They lived a thousand miles apart, but still swapped keys. Jax had a set for Max's Vegas apartment.

He put the key in the lock, calling out at as he walked in. There was always the possibility Jax was home and just didn't want to answer the door. God forbid Max walk in on his brother with some woman. They were close, but he didn't need to see Jax having sex.

"Jax! You around?" Silence echoed back. Max dropped his bag on the floor and stopped. Something was off. He scanned the room. Nothing blatantly out of place, no cushions overturned or pillows unstuffed but damn, it looked like Jackson's house had been searched. It *felt* like the room had been tossed.

Jax was almost fanatical in his need to be organized. It helped his sense of control.

Max pushed the door closed behind him and sniffed the air, letting his wolf senses come to the front. His vision turned black and white. The loss of color sacrificed in favor of crisp sharp focus. Human sweat lingered in the room—surface scents, not imbedded in the furniture. Papers were scattered across the dining room table. Books were misaligned on the shelves. Not that Jax was completely OCD, but he had obsessive tendencies. He never would have left his place like this.

Max closed his eyes and listened. He was alone in the house. At least as far as living creatures.

If Jax is here, his heart isn't beating.

Reining in the wolf's volatile emotions, Max forced himself to move methodically through the house. If Jax were still here, he was beyond human help. Letting the anger simmer in his chest—that someone dare threaten his twin—he checked the kitchen, newly remodeled and gleaming. Nothing out of place. Whoever had come in, they hadn't bothered to search this room.

Max finished examining the first floor then moved upstairs. He stopped at the top and sniffed again. The human smells continued. Jax's scent lingered beneath the intruder's. *You know he was alive two days ago,* Max reminded himself.

Strangely reluctant to continue the search, Max forced air into his lungs and urged his feet around the corner, moving to Jackson's bedroom first. Empty. The bedside tables had been opened and not closed properly. So had one of the dresser drawers. Not like Jax. A quick peek in the master bath told him it was empty as well.

He retreated, not touching anything, and went to the next room. Jax's place wasn't big and he used the second room as an office-guestroom. Max pushed open the door and sighed. Empty. Thank God. But here the disarray was more pronounced—files opened and emptied onto the floor.

What had they been looking for? And had they found it?

Questions that Max wanted answers to, but first he needed to answer the most critical one—where was Jax?

He flipped open his phone, ignored the message indicator—another call from Mik, one from Dad—and hit speed dial one. His heel bounced restlessly on the ground as he listened to the buzzing ring in his ear…and heard it echoed downstairs.

Sighing, Max followed the sound and found Jax's cell phone on the kitchen counter. Wherever he was, he didn't have his phone.

Max shook his head. Jackson appeared to most of the world as the stable, organized methodical brother. Only their family knew the truth. Jackson had to be organized. He'd forget his head if wasn't attached—as their mother used to say.

Max paced the living room and debated whether to call the police. Would they even care? It wasn't obvious unless you knew Jax that the house had been searched and for all Max knew, his brother might be on a plane flying into a remote Alaska village. Jackson consulted with a couple of the Alaska Native Corporations and sometimes had to fly to Nome and Bethel.

Not caring that he invaded his brother's privacy, Max went to the phone and picked it up. The tone beeped in his ear indicating he had messages. He dialed in to Jax's voicemail and waited. One message left two hours earlier.

"Jackson, it's me." He didn't recognize the feminine voice. "I'm just calling to remind you about tonight. I know you won't forget—you never do—but I'm compelled to remind you. If anyone understands that, it's you, right?" She laughed like it was a joke between them. "Anyway, eight o'clock at Gideon's. I'll see you there."

Max hung up the phone. Whoever the woman on the phone was, she was right about one thing—Jax didn't forget appointments. If he was supposed to be there tonight, he'd be there. Or Max could officially panic.

* * * * *

At seven fifty-five Max sat down at the bar in Gideon's. It was a restaurant-bistro kind of place. The dining area was down a short, dim hallway, leaving the bar in an intimate corner of the building. So far, Max liked the atmosphere—dark but not depressing. It was the kind of place he and Jax would have hung out in—if they lived in the same city. It had an elegance that would appeal to Jackson and a sensuality that called to Max. And based on the top-shelf liquor that lined the back of the bar, they probably had a great wine list. That sparked Max's interest.

The female bartender approached. Before he could ask for a wine list, she placed a glass in front of him—filled with clear liquid and ice. He sniffed. Gin. Tanqueray and tonic, if Max had to guess. Jax's drink.

"Evening, Jackson."

Max thought to correct her but something stopped him.

"Alone tonight?" She leaned forward, the motion pushing her breasts together and straining the top of her t-shirt. Along with the interesting display of cleavage, it gave Max a chance to read her name tag. Jackie.

"I'm meeting someone."

A smile bent her lips, tainted with disappointment but more arrogant than anything else. As if she knew Jax would reject her...and he didn't know what he was missing.

"Aren't you always? Oh and I think she's here now." Jackie tipped her head toward the entrance.

Max turned and followed the direction of her gaze. A woman stepped in the doorway and scanned the room with an almost computerized precision. Starting at her left, she observed, catalogued and dismissed the four other parties in the room.

Her gaze landed on him and she nodded once, the movement brisk before she walked forward with efficient steps.

He took the few seconds he had before she reached him to check her out. She was on the taller side of average. A gray cardboard box suit camouflaged most of her body so he couldn't get a precise read on her form. It looked like she had some curves but he couldn't tell through the ugly clothes. The loose skirt ended just below her knee and the matching jacket hung down past her hips, hiding both her ass and her breasts.

The way she moved indicated efficiency and competence. And the combination made him want to muss her up—see her with her hair hanging around her face, panting as he fucked her, begging for him to come inside her.

But the prim set of her mouth killed that fantasy. She looked like the warden of a women's prison. A real prison—not one of the fun, sexy versions so popular in porn videos.

Her blonde hair was pulled back in a tight bun that rested against the nape of her neck. It left her face completely bare and made her cheekbones stark, harsh lines on her skin.

On any given day, Max would have looked past her. Not because of her average appearance but because of the dull, repressed aura that surrounded her.

On a bad day, this would be the kind of woman Jackson would choose. Personally, Max had always thought Jax needed to find a wild woman, someone to loosen him up, not encourage his control-freak tendencies.

Not that the woman wasn't pretty—she was in a rounded, comfortable sense—but the serious set to her eyes and firm line of her lips screamed she'd be no fun in bed.

"If you ever get tired of vanilla," Jackie the bartender whispered, "call me. I'll give you a great ride."

Max nodded, thinking he might take her up on that. Of course, he'd have to come clean about not being Jackson. But that was for later. First he needed to meet this woman who was expecting Jax.

"Hi," she said as she got close. There was no intimacy in her greeting, nothing to indicate she and Jackson were anything more than friends. Her voice was husky and low, a little breathless, the kind of voice that would deepen while she was being fucked. The sound reached inside him and triggered an unexpected fantasy—the two of them naked, fucking hard against the wall. Her legs wrapped around his hips, her mouth open, moaning his name as he pounded into her. The image shook him and he drew in a long breath, trying to slow his thumping heart, maybe clear his mind. Somehow she didn't look like the type to want it hard against the wall.

The bartender. That's your kind of woman, he reminded himself. Tough, cocky and wouldn't squawk when he crawled out of bed in the middle of the night.

But even as the fantasy faded, a delicious, sexual scent wafted toward him—making him hungry and hard in one breath. He tipped his head to the side and inhaled again, searching for the source. Sweet and intriguing. Hmm. It came from the woman before him. His cock twitched and the wolf growled. Great. Getting hard in a public place. Not what he needed. A week without sex and his wolf was getting tense.

She leaned back and did a quick glance at his body.

"This is a new look for you."

"Uh, yeah." Max hadn't planned to impersonate his brother when he'd left the house. And he still had some hope that Jax would show up. They could all laugh and Max could try out the bartender. Though the idea didn't sound that appealing now. He took another breath, capturing more of the seductive perfume that tantalized his nose. *More.* He licked his lips. More, yes. On his tongue.

His cock swelled, nudging the fly of his jeans.

"It looks good." He jerked, then realized she was talking about his clothes. "Are you ready for this?" She blinked and looked at him, her eyes glittering with emotions he couldn't classify—excitement, fear, hunger. They all blended together, linked somehow to his brother.

"Yes," he said, infusing the single word with confidence.

Relief eased the back of her neck and her shoulders relaxed.

"Good. I saw Gideon as I came in. He says they're already in there. Just go with what we planned and everything will be fine."

Max nodded, the cryptic conversation intriguing.

"Let's go." She tipped her head and started to walk away.

He looked at his drink—untouched.

"I'll bring it in to you," Jackie offered.

Max shook his head. Gin made his stomach revolt and his head spin. He had a feeling he needed his wits tonight.

He tossed money on the bar and followed the woman in gray.

She waited for him in the hallway leading into the restaurant. Her fingers fluttered along her purse strap. *Tell her. Tell her you're not Jax.*

"Listen—" he asked.

She shook her head. "We've been through this. You're not talking me out of it."

"No, I—"

"It was your idea in the first place. Now let's just do it." She hesitated, her gray eyes drilling into his, a strange mix of determination and uncertainty.

"Just one more thing," she said. She rolled her shoulders back as if bracing herself for an unpleasant task. The movement separated the edges of her jacket and he could almost, almost see the shape of her breasts. The sight distracted him enough that he didn't notice that she'd stepped close. Very close.

She wrapped her fingers around the front of his shirt and pulled, dragging him down, drawing her up until their lips were inches apart. She hesitated then closed that short distance, pressing her mouth to his. The awkward connection registered in the corner of his brain moments before it short-circuited.

A faint voice he recognized as his conscience warned that she thought he was Jax, but when he moved to speak, his lips brushed hers and the silk of her skin was too tempting to not sample again. He rubbed his mouth across hers, the seductive scent of her skin sweeter and stronger close up. Needing a taste, he opened his lips, just a little. He almost groaned when she did the same.

The crisp clean flavor—like she'd just eaten an apple—clouded his already confused brain, making him want more. He licked her upper lip, tempting, teasing her into inviting him inside. Her eyes blinked and she looked up, the surprise forgotten as she opened her lips. Unable to resist the pure temptation, he drove his tongue into her mouth and growled, the delicious taste swelling inside him. Perfect. Sweet but not too much. A hint of spice to make it interesting.

His cock strained against his jeans, the zipper digging into his skin. Damn he couldn't remember when he'd been this hard, so ready to fuck so fast.

He twirled his tongue around hers, feeling her tension then the sweet power of her submission. The wolf came alive, howling and filling his head with the need for more.

She was delicious, addictive.

Heat flared between them. She moaned and moved closer, her breasts pressing against his chest. He grabbed her arms and turned placing her back against the wall and moving closer to cage her with his body. The fantasy from moments ago reverberated in his brain. She tipped her head back and looked up at him, her lips open, her eyes flashing with hunger. Why had he ever thought she wouldn't be the type to fuck against the wall? Naked. They needed to be naked.

He slid his hand down her back and squeezed her ass, loving the way her flesh curved beneath his hand, urging her against his body, easing her onto his cock even as he pressed forward.

She gripped the back of his neck and drew him back to her, her lips opening, offering.

That's it, honey. He covered her mouth with his, tasting her. Hot slick pussy juice flooded her cunt. He could sense it, almost taste it. The wolf in his head growled his approval, wanting that scent on his body, his mouth, branded on his soul.

He slid his hands up her sides but the thick jacket blocked the access to her skin. He snarled, knowing her nipples were getting hard, wanting those tight peaks in his mouth, sucking while he fucked her. He groaned and she took the sound into her, accepting it with hungry surprise.

A voice—he supposed it was his conscience—reminded him that she thought he was Jax, but fuck, he couldn't pull away. Not yet. He pressed his hips forward, the wall and his hand on her ass holding her in place as he pulsed against her, gentle taps to her pussy, a slow grind. Fuck, he needed to be inside her. She dragged her mouth away, gasping for breath. The wolf growled but before the sound had the chance to make it to the surface, she smiled—a wicked twinkle sparking in her eyes.

The light ignited his dick. Damn. The prim, serious woman had disappeared and pure hunger stared back at him.

He clamped his hands on her ass and held her in place as he ground against her, harder, longer, fighting their clothing to make sure she felt him. Her eyes widened and a delicate hitch sounded from the back of her throat.

"That's it," he whispered, leaning down and speaking against her mouth. "I'm going to be right there, fucking you, riding you hard."

She groaned and her eyelids fluttered shut as he repeated the motion. She tipped her head back, baring her throat, offering it to him. His gums tingled, warning that his teeth were ready to drop, to plunge into that soft skin and mark her.

He licked his lips, tasting her, ready to—

Instinct alerted him to the newcomer moments before he heard the sound—a throat clearing, a warning that they weren't alone. Fury and dominance surged through chest, clearing out the sex and leaving behind the overwhelming desire to protect his mate. He spun around and put her behind him, placing his body between his mate and the danger.

Wait, what the hell? His mate?

The word finally connected in his brain. He didn't have time or focus to swear at the wolf. Max's body, his instincts demanded he guard the woman.

His lips twitched with the urge to snarl, warning other predators away from his prize. The tall man at the end of the hall didn't seem threatened by Max's display. His mouth spread wide with a smile.

"Sorry to interrupt—because it looks like more fun than I've had in months—" He winked. "But *your* guests are waiting and *my* guests don't expect a show with dinner."

His words took a moment to penetrate as reality returned. Max looked down, his body was in full battle mode, the woman—fuck he didn't even know her name—crushed behind him. He ground his teeth together and straightened, signaling to his wolf to back off. There was no threat. This guy seemed to know either Jackson or the woman. Maybe both.

"Sorry about that, Gideon." She apologized as she slid out from behind him smoothing her hand across her hair, making sure that the tight strands were still in place. In the dim light he couldn't see her blushing but the embarrassment in her voice told him she was. She pushed her shoulders back and started forward.

If it hadn't been for the scent of her pussy, warm and wet—damn, he'd bet her panties were soaked—Max thought he might have imagined the kiss and grope. He knew better. She was aroused, her pussy slick and ready for his cock.

Fuck.

Hard like he'd never been before, ready to bend her over the nearest flat surface and pound his cock into her...and she thought she'd been kissing Jackson.

Perfect.

Following the woman, he reached the end of the hall. Gideon hadn't moved. Laughter and a touch of confusion glowed in the man's eyes. Max couldn't help but size up the other male. It was instinct—human and animal. An inch or so taller than Max's six-foot-two-inch frame, Gideon's body was long and lean. Like a swimmer or a runner. In a battle of sheer strength Max was pretty sure he could take him but if it involved speed, he had a feeling Gideon would take him down.

Dark eyes stared at him, amusement radiating from the man's gaze.

"That was a pretty hot display." He glanced back over his shoulder then dropped his voice. "I didn't expect that kind of heat between you and Mandy."

Max straightened his spine. "Why not?" he demanded, feeling the compulsion to protect his twin.

Gideon chuckled. "Untwist your knickers." He patted Max on the chest, the touch familiar, almost a caress. "If it's working, I'm thrilled for you."

The words dripped with insincerity and laughter.

He was mocking Max. Or Jackson, really. And Max hated the thought that anyone would make fun of his brother.

"I'll sleep better knowing we have your approval," he snapped. "Our table?" The laughter disappeared from Gideon's stare.

"You *are* in a mood." He flipped his head around like a pissed off princess and strolled away, leading Max and Mandy—at least he had her name now—to their table. Two men already occupied it. They stood when Max and Mandy approached. One of the men smiled and gave Mandy a hug. She grunted as she fell against him. The forced laughter as she pushed him away sent Max's nerves on alert. Despite the familiarity, she didn't like that man touching her. And neither did Max.

Eyes and lips tight, she stepped back and pulled Max forward. "Jackson, this is Sean Baldino, Brian Mickelson. Uncle Sean, this is Jackson, my fiancé."

Chapter Two

ꕥ

Mandy felt Jackson's hand—the one resting so protectively on her back—flinch. She took a deep breath and silently begged him not to blow it. But when she glanced at his face to make sure his panic wasn't showing, she calmed. He looked a little irritated but didn't look ready to run for the door. Maybe it was just the natural masculine reaction of hearing the word "fiancé" in connection with his own name. He still wasn't used to it but he'd agreed. Finally.

"I hope you don't mind that I brought Jackson along." She looked at Sean and Brian, knowing it would now be impolite for them to say that they did. She didn't want to do this by herself. She needed Jackson by her side. It had been his idea in the first place. Of course, that had been after a few drinks and he'd only suggested she play Nancy Drew to make her feel better.

"Since we're engaged…" She lifted her chin and stared down the man her father had considered his best friend. "I wouldn't want to make any decision without consulting him." Sean's eyes tightened at the edges but he nodded.

"You're an accountant too?" Sean asked.

"Yes."

The clipped one word answer vibrated with aggression and Mandy knew she had to take control of the conversation. Keep things smooth and easy. She wasn't here to antagonize these guys.

"He's brilliant." She leaned in, grinned and actually fluttered her eyelashes, trying to ease the tension that hummed between the three men. "Phenomenal with numbers."

That was no lie. Jackson could calculate, twist and turn numbers. It amazed even her. It was the thing that had first drawn her to him.

She turned and looked up at Jackson. Instead of giving her a shy smile to thank her, he nodded, just once.

"Maybe we should sit," he said, the suggestion more like a command. The others reacted to it as well, taking their seats.

He guided her into her chair, his body shielding her as if he protected her, a threat to anyone who came near. Her lips pulled up into a wide uncontrolled smile. Right. This was Jackson, accountant, gentleman and all-around good guy. Not exactly a warrior.

But there was something different about him tonight. A dangerous energy surrounded him. The clothes, the glint in his eye and that kiss. She mentally fanned her face. Where had that come from? She hadn't known he had anything like that in him. Of course, she'd been a bit more aggressive than normal as well, the adrenaline probably. It wasn't every day she propositioned criminals.

They all shifted in their chairs, unconscious adjustments while each decided who would begin.

"Are you the assholes who searched my house?" Jackson asked, his gaze challenging as he stared across the table.

"Jackson," she gasped, then the words became clear in her head. "What? Someone searched your house?" She turned Sean and Brian and tried to force a smile. "You wouldn't search his house, would you?" She'd never even considered that. These guys were white-collar criminals, not gun-toting thugs. At least that's what she'd assumed.

Her heart did a little leap in her chest. This could be a bad idea. She wasn't Nancy Drew and the police certainly weren't going to help her.

Sean looked at Brian as if to get his approval for speaking then shook his head. "Why would we search your boyfriend's house?"

She might have believed him. Except for the twitch above his eyebrow and Father's tales of late-night poker games. Whenever Sean bluffed, his left eyebrow twitched.

She opened her mouth to call him on it but Jackson's hand on her leg stopped her. He squeezed, just above her knee, just hard enough to get her attention and keep her quiet.

She got the message and pushed her shoulders back. "Well, that's horrible." She glanced at Jackson. "Did you call the police?"

He shook his head. "No. I can handle it."

The threat rumbled beneath his words. Sean swallowed as if trying to clear a lump from his throat. A tiny spark of satisfaction swirled through her chest. Sean was actually frightened by Jackson. Good.

Feeling more in control, she slipped her hand beneath the tablecloth and patted his thigh, a light touch, a thank you and a warning to behave that was more teasing than serious. His eyes met hers. He didn't smile—but she could see the laughter flickering his gaze. She fought the urge to grin, knowing this was serious business. She rubbed his leg again and the light in his eyes changed. For a moment they almost seemed to glow red. A shiver raced across her neck making the little hairs stand up. Tension zipped around the table, encompassing all four of them.

This was not going as she'd planned. She took another slow breath, hoping her nerves didn't show.

The heat under her hand helped calm her. Her fingers rested above his knee, her mind processing the sensation beneath her fingertips. Solid muscle, rock hard, strong. Wow, she knew Jackson worked out but this was more than just gym-muscles. Her palm tingled with the desire to slide the full length of his thigh, and higher, between his legs.

Her mind, desperate for any distraction from the stress, created a wicked fantasy—her kneeling before Jackson, those rock-hard thighs spread just enough, her hands behind her back, lips open, wrapped around his cock. Heat rushed through her pussy and the strange tingling in her hands shifted locations, sinking deep into her sex. This was so strange. She'd had sexual thoughts about Jackson before but never those dark submissive fantasies she hid deep inside.

Jackson shifted in his chair, turning his body toward hers. A subtle challenge flashed in his eyes and for one desperate moment she feared he could read her mind. She shuddered at the thought of anyone knowing those wicked dreams.

Now is really not a good time to think about sex. Save it for later. When you're alone. With your toys. The mental reprimand helped draw her attention back. These were bad guys and she had to stay focused. She took a shallow breath and willed the desire away.

The table was silent and she realized they were waiting for her. She had called this meeting after all. But how did one proposition a criminal? She was too new at this and the first thing that popped into her head was food.

At least it replaced the thoughts of sex.

"Would you like something to eat?" Food relaxed people, didn't it? Or maybe it was just her and that's how she ended up carrying an extra fifteen pounds.

Sean and Brian shook their heads.

"Dessert sounds good," Jackson drawled. Wow, had she ever heard him drawl before? It sounded wonderful and sensual and damn she was getting hot again. "Something sweet." As he said the words, he put his hand on her knee, crossing his arm over hers, his fingers sliding between her legs. He wasn't aggressive or lecherous but there was no mistaking the sexual aspect to his touch, the way his fingers whispered on her skin, warning they weren't going to be content with the modest caress to her knee for long. She squirmed and looked over her shoulder, begging Gideon to appear and thank God, there he was.

He stepped forward, stopping beside Jackson, looking poised and calm—gorgeous. She tried not to stare at the two men but it was more than her feminine hormones would allow. They were striking together. Gideon with his dark eyes and dark hair, long enough that she could imagine trailing it through her fingers. Jackson's strength and heat. A small flutter teased her pussy and fought the urge to squirm in her seat. Between Jackson's hand on her leg and Gideon's smile she was going to have an orgasm right here.

Gideon winked at her, not in a sexual way, but as a friend. She smiled back. She didn't know Gideon well but Jackson trusted him. That's why they'd picked this restaurant. A little backup if they needed it.

"Have you had a chance to look at the menu?" Gideon directed his question to Jackson, one side of his mouth pulled up like he was fighting a smile. He blinked his eyes and Mandy saw the laughter twinkling in his dark gaze. "See anything that looks good?"

The grip on her knee tightened for a moment and Jackson lifted his chin, daring Gideon with his stare. What the heck was going on? Jackson was behaving like a thug, which was probably appropriate but not what Sean and Brian were expecting. They were looking for a mild-mannered accountant.

And what the heck had happened to her mild-mannered accountant?

Not wanting to startle Jackson by squeezing his leg, though the urge to pinch him almost overwhelmed her, she rubbed her fingers up his thigh, distracted by the hard muscles beneath the black denim he wore. Her subtle touch captured Jackson's attention and he pulled his insolent stare away from Gideon, directing the power to her. The irritation faded and it was lust and hunger that flowed from him.

"What would you like, honey?"

You on the floor, naked, now. Or even better, me, naked, on the floor, hands tied—

She opened her mouth, praying that those words didn't actually slip out. The sexual tone of his voice curled through her core, her pussy clenching with anticipation, as if he invited her to debauchery with every word. Weird. Jackson and debauchery were not two words she'd ever thought of together. Until tonight.

His fingers did another little slide beneath her skirt and she sat up a straight.

"Honey?" This time there was laughter.

She glared at him and smiled at Gideon. "I'll have the key lime pie."

"Excellent," Gideon said with the perfect precision of a longtime restaurateur. "Gentlemen?" He looked to Sean and Brian.

As Gideon turned to Sean and Brian, Jackson shifted, the movement pushing his fingers a little deeper between her legs, inching her skirt up until her thighs were visible. Warmth from his palm curled over her skin but he didn't stop. She snapped her knees together. The corner of his mouth bent upward and with seemingly no strength, he slid his hand higher, leaving her knees and teasing the inside of her thigh.

She heard him speak, vaguely aware he'd ordered the Chocolate Indulgence, his voice lazy and smooth, even as he continued to stroke her, the movements subtle but determined, inching higher. What the heck was happening? Jackson had his hand under her skirt. In public. And if she didn't do something soon he was going to get close enough to know her panties were drenched.

Mandy pulled her shoulders back and nudged her chair forward. Surely that would stop his teasing. Instead he just moved with her, adjusting the tablecloth to cover her lap.

Feeling as if she'd been doing nothing but taking deep, calming breaths all day, she tried another one. She had to stop him. It just wasn't right for him to—he twirled one finger, rubbing a hot little circle.

She froze, her mind blanking for a moment. When her thoughts reengaged, it took a moment to remember what she'd been thinking. Oh right. Making Jackson stop. Except that she wasn't sure she wanted him to stop. She hadn't been this hot since…okay, she couldn't remember but surely it had taken more than fingers on her thigh to make her ready to pounce. Or even better, be pounced on.

Still, it wouldn't do to make a scene. Not in front of Sean and Brian. She and Jackson had to appear a unified team.

She blinked and realized Gideon had left and the conversation had stalled. All three men were looking to her.

"Have you given my idea any thought?" she started, leaving the floor open for "Uncle" Sean or Brian to begin.

Brian looked at Sean and there seemed to be a silent communication between them. Brian was definitely the one in charge. Sean just seemed to be carrying out his instructions.

"Not that we don't trust you," Sean said. He raised his hands to stop her protest. "We do. I knew your father too long not to trust you. But him." Sean lifted his chin toward Jackson. "We've had so many problems, we just want to be sure that's he's not, you know, working for the cops."

"Cops?" Her voice squeaked next to Jackson's snarl.

"Cops? What the hell?"

"Cops. Feds. Can't be too careful." Brian nodded his weaselly little head. "You're family. He's not. We want to check to make sure he's not wearing a wire." He caught Mandy's stare. "It's happened before."

She knew that from personal experience. Her father's indictment had been based on a recorded conversation.

Jackson's fingers twitched against her skin but he didn't remove his hand from between her legs. She'd warned him about this. It would be a simple thing. They could slip into the bathroom and prove that Jackson wasn't—

He sat forward, the movement slow and predatory. Sean and Brian seemed to recognize the animal strength and they both leaned back. Not enough to be called a retreat but the movement acknowledged the other male's power. It was like watching an episode of Animal Kingdom.

"You want me to go into the bathroom and strip so you can prove I'm not wearing a wire?" Jackson's words were more threat than question.

Brian's lips got white around the edges. "Yes."

"No."

"Jackson—"

"I'm not stripping for these guys unless they're willing to do the same," he announced. "And frankly, I'm not that interested in seeing you two naked." He paused and Mandy realized the power at the table had shifted to him. "We'll just have to trust each other."

Mandy had no choice but to sit quietly and add her support to Jackson. It wouldn't look good for her to nag or contradict him, not in public, but as soon as they were alone, they were going to have to talk.

She offered a weak smile and shrugged.

Brian gave another speaking glance to Sean then turned back to Jackson.

"Okay, we'll let it pass but you know what happens to people who cross us."

Max listened to the barely veiled threat and didn't know what the hell to think—either he should be worried about his brother or worried that the two wiseguys sitting across from him were walking, talking clichés. Either way, what the hell had Jax gotten himself into?

A server appeared beside the table with Gideon approaching from the other side, a bottle of wine resting against his forearm. It was an excellent wine, a perfect complement to the desserts being placed on the table.

"I thought this would go well with your desserts."

The one Mandy called "Uncle" Sean—Max thought of him as Baldino—grimaced as if irritated by another interruption.

Max did what he did best and took control. "That would fine."

Gideon eyes widened for a moment, laughter twinkling in his dark eyes, and he bowed his head. "Very good, sir."

Asshole.

Gideon moved around the table, pouring wine into the glasses of the other three. He pulled back when he came to Max's seat, pausing. A spicy scent flowed from Gideon, a flavor that had nothing to do with the food in the room. It was his natural scent. And fuck, it blended perfectly with Mandy's sweet perfume. He licked his lips imagining the two tastes on his tongue.

"Wine, sir?"

Needing something to mute his senses before he dragged the tablecloth away and buried his face between Mandy's legs, he nodded. Gideon paused a fraction of a moment before pouring the deep red wine into Max's glass. The bouquet filled the air, combining with the sexual scents from Mandy and Gideon and invading Max's head, making him drunk just from breathing.

His cock throbbed, needing to be released. It made no sense. He'd never been attracted to another male before but something about Gideon not only pissed Max off, it made him hard. And Mandy…when she'd walked into the bar, he would have classified her as no-fun, too uptight to hold his interest. Now he couldn't keep his hands off her.

The knowledge that he was behaving out of character not only for him but for his brother didn't help much. He kept his fingers firmly fitted between Mandy's thighs and used his free hand to reach for his wine. He moaned as the slightly cool liquid slid down his throat. His cock twitched. Fuck, good wine, chocolate and a sexy, aroused woman. Damn, the only thing better would be to have her cunt juices on his tongue as he sipped the wine.

Heat radiated from her pussy invading his skin. If she hadn't been wearing underwear, and he was pretty damn sure she was, he knew she'd be wet, smearing her cream down her thighs as she sat there so properly.

Not wanting to scare her or push her too far too fast, he left his hand where it was and turned back to table, his attention captured by the chocolate cake before him.

He reached for his fork, thankful that he was functional with his left hand because he had no intention of taking his right away from Mandy's thigh. If nothing else, it kept her off balance and he had a feeling she didn't allow many people to see her in that state.

The fork slid through the cake like it was heated. He carried it to his mouth and groaned. He tipped his head back and savored the flavor as it slid down his throat. Mandy's eyes widened as she watched and a soft, almost inaudible hitch caught her breath. He licked his lips and stared at her mouth. Oh yeah. The cake and Mandy, naked, licking the thick chocolate off her breasts, sucking on her pretty nipples as he fucked her.

Every sense came alive until he was surrounded by sex.

The wolf howled in his head. Max crushed the hungry noise and tried to focus on the obscure purpose for this meeting. There would be time for fucking later.

Allowing the first delicious bite to settle, he glanced at the two men across the table. Definite lowlifes. Possible crooks. What was Jackson doing meeting with these people? And what about Mandy? She'd set this up. His heart did a little jump that she might be a crook but his dick didn't seem to mind. And his wolf had no problems with women of questionable morals. The more of a slut she was, the more his wolf would like her.

Unfortunately, Mandy didn't come across as a slut. Too controlled. The edge of Max's mouth pulled up as he thought about how much fun it would be to bring out the inner slut in Mandy. Seduce her until she was begging to be fucked. Needing his cock. The wolf's impatience came forward, the animal eager to move on to the fucking.

But first Max had to figure out why his brother was meeting with thugs. Mandy obviously knew them well enough to call one Uncle Sean. Surely Jax wasn't so desperate for money or God forbid, entertainment, that he'd decided to work for The Mob. Not that these guys were part of The Mob. It was Alaska for God's sake.

He let his mind circle as he ate his cake. Every bite was perfection. No wonder this was Jax's favorite restaurant. They had different tastes in a lot of things—women, alcohol, clothes—but one thing they agreed on was chocolate.

Everything seemed to settle and Mickelson sat forward.

"I have to say I was surprised when you contacted me."

Mandy nodded and her cheeks pulled up in a strained smile. "It seems a little strange, I know." She looked at Max. He tipped his head forward, trying to give her whatever support she needed. He didn't understand what was going on but until he could figure it out, he was on Mandy's side. "It's just with everything that's happened, our business..." She inhaled through her nose, the sound strained. "Has suffered."

Mickelson sat back, his eyes squinting down at the corners. He crossed his arms over his chest.

Mandy's thigh jumped beneath his hand and he tightened his grip, willing her to breathe. She seemed to hear his silent command and gave a weak shrug.

"No one wants to hire the daughter of an embezzler." Tears filled her eyes. The wolf howled and Max struggled to keep the sound from entering the world. His soul demanded he distract her from whatever was causing her pain. He slid his hand higher up her thigh. Red stained her cheeks but she didn't pull back.

Baldino and Mickelson sat forward, their eyes sharp and still cautious.

"People are still looking hard at our company," Mickelson said in a low voice. "Federal indictments are coming down all over the place and we need to make sure we're clean as a whistle"

Max fought the urge to roll his eyes at the cliché and focused on the cryptic conversation. He didn't track Alaska politics much but he knew there had been several businessmen and government officials accused of bribery.

"If there's a chance something like that might happen, I'm not sure I want Mandy involved in this."

The tablecloth he'd used to cover his hand between legs also camouflaged the swift kick to his shin, a hard thunk that hurt, damn it. The clunky heels she wore left a dent in his flesh.

"We're thinking of starting a family soon so Jackson is worried about me working too much." She fiddled with the crust of her key lime pie. "I don't think it should be a problem. And we will need the extra income with a baby on the way." Her voice came out confident, a touch hard. She kicked Max again, this time more warning than punishment.

Max didn't allow himself to smile. She had a bit of fire in her. He liked that. Didn't mind prickly women at all. Made them more fun to dominate in bed.

"Do you understand your father's accounting system?"

"Oh yes. He trained me." She laughed. "He used shortcuts and abbreviations that no one else is going to understand."

Mickelson nodded, an irritated grimace on his face.

"Yeah, we had another bean counter look at it and he couldn't figure out what your dad had done."

"He was very cautious. Diligent."

Baldino blanched but nodded. It took Mickelson a little longer to agree but finally he nodded as well.

Mandy sighed, her relief a little too obvious. His hand still lodged between her legs, he gave her thigh a squeeze. The movement put the starch back in her spine and she sat up straight.

"I'll do my best to finish what my dad started."

Max listened for tears or pain in her words but they were calm and confident.

"I was sorry to lose him. Despite what they said, I never believed a word of it," Mickelson said, though there wasn't an ounce of sincerity to his words.

This time, Max caught Mandy's reaction. It was small, just the merest tightening of her lips.

"Thank you."

"When can you start?" Mickelson asked.

"Monday? I'm still going through my father's old papers. He kept books on all his clients and I want to be up to speed when I show up."

Mickelson and Baldino looked at each other—their little rat ears practically twitching with interest. They turned back to Mandy.

"Papers?"

"Books?"

She nodded, smiling angelically at their response. "My father liked to keep a copy of his clients records." She paused and he could hear strength behind the serenity of her voice. "In case something happened to him or something damaged your records." Damn that almost sounded like a threat. Fuck, he wished he knew what was going on.

More meaningful looks bounced between Mickelson and Baldino. This time it was Baldino who spoke—obviously playing on Mandy's "family" connection between them.

"Maybe you should bring them with you on Monday," Baldino said.

She forced another smile. "I'll have to see if I have them. I still have boxes of my father's business things to go through.

"I could stop and help."

Something about Baldino's offer made Max's stomach turn.

Her mouth opened and a soft "uhh" slid from her throat.

"No." All three heads turned to him. Time to retake control. He didn't know what he was blundering into but there was no way Mandy was going to be alone with these guys. "Mandy's still going through her father's things. It's very emotional. You understand."

"Jackson..."

"No."

He waited for Mandy to protest. Dani would have ripped his lips off right there in the restaurant if he'd made that sort of announcement. Mandy blinked and offered another half-smile and a shrug.

Disappointment lodged in his chest. He really did like a little heat, a little confidence in his women. The flicker of attitude he'd sensed earlier was gone.

Then, as Baldino and Mickelson talked quietly between them, Mandy looked at Max. Anger and irritation flashed in her eyes. So, she wasn't acquiescing so easily. He would hear about this later. For some reason, she was determined not to rock the boat in front of Mickelson and Baldino.

Jax, what the hell have you gotten yourself into?

He needed to find his brother. He didn't understand what was happening but even he could tell this was a bad situation. If by some chance Jax was actually thinking of working with these assholes, Max would just drag his ass back from the brink of insanity and smack him around until he came to his senses. And if that didn't work, Max would tell the rest of the family. He'd love to see that—their mother, father, brother and, God, their sisters would rip into Jackson so badly he'd be limping but he'd be walking the straight and narrow.

"I really appreciate you giving me this chance," she said with a smile. "I need the work...and you need someone who can take up where my father left off." He tried to listen to what she was saying to understand the subtext beneath her words but damn, all he could hear was her voice, low and husky and wrapping around his dick like a fist.

Made no sense. He liked his women tall, lanky and wild—not repressed and *efficient*. Still the idea made him want to debauch Mandy just a little. He almost groaned when he thought about it. Mandy, stretched out on his bed, her hands tied above her head, her legs bound open. Her pretty lips begging for his cock.

If she tasted half as sweet as she smelled, he'd spend hours between her legs, sampling every bit of the pussy juice dripping from her cunt.

Her fingers tapped the back of his hand and he opened his eyes, unaware he'd closed them to better enjoy the fantasy. He looked to where his fingers were nestled so comfortably between her legs, mere inches from her sex, her skirt scrunched up, revealing soft rounded thighs.

"We have to go, Jackson," she said through clenched teeth. He dragged his gaze away from her legs and met her stare. With a smile he knew would infuriate her, he let his fingers trail away, but before he completely freed her, he tugged down the hem of her skirt. That part of her belonged to him.

Jackson. Your brother. Remember him?

The mental slap back to reality helped a bit and he pushed his chair back, following Mandy toward the door.

She belongs to Jackson. There will be no stretching out, no tying her up and watching her tits shimmy as she begs to be fucked.

The wolf howl rattled his brain, weakening his resolve that she didn't belong to him. He needed to get away. Needed a little space...before he bent her over the closest table and fucked her in front of the entire restaurant.

They reached the front counter and stopped. He didn't know the etiquette for something like this. Was the thug or the sleazy accountant supposed to pay? Hell, he didn't want to owe these guys anything.

"I'll just go pay the bill."

"Fine." Baldino said, putting his hand on Mandy's arm. Max's lips trembled. The urge to rip them back from his teeth and snarl at the asshole touching his woman was almost too strong to resist. "Can we walk you to your car?"

"Of course." Again, the precise words should have chilled his soul but instead he just got harder. She blinked and looked up at him. "I'll see you later?"

He nodded, not trusting himself to speak. He was too keyed up, too ready to pounce. He grabbed hold of the howling wolf inside him and yanked him back from the edge, forcing the animal into his mental cage.

"Good to meet you, Jackson," Mickelson said.

Liar. But considering he felt the same way, he lied right back.

"You too. Have a good night." He could do insincerity as well.

Mickelson and Baldino followed Mandy out the door. The hair on the back of his neck stood up. He didn't like those guys. They hadn't done anything overtly criminal but something about them made his teeth ache. And Mandy was going to work for them.

Max walked to the doorway, tracking the three of them across the parking lot. With a casual wave, Mandy climbed into a silver SUV and pulled out of her parking space. Mickelson and Baldino stood in the shadows and watched, their heads drawn together in discussion. They didn't follow her but Max didn't like they way they looked at her. He didn't want her anywhere near those two.

Her car turned onto the main drag and picked up speed. A vague dissatisfaction rumbled in his stomach as her taillights disappeared. Not with the strange meeting. The discontent surrounded Mandy. He licked his lips. *Kiss her.* That was it. He hadn't kissed her goodnight. It left the evening unfinished. He wanted her flavor imprinted on his lips.

But she hadn't offered her mouth, hadn't hovered near him with the intent of one more kiss before she went home. Did she expect Jackson to follow her home? It was clear from the masculine state of Jax's place that she wasn't living there.

If she belonged to me, she'd never sleep alone. His cock jerked at the idea and Max knew that if she belonged to him, she wouldn't sleep much at all for the first few nights. He had a short attention span when it came to women so after a few nights of hard fucking, he'd probably work her out of his system.

Yeah, a few long *nights of hard fucking. And maybe a few afternoons.* The wolf inside his head leapt like he was trying break free and chase after the disappearing taillights.

What are you thinking? She's Jackson's girlfriend. His fiancée. No more thinking about fucking.

Right.

He looked up, his eyes tracking across the restaurant's entryway to the back hall. Gideon stood in the shadows watching him. He tipped his head to the side then disappeared into an open door, expecting Max to follow.

Better see what this is about.

He confirmed the hallway was empty and started down the dark passage. The sounds of the kitchen rattled through the wall on his left. At the end of the hall, an office door stood to the right. Max pushed it open and stepped inside.

The door snapped shut behind him and Gideon was there, up against his body, his mouth on Max's, his hand on Max's hip.

He froze, expecting the rage, the panic—the instinctive reaction of a heterosexual man when another male kissed him.

Instead that spicy masculine scent filled his head, demanding a response. Gideon's lips moved, warm and soft across Max's. He wasn't going to react. Hell, this was another guy kissing him. But then Gideon licked his tongue out, flicking across Max's upper lip, a subtle invitation for Max to let him inside.

Telling himself he was only responding because he was playing the part of Jackson and for all he knew, Gideon and Jackson were lovers.

And if he was supposed to be Jackson, Gideon expected a response…Max opened his mouth. Gideon pressed inside, hard and fast.

The strong thrust into his mouth snapped Max out of his frozen silence. He groaned and his tongue met the invading presence, twining around it. He turned his head to better meld their mouths together, his eyes drooping shut, spots forming behind the lids. Fuck, what was happening?

The wolf's growl echoed through his head, the animal making its hunger known. It wanted more of the powerful taste and texture, the sexual touch of this male.

Max dragged his head back, needing a breath, needing a moment to think. He didn't understand any of this. His wolf had never reacted to a male before but there was no mistaking the animal's desire. He inhaled. Gideon distinctive scent filled his head, intriguing, compelling.

Gideon didn't let Max go for long. He cupped one hand to the back of Max's neck and pulled him close, realigning their lips. This time there was no hesitation on Max's part. He opened his mouth and kissed the other man, sinking his tongue into Gideon's mouth, commanding a response.

Heat surrounded his cock and the barely coherent corner of his mind realized that Gideon was touching him, rubbing him. The erection that had remained while sitting next to Mandy swelled under the hard caresses. He couldn't stop his hips from rolling forward, moving into the powerful cock massage. *God, that feels good.*

Finally the panicked, slightly homophobic side of him came to the surface and Max backed away, pushing against Gideon's chest to break the contact. Gideon released him easily and took a step backward, leaning his hip against the desk.

Max inhaled through his nose, trying to calm his pounding heart and slow his racing mind. The two most incredible kisses of his life had occurred on one night—one from a woman, one from a man.

What the fuck is going on?

He didn't have a chance to answer his own question. Gideon folded his arms across his chest and smiled, looking smug and too damn confident.

"So," he said. "I know you're not Jackson. You must be the twin brother, Max."

Chapter Three

ꟗ

Max hid his surprise. Gideon had been able to tell the difference when even Jackson's fiancée hadn't noticed. Did that mean Gideon knew where Jax was? Knew that he wasn't able to keep the meeting with Mandy and the petty criminals she seemed to be courting? Or did Gideon just know his brother better than Mandy?

Max shook his head. What was going on with Jax? *First, he's associating with crooks and now, he's fucking a guy?* These were things a twin brother needed to know. Still, Max decided to play it cool, at least until he figured out what else to do.

"Why would you say I'm not Jackson?"

Gideon laughed. "Well, while I've teased Jackson for the last year about his questionable sexual orientation, he's never once let me put my tongue in his mouth. And he sure as hell wouldn't let me touch his dick."

Max felt himself blush. That was as good an explanation as any. Now if Max could only forget how it felt to have Gideon's hand rubbing his cock.

"I only went along with it because I didn't know what your relationship with Jax was."

"Right. Didn't enjoy it in the least."

The gentle mocking in Gideon's reply told him the other man knew the truth. The blush grew worse until Max was sure his cheeks were on fire. What the fuck? He hadn't blushed since he was fifteen years old and his mother found him the bathroom with a Playboy magazine—a situation that had mortified them both for months.

"What gave it away?" he asked ignoring the thoughts in his head.

"Red wine gives Jackson headaches."

Max sighed. "I know, but gin makes me throw up so I went with blowing my cover instead of puking my guts out all night."

"Probably best. No one else seemed to notice." Gideon fiddled with the stapler on his desk before looking up. "Seems kind of 'high school' for you two to be switching places." Max shrugged. They hadn't even done that in high school. Fear of their mother's wrath had been enough to keep them from even attempting it. "Where is Jackson tonight?"

"That's what I'd like to know."

Gideon seemed to catch the seriousness in his voice and straightened. "What's that mean?"

He considered the other man. Jax had talked about Gideon—had said he was a good guy and a great cook. But really, what kind of judge of character was Jax when his fiancée was setting him up with white-collar criminals? But Max needed to trust someone. Needed to talk to someone.

"I can't get a hold of him. His house has been searched—"

"What? What were they looking for?"

"Don't know. He hasn't been around and he left his cell at the house."

"You don't really think something's happened, do you?" Gideon's voice held the kind of concern Max appreciated—the "I'll stay logical and believe the best while still trying to find the truth" kind of concern.

"Probably not. You know Jax. He flies around Alaska."

"Yeah but doesn't he usually call you?"

Max nodded and then looked at his phone. *Fuck, there was a message.*

"It didn't ring."

Gideon grimaced. "It's Alaska. Weird cell coverage, even here in town. Check it."

Max called his voicemail, hit the appropriate buttons. Jackson's voice—healthy and well—rang through the line.

"Max, where are you at? Listen, I left my cell at home and I'm, uh out of town so I'll have to call you. Step away from the woman and pick up the phone next time." The teasing washed over him like a cool breeze. His eyes burned and damn if he didn't feel like he was going to cry. The knot in his chest unraveled and he let out a long breath. "Talk to you later, Brother."

"Him?" Gideon asked.

"Yeah. He's okay. Says he's out of town."

Gideon put his hand on Max's shoulder, a comforting squeeze. Max had the most ridiculous urge to turn into the touch, put his body against Gideon's. The wolf paced inside his mind, wanting to be released, wanting to rub against the male beside him.

He shook his head and tried not to acknowledge the disappointment when Gideon took his hand away. It had to be the stress of worrying about Jax. Had to be. His wolf snarled his irritation but Max shut down the animal, slamming him behind an invisible door. He didn't need the added distraction.

"Great. Glad to hear it." He waved to the phone on his desk. "You're welcome to call Mandy. She must be worried as well, yeah?"

Max winced. "I don't think she knows he's out of town."

"But what about..." Gideon choked. "She doesn't know you're not Jackson?"

"Uh, no."

"And the fact that you had your hand under her skirt all night was just part of the act?" Max felt the heat rising in his face again. He hadn't meant the caresses to go that far but damn, she'd smelled so good and her pussy was so tempting that his hand on her thigh had been a better choice then dropping to the floor and burying his face between her legs.

"I was acting like an engaged man."

Gideon grinned. "Right. Jackson isn't quite that open with his affections. In fact—" Confusion screwed up Gideon's face. "I was shocked as hell when she introduced you, uh, him, as her fiancé. I didn't even know they were a couple." He shrugged. "Guess you can't tell, huh?"

"She's the kind of woman he usually goes for."

Gideon sighed—and Max couldn't tell if that was because he was upset that Jax was dating a woman like Mandy or that Jax was dating a woman at all.

It did give Max comfort to know that Gideon and Jackson weren't lovers. Not that he would have minded his brother being gay. But he'd have been pissed that Jax hadn't told him about it.

Of course, Max hadn't known about Mandy either. Casual women, he couldn't care less about, but this was the woman Jax was going to marry. He would have at least liked to know his brother was dating someone. Max had told Jax about Dani and gotten his advice before they'd gotten engaged. Of course, he hadn't yet told Jax they'd broken up, but that might not be permanent so no need to reinforce the family's image of him as a "do 'em and dump 'em" kind of guy just yet. Besides, it was Dani who'd dumped him—or suggested they go on a break.

"Here." He flinched, Gideon's voice invading his thoughts. Gideon held out a business card. "If you need anything while you're here, call me." He winked. "Or if you find yourself alone..."

Max shook his head. "Don't go there." But he didn't say it with any heat. Possibly because his cock was still hard from the press of Gideon's fingers and damn, the way his wolf was reacting to the male, there was always the chance he could end up in bed with him and wouldn't that freak out his family? Suddenly the breakup with Dani didn't seem like that big of a deal. Not if he had to reveal he was sleeping with a man. His parents would collapse at the thought.

Gideon just chuckled and Max decided he liked the sound—it was deep and personal, resonating in Max's chest.

"I'm just teasing. Seriously, if you decide to hang around until Jackson gets back, call me. I belong to a great gym you can use and I know where the best restaurants are. Hate to think of Jackson's brother sitting all alone in his house."

Max nodded, understanding why Jax considered Gideon one of his best friends. He could almost forget that moments before Gideon had had his tongue in his mouth. Except for the lingering taste of spice on his lips.

"Thanks, I might take you up on that." He tapped his fingers on his thigh.

"Want to give me your number, in case I hear from Jackson?"

"Yes." He pulled out his own card and handed it to Gideon. "If he does call you, have him call me. Again." He looked around the room, his mind clouded by Gideon's scent, the lingering taste of his lips and the memory that moments ago he'd been stroking the inside of Mandy's thighs. Fuck. Mandy.

"You going to tell Mandy?"

Max shrugged. There was really no reason. He could explain it to Jax and *he* could tell Mandy. It wasn't like they'd had sex. It was just a kiss and okay a few caresses but he hadn't actually touched her pussy.

"Don't know if it's necessary."

"What if Jax calls her?"

"Fuck." Max closed his eyes and moaned. He didn't want to screw up Jax's life like he had his own.

"And it wouldn't be a bad idea considering that kiss in the hallway," Gideon added. "She might expect that same response the next time she sees Jackson and I've never seen those kinds of sparks between them."

Max's wolf, smug beast that he was, chuckled in the way of a wolf.

Max the human had to admit he found that information fascinating as well. She'd been hesitant at first but then she'd responded to him deliciously, melting in his arms. The memory of her taste and the wolf's screams in his brain blurred his world into pure sensation. He shook his head trying to clear it.

"Do you know where she lives?"

"I don't."

"Last name?"

"Jensen?" Max looked at Gideon who shrugged. "Pretty common name." He snapped his fingers. "You have Jackson's car?" Max nodded. "He's got a GPS in there and I'm betting he has her address programmed in. You know he has no sense of direction."

"No kidding. Thanks." Max headed toward the door…and had the strangest urge to lean in and kiss Gideon as he passed by, even felt his body slowing, the wolf begging for one final connection. Seizing control, Max held out his hand. "It was nice meeting you." Gideon's palm slid against his, strong and a little soft and damn if the image of those fingers stroking his naked chest, wrapping around his cock didn't fill his mind. *What the hell is going on?*

"Nice to meet you too."

Max nodded and dropped his hand, practically lunging for the door. He had to get away. Maybe getting away from *all* people was a good idea.

He stepped into the hall and took a deep breath. The scent of food inundated the air and for the first time all night Max didn't feel like he was inhaling pure sex. It helped, calming the animal inside him.

That had to be the problem. The wolf hadn't been allowed to run in months. The animal was probably going a little crazy. Hmm, this was Alaska after all. There had to be a place Max could find to release his inner wolf.

Setting the wolf free was almost mandatory if he wasn't getting frequent sex. Which he had been up until the breakup with Dani. He closed his eyes and pictured his on-again, currently off-again lover. Talk, sleek, long straight black hair with nice round breasts that overflowed his hands…and why the hell wasn't his wolf reacting? The damn thing should be leaping like a dog going for the fence.

A footstep on the tile floor forced him to open his eyes. Jackie, the bartender from earlier, walked toward him.

"Hi, you okay?"

"Uh yeah."

She kept coming, close, a little too close. The smell of splattered alcohol coated her skin. Max forced his senses through the alcohol and tried to scent the woman beneath it. She wore a floral perfume that made his nose itch and did nothing for his wolf. The animal stayed annoyingly silent. Damn, if it was just the need to fuck, any woman would do.

Unless his wolf had turned gay on him?

"Fuck," he muttered.

"Uh thanks." Jackie backed away and stalked down the hall, disappearing into the kitchen.

Great. Next time Jax comes in, she'll probably poison his gin.

He was doing wonders for his brother's life.

* * * * *

Mandy circled her couch. Again. She had things she should be doing—making notes about the night's meeting, going through her father's papers. Something. But she couldn't sit. Couldn't concentrate. Energy surged through her veins like electric pulses, spiraling through her body, igniting nerve endings until she thought she might explode. She needed something to burn off the stress. And the random pacing around her living wasn't helping. She needed something stronger, harder, faster.

Jackson. Her stomach dropped and she grabbed the back of the couch, keeping her knees steady. *Oh yeah, that would be a way to burn off the energy.*

Except no, Jackson was part of the problem.

What had he been thinking? He'd gone off plan. And it had been *her* plan.

In the end, it seemed to have worked—that arrogant "I'm not some weak ass accountant" persona appeared to resonate with Brian and Sean. That bad-boy image appealed to men and women it seemed.

But still—they'd had a plan going in. The point had been to get Brian and Sean to trust her, not make them adversaries.

"What was he thinking?" Her irritation rang through her voice filling the empty room. He was supposed to be her support, but he'd challenged them, just by being there.

There had been something different about Jackson all night. Not just the attitude but the clothes and the kiss. He hadn't been himself tonight.

She sighed. It was probably because he was dealing with guys like Brian and Sean. Criminals. It no doubt called to some deep-seated macho part of him that he'd never known existed until now. Great. Now instead of just watching Sean and Brian, she was going to have to keep an eye on Jackson. Make sure he didn't go too far. He'd never make it as a real crook. Didn't have the constitution for it. The Jackson she knew was methodical, precise. Exacting. A good crook probably needed a reckless streak that Jackson lacked. He was the only person more organized than she.

She eyed her phone. She could call him.

Right, but are you calling him to yell at him or to see if his voice really sounded that deep and sexual? She closed her eyes and sank her hip against the back of the couch.

I'm going to be right there, fucking you, riding you hard. The memory filled her head and dropped down into her pussy. She slid her hand down her stomach to the vee between the thighs, letting her fingers flutter against her mound. *Fucking you, riding you hard.* She groaned and bit her lip. It had been well over two years since she'd been on a date. Longer than that that she'd had sex. Maybe the deprivation was finally getting to her.

Or maybe she'd finally found a man who tempted her to fulfill all those wicked fantasies. She clapped her hand across her forehead and moaned. Women like her didn't get tied up or spanked or fucked by two men. Women like her had nice solid relationships that involved infrequent mediocre missionary position sex. At least that had been the pattern in the past and she didn't see it changing anytime in the near future.

She had a good addition to her fantasies though—Jackson's voice. She tipped her head back and licked her lips, the images coming at her hard and fast—Jackson standing before her, naked, commanding her to suck his cock. Or her, bent over the end of her bed, her ass—

Heavy steps on her front porch jolted her out of her dream. She spun around and stared at the door, knowing who was on the other side.

The man had his hand between your legs an hour ago. What did you expect? She demanded the answer from herself.

I expected him to lose interest. Or that it had all been part of the act.

The firm knock made her heart beat a little faster. She shook her head and pushed her shoulders back. Really. If it was Jackson on the other side of the door, he'd been here a dozen times. No reason to expect tonight would be any different.

Except she was wearing pajamas, no bra and he'd had his hands on her ass earlier in the evening.

Lifting her chin to give herself a little boost of confidence, she walked to the door and peered through the peephole. Jackson. Looking strong and masculine and irritated. Sexy. Why had she never seen this side of him before? She, of all people, should have noticed it.

She glanced down at her body. Not exactly seduction clothes. Long plaid flannel pajama bottoms and a lightweight Dallas Cowboys t-shirt had been her choice after a day in skirt and heels.

She glanced down. Her nipples pressed against the Cowboys logo.

Just as she was considering grabbing a coat to cover up her chest, Jackson knocked again, the annoyed twist of his mouth warning her he wasn't going to give up. Well, good. Because she had some things to say to him.

Gathering her own irritation, she took in a bracing breath and opened the door.

Max pulled Jax's car into the driveway. The house had been simple enough to find. Gideon had been right. Jax had Mandy's address programmed in. Her house wasn't far from Jax's place and looked a lot like it. Solid. Stable. Probably had a good resale value.

Mandy and Jackson obviously made a good match. They were similar in so many ways. Except for Mandy's tendency to proposition crooks. Max didn't understand what had happened at the restaurant, but those guys were shady. That he would bet on. And living in Vegas, he knew how to tell a good bet from a bad one.

He started up the walkway, the words not quite set in his mind of what he was going to say. How he was going to explain he wasn't Jackson.

I'm not Jackson. I'm his twin brother, Max.

It shouldn't be that hard. He could even justify the deception. Once she heard that he'd thought Jax might be in danger, she'd probably accept it. She might be irritated but she'd get over it. She was his fiancée. She should have been worried too.

The only part he wasn't quite sure he could justify was the whole hand up her skirt. How did he explain that? *You smell sweet and hot and I couldn't resist the chance to touch that soft skin while imagining my face between your legs and licking your pussy until you screamed my name.*

Yeah. That would work.

His fingers curled up into a fist and he squeezed, letting his knuckles turn white, fighting the growing cock in his jeans. Showing up with a hard-on wasn't going to help the situation. Of course, if she'd looked down at all during the evening, she would have noticed he'd been half hard all night.

Just get this over with.

He raised his hand, hesitating just a moment, before rapping his knuckles against the wood. The wolf had been silent during much of the drive over so Max had weakened the hold on him, opening the cage to let the animal free. Now, so close to Mandy the wolf subtly pushed to foreground. Max barely noticed his vision turning black and white. His ears practically twitched at the soft padding of her feet across the floor. The faint feminine scent grew stronger as she approached the other side of the door.

He waited, knowing she was inches away. Hesitating. He pressed his hand against the door, willing her to feel the heat, the need. The wolf growled and Max felt his muscles tighten, in preparation for breaking down the barrier to get to his woman.

Another moment passed and the doorknob turned.

The tension in his body shifted moving from fight to fuck. His feet moved almost without his command, driving him forward even as Mandy opened the door, the need to be next to her overwhelming societal conventions.

"Jackson—" Her yelp filled the space between them as she stumbled back, inadvertently clearing a path for him. Her arm flailed and he reacted, reaching out and grabbing, pulling her upright, hard against his body.

When he looked back later, he knew this would be the moment when it all went wrong. When he made the leap off the cliff and into heaven.

He slammed the door shut, blocking off any means of escape, closing out the world. The perfume of her skin flooded his senses, binding him until he wanted to taste and touch. Only the vaguest sense of responsibility stalled him from spinning her around and fucking her against the wall.

Jackson's woman. You're just here to explain.

With that logical, conscientious voice in his head he found the strength to ease back. He looked down, immediately meeting her gray eyes, made brighter by heady lust flowing through her veins. He could sense it, even as her cheeks turned a pale beautiful red.

He bit his lips together pressing hard to hide the extension of his teeth. The tight t-shirt clung to full, round breasts. Just like he'd imagined. The blue star logo muted the tight tips of her nipples. Baggy pajama bottoms hung from her hips and he knew with one quick pull he could have her naked. A frightening red fog pressed at the edges of his vision—hot and intense, sending a shaft of fear into his brain. *This isn't normal.* Even as he thought the words, her lips opened, just a hint, just enough to tempt him. Ignoring the foreign presence hovering just beyond his control, he moved close, unable to stop his slow approach.

"Jackson?"

Her voice came out as a squeak but Max pushed the sound aside, making the noise insignificant in his brain. He bent down bypassing her lips and heading for the sweet line of her throat, the perfect stretch of muscle and blood, the pulse throbbing just beneath the skin. The pounding resounded through his head and dropped down into his cock.

He moved, not thinking, just acting. Taking what he needed.

He clamped his hand down on her ass and pulled, drawing her close, rubbing that sweet cunt against his cock. A low growl erupted from this throat. The sweet curve of her ass led him down, until he could cup her thigh and pull, draping her leg around his hip. The sweetest gasp echoed through his ear, ringing into his cock.

"That's it, honey." The image from earlier—hell, the reality—of having her pressed against the wall, her pussy wet and hot, slick. Even without touching he knew, he could tell that she was ready. She could take him.

He ground his teeth together and drew back, fighting the beast inside him, straining every muscle.

And the faint, faded voice of conscience that nagged at the base of his skull.

He might have made it. Might have managed to pull back.

If only she hadn't touched—her fingers stroking the taut muscles of his throat, almost scratching. As if she felt the same intense, vicious need. He stared down at her, those wide gray eyes flickering with lust and a hint of fear. The predator in him rose up, loving that bit of uncertainty, needing the chase. She would yield nicely to him.

Her lower lip trembled just a little, capturing his attention. The memory of her taste echoed through his senses and he needed more. He moved slow, not wanting to startle her, bending to brush his lips against her. Not a kiss. Just a breath, savoring the anticipation running through her veins. The hand at his neck gripped the collar of his leather jacket, as if she was using his strength to keep herself still. To resist the flight instinct.

A low rumble came from his throat, the sound more of a purr than a growl. The shy exterior hid a hunger, a need, that resonated in him.

Unable to deny himself any longer, he pressed closer, his body moving to trap her, pressing her back against the wall, his hands locked on her hip and ass.

He tilted his head to the side and pressed his mouth against hers, lips open, the need to taste building. Her tongue met his as he dipped inside, a tentative welcome that only made the wolf crave more. He groaned. The memory had been weak, insignificant to the reality of tasting her again. He drove his tongue into her mouth, conquering with the kiss. Her fingers tightened, every muscles tensing. For a moment he thought he'd pushed too far. Then a soft whimper, filled with hunger, slipped from her throat. She twirled her tongue around his and fell into the kiss. She matched him, giving as good as she got and then submitting, allowing him to take and lick and linger over every point in her mouth.

His cock throbbed, the persistent need exploding with the simple touch of her lips on his.

Fuck. There had to be something going wrong with his wolf. The full moon so close. The animal too long constrained. *Something* because he shouldn't be this hard from a single kiss. The brief moment of clarity evaporated as she moaned, her fingers biting into his arms. Heat tempted him, drawing him in, deeper, until he was surrounded.

The red at the edges of his vision turned bright but didn't overtake his senses. The still functional corner of his brain guided his body, leading him to where he needed to be.

He pressed against her, grinding his cock against her pussy, feeling the wet soak through her pajama bottoms, dampening his jeans. The fluid scent filled the air, clinging to his skin. He growled, wanting that perfume all over his body.

He sank his fingers in to her hair and tugged pulling her head back until she looked up at him. Her lips were already red from his kisses, open and wet.

This was the second time he'd had her in this position tonight and there was no one to interrupt. No one to stop him. He rolled his hips, pulsing against her clit, moving one hand to cup her breast, squeezing the full mound, testing her.

A delicious sound caught in the back of her throat. Good. She liked a strong touch. Her nipple pressed into his palm and he pulled back rubbing a circle around the tight peak. Her back arched and she arched forward, the line of her body curving and moving, wanting more.

Leaving his hips pressed against her, he leaned back, watching his hand on her breast, the blue star on her chest moving with each breath.

He growled. "This isn't going to work."

She blinked and looked up, confusing snapping the desire from her stare.

"Wha—?"

He shook his head, fighting a grin.

"I hate the Cowboys." He grabbed the top of her t-shirt and pulled, ripping the material in two.

Chapter Four

ꟗ

Her offended gasp gave him a moment's pause but then he looked at her naked tits.

The remnants of cloth were immediately forgotten. He dropped the edges and cupped her breasts, his large hands still barely able to hold the full weight, thumbs moving to the nipples, tight and begging for his mouth. The ugly suit she'd worn at dinner had completely hidden her curves. Now they were visible, available. His to touch. Suck.

He wrapped his arm around her back and arched her up, drawing those beautiful breasts up to his mouth. He bent lifting the tip to his lips. A restrained gasp shattered the silence. He growled, the sound muffled against her skin. He wanted her to be lost in him, submersed to the point of drowning, so consumed by his fucking that she couldn't control her reactions. He swirled the tip of his tongue around her nipple one more time then drew the peak into his mouth, slow, monitoring every reaction, absorbing it.

Gentlemanly restraint battled with hunger. Hunger won. He sucked her nipple into his mouth, loving the shivers coursing down her spine, the delicious moan that slipped from her throat. Her hips rocked against his. He wanted to linger, to spend hours teasing and tasting her pretty tits but the lure of her pussy was too strong. The need to sample her flesh—and the wolf's desires—overpowered him. With another whispered kiss to her nipples, he slid his hands down, the smooth curves of her hips captivating him.

But everything about her tempted him to indulge. He couldn't resist another taste of her skin, a nip to her earlobe, loving the way her pussy creamed when he bit her, a quick scrape of his teeth to her neck, another sampling of her pretty tits.

The flavor of her desire sang on his tongue and his cock leapt in his jeans, wanting its freedom, wanting to be buried in her cunt.

He hooked his thumbs in the waistband of her pajama bottoms and dragged them down. Once over her hips, they fell with a quiet thump the ground. The scent of her pussy flooded the room, filling his head, drawing the wolf to the front of his brain.

Her pussy was almost bare—not fully waxed but trimmed and slick, the rosy pink of her pussy lips flushed deep red and glistening with her juices.

"Fuck."

Subtlety left him. He dropped to his knees and lifted her thigh, draping it over his shoulder, opening the sweet space between her legs. Delicious perfume covered him. Honey. She smelled like honey. He watched his hands moving across her skin. He spread his fingers across her stomach and slid down, trying to touch all of her but the liquid heat from her cunt called to him.

He had to grit his teeth to keep from howling.

Her thighs were drenched with her pussy juices and he couldn't resist lapping, capturing that spicy liquid on his tongue. He swirled the tip of his tongue across her smooth skin, a delicious detour before he plunged in, sliding his tongue between the slick folds her cunt.

Her cry bounced off the walls as her fingers grabbed his head, using him for support. Loving the strength in her hands, the power she used to hold him, he growled and went deeper driving his tongue into her entrance, sinking as far as he could, preparing her for his cock. The wolf's ears perked up, catching her breathless moan. She squirmed, trembling in his arms, the sweet flesh of her pussy slick beneath this tongue. Needing to feel her come, he fucked her with his tongue, short shallow pulses. Her thighs tightened, squeezing his head as her fingers slid through his hair, holding him close.

The wicked animal's purr vibrated through her pussy lips sinking deep into her core. She dropped her head back against the wall and closed her eyes, every sense in her body centered on the tongue pumping in and out of her pussy. Each stroke ignited delicious tingles, blurring her mind until she couldn't think.

He eased back and slid his tongue across her clit, a light teasing stroke that jolted her eyes open. He grunted, the pleased satisfied sound of a male who'd been proven right. The revelation hit her brain moments before the orgasm flooded her pussy, hitting hard and fast and with no warning. She cried out and absorbed the delicious little shocks.

The self-satisfied sounds turned to hungry growls and she thought she heard him snarl "more" against her skin before he drove his tongue back into her passage, the hard sharp penetration sending a new spike of renewed need through her pussy.

Strength-stealing shudders rippled through her core as he licked and kissed her sex, dipping his tongue into her opening, drawing back, lavishing seductive attention to her clit. He seemed to be testing, exploring her responses, finding those places that made her breath catch.

Swallowing deep, she braced her standing leg hard against the ground using his strength to hold her upright, the bite of his fingers cupping her ass and hips, moving her against his mouth, slow shallow pulses as he fucked her with his tongue. The first sensitive inch of her pussy sizzled with tension.

"Please." She wasn't sure what she was begging for—more, deeper, harder. *Jackson.* His name echoed through her mind but it didn't fit, didn't match the man with his face between her legs. He seemed different, stronger, more dangerous. Wicked.

He gave another flick to her opening then drew back, lapping at her pussy lips, the intensity shifting as he teased. She fought for breath. Every nerve still tingled but there was no pattern—he flicked and licked, swirling his tongue around her clit before drawing back and placing a hot hard kiss on the inside of her thigh. The need spread, moving in streaks from her pussy into the rest of her body, making her breasts throb. She dragged one hand off his head and grabbed her breast, needing something to ease the ache. Her fingers slipped down to pull on her nipple. A tiny jolt zipped into her pussy, tracking from the tight peak.

He raised his eyes and watched, the low growls of approval urging her on. Delicious vibrations slid into her sex but before she could enjoy the subtle sensations, he drove his tongue into her entrance again, reaching the nimble tip deep before pulling back. He lashed her clit then plunged into her pussy again. He stretched so far, teasing the top of her passage, before retreating and circling her clit, this time soft and light, mere whispers that moved as wild caresses through her core, into her chest. She squeezed her breast, pinching the nipple almost to the point of pain, matching his thrusts as she rocked against his mouth.

He jerked his head back, flipping his hair out of his way, looking up at her. A strange red light flashed in his eyes.

"That's it, honey." As she watched he stretched out his tongue and stroked the top of her crease, flicking past her clit while his eyes burned. "Touch those pretty tits, imagine I'm sucking them while I fuck you."

Following his instructions, unable to do anything else, she squeezed her breasts. The frantic touch made it better and worse. A low, harsh groan ripped from her throat. Too much and yet not enough.

"Damn," he whispered, his tone reverent. The right side of his mouth pulled up into an arrogant smile. If she'd been in her right mind, the sight might have irritated her, but she wasn't. Wasn't anywhere near her right mind.

She pumped her hips forward, trying to tempt him to return. "More?" Her plea was almost more than her sex-drenched mind could handle.

But she saw the reaction, watched it flare in his eyes.

"More." His answer was definite. Strong. Powerful.

She blinked, staring past her own hands on her breasts, the hunger flickering in his gaze as he turned his attention back to her pussy. Tension did a wicked little zip through her body, ripping from her breasts to her cunt. Even before he touched, licked, she felt the edge of the blade teetering. Held breathless for a heartbeat, she waited, needing, anticipating.

Time slowed as he leaned forward, giving her the lightest touch, a quick flick of his tongue. He looked up as if to confirm she was still watching, then eased forward, sliding his tongue between her pussy lips, letting her feel every inch as he approached her entrance.

Vaguely aware that she was panting, she reached for him. Silky soft hair, just long enough to slide through her fingers, stroked her skin, mirror images of the delicate touches to her clit. A sound that was part grunt, part groan broke from her lips as she pumped her hips forward, trying to find a harder contact. He groaned and licked, sinking his tongue between her folds like a starving man, as if he couldn't taste her fast enough, deep enough.

He lapped at her clit, a quick, delicious taste before he returned to her opening, driving his tongue into the tight passage, not deep but just enough to make her insane. She grabbed the back of his head and tried to guide him back to her clit.

Frustration bloomed inside her as he resisted her direction. Not that he didn't know what he was doing. Or that what he was doing wasn't amazing, sexy, and fucking wonderful but she wanted more. Wanted to come. And every stroke of his tongue, every thrust just made the need worse.

"Please." She dragged in a frantic breath. "Fuck me."

This time he seemed to hear her. He drew back, wrapped his lips around her clit and suck, slow rhythmic pulses. He slid a single finger between her pussy lips and slipped it into her opening, slowly fucking her as he worshipped her clit. The dual caresses sent her flying, delicious zings running through her pussy, threading into her limbs.

She cried out, releasing her breast and putting both hands into his hair, fingernails biting into his scalp. A low hungry growl reverberated from his chest and throat, flowing into her pussy, as if the little bit of pain she gave him made it all the better.

Her body pulled tight, consumed and condensed by the steady, intoxicating thrust of his finger, sliding in and out of her pussy, fucking her until she couldn't take it any longer. Until she needed more.

"Damn it. Fuck me!" The command filled the room.

He gripped her ass and tipped her forward, driving his tongue into her one more time, trailing kisses along her slit, returning to her clit, no seduction, no hesitation. He took the tight bundle between his lips and sucked hard, pulsing caresses that shot into her pussy.

"Ah!" Her cry reverberated through her entryway, the delicious tension rippling from her clit and racing into the rest her body, draining the strength from her muscles.

He hummed, the sound so low it became a growl, and continued to lick, long lush strokes that worked the orgasm deep into her core, making her body shudder. She closed her eyes and breathed, her mind blank, the only sounds her breath and heartbeat.

Through her eyelids, the world spun. Dizzy and satisfied, she clung to the one constant in her world—Jackson. Hot kisses whispered across her thighs. Subtle flicks of his tongue, higher, along her stomach and up, pausing between her breasts.

"Gorgeous." She blinked her eyes open. The glitter of her pussy juices sparkled around his mouth. He licked his lips. "Delicious."

Her heart pounded loud in her ears. No one had ever told her that before. No one had ever meant it before.

Heat—pure, animal desire—stared back at her. She swayed but he was there, catching her, warmth and strength covering her body.

He pressed close, nudging his erection against her bare pussy. Her clit—sensitive from coming—vibrated but he backed off before it was too much. Fire streaked along the tight muscles of her throat as he teeth raked her skin, almost painful but still not quite enough.

She turned her head, silently begging for more. Something burned inside her to feel that delicious pain again.

Max stared down at the pretty female, baring her neck, offering herself. He clamped his lips closed, hiding his teeth. The sharp canines filled his mouth and were clearly nowhere near human. The taste of her cunt lingered on his tongue, his mouth, driving him insane. The wolf screamed in his head, demanding he fuck her, claim her.

Max shook his head, fighting the animal's instincts. He was human. He was stronger and fucking more logical than the beast inside him. Red once again teased the edge of his vision but he blinked it away. He licked his lips and tried to force his body to retreat. Just a few inches. If he could get the distance, he might, just might be able to escape.

Mandy tipped her head back to meet his gaze.

Fuck. Her eyes were hazy from the double orgasm, her cheeks flushed a delicious red. And her lips…fuck she kept licking her lips, as if she was imagining his cock in her mouth. Or her taste on his lips.

Drawn by the image, he bent down, placed his mouth on hers, blending the flavors of her cunt with her mouth. The wicked spice and sweet exploded on his tongue. He grabbed her ass and pulled her hard against him. Heat surrounded his dick as he pressed against her pussy, liquid practically burning him through his jeans.

He grabbed the back of her torn t-shirt and dragged it down, leaving her naked, bare before him.

The faint voice of his conscience tried to insert itself but before the sounds could make sense in his brain the wolf howled its need, its intent.

He pulled back, enough to capture a breath, thinking it might be enough to clear his brain. But the scents of their bodies together only made it worse. And the hint of uncertainty that flickered through Mandy's eyes.

She grabbed her lower lip between her teeth then let it slide away, as if bracing herself for the rejection. A burst of anger throbbed at the base of his skull. That Jackson would have left her insecure. If she belonged to him, she'd always know she was the sexiest woman in the room. He bent down, cupping her cheek in his palm, covering her mouth with his, slower this time, savoring the softness of her lips.

When he lifted his head, she looked up at him, her mouth red from his kisses, her eyes glazed with passion he created. The driving urge to be inside her flooded his chest. The need pushed aside any hesitation. He scooped her up in his arms and headed toward the stairs.

Mandy gasped and tried not to scream like romance novel heroine. The world shifted beneath her jolting her out of the lovely stupor two orgasms in quick succession could cause.

His strength eased her panic and the languid satisfaction returned to her muscles, leaving her limp and draped against him. She turned her head and buried her nose in the nape of his neck, inhaling the masculine scent. She'd always thought Jackson smelled good—crisp and clean scents from his aftershave—but this was different. Earthy, male, intriguing. It made her want to taste.

Unable to deny herself the pleasure, she stroked her tongue across his skin and lapped at the base of his neck. A growl rumbled beneath her tongue—a clear warning. She giggled, feeling no threat. Instead she repeated the caressed a little longer, harder. His taste was as delicious as his smell.

He tipped his head back and looked down at her, the red glow returning to his eyes.

"Be careful, honey." The warning was lost in the endearment, the sexy way he drawled the word. "It's not wise to tease the beast."

The thought of Jackson being "a beast" drew another giggle.

"Maybe it's not wise," she whispered, letting the words brush against his skin, emboldened by the lust that emanated from him. "But it's kind of fun."

A quick snap filled the air moments before she felt the tap on her ass and the bright bloom of pain. Her head snapped back and she looked up at him, blinking, her body vibrating between shock and desire.

"Wha—?"

"Naughty girls get punished."

"P-punished?" The word caressed her pussy sending a rush of liquid through her cunt.

"Yes." He reached the top of the stairs. "Good girls get fucked. Naughty girls get punished." He set her feet on the ground and she stood, using him to support her shaking knees. He placed his fingers beneath her chin and tipped her head back so she had no choice but to look at him. "Do you understand, Amanda?"

The firm, almost paternal way he said her name sent shivers down her spine.

"Yes."

"Repeat it back to me."

She forced her lungs to take a shallow breath. "Naughty girls get punished."

"And…?"

"Good girls get—" She swallowed. It wasn't like she hadn't used the word before but, standing here, she felt very much like a schoolgirl in the principal's office. He stared down at her, the stern set of his mouth warning her she was quickly entering the dangerous realm of "punishment". "Fucked. Good girls get fucked."

"That's right." He stroked the backs of his fingers across her temple, lightly touching her hair. "And you want to get fucked don't you, Amanda?"

She dropped her gaze and nodded.

"You must answer me, Amanda. Do you want to get fucked?"

"Yes." The word burst from her throat, almost defiant. A sexual energy crackled between them making her nerves sing. Every wicked fantasy she'd ever had—since she was old enough to know better—involved a strong, dominant male, ordering her, fucking her, commanding her to take him. She'd just never imagined that man would be Jackson.

"Very good, Amanda. Now go get on the bed and spread your pretty legs. I want to see your pretty cunt."

Her legs wobbled and she was glad he was holding her up.

She pushed her shoulders back and turned, walking the short hallway to her bedroom, trying not to think about the fact that she was naked and he was still fully dressed and she was walking away in the full light of the hall.

Insecurities assailed her as she pushed open the door. Her ass was too big, her hips too big. Hell even her breasts were too big—though some guys obviously liked that. She stopped beside the bed, not sure she had the emotional strength to climb onto the mattress and spread her legs, bare herself to him so blatantly.

Her throat tightened like someone had a fist around it. But even as her mind fought the fear, her body reveled in it. Her clit aching. She squeezed her knees together. The subtle movement only made the need worse. A few hot words and she was ready for more.

Ready to be a good girl.

"Get on the bed, Amanda." Lust and command filled his voice and pushed aside some of the fear. The sight of her naked ass walking down the hall hadn't turned him off. He still wanted her.

Still, her body struggled to follow his instructions. Moving slowly, she placed her hands in the middle of the bed and put one knee on the mattress. The image of how she must look overwhelmed her and she froze, not sure she could go on. She opened her mouth, thinking to tell him no, that maybe they could turn down the lights and crawl under the blankets.

Heat enveloped her pussy, warm fingers dipping into her cunt. The caresses locked her muscles in place and she froze, afraid to lose the intoxicating touch.

"I told you not to tease me, honey. And the sight of this gorgeous ass is too tempting." He scraped his teeth across her hip. The thin streak of pain translated into pleasure by the time it reached her brain. The fire from his bite pushed her hips forward, rubbing her pussy against his hand, the shallow movement pressing her clit against the heel of his hand and she groaned. *More.* She rocked her hips again. And again. It would be so easy for her to come.

Max watched the beautiful woman fucking his hand, her ass pushing back and forward, her juices coating his skin. The wolf growled and that freaky red haze threatened his vision. He pushed it aside, fighting his wolf for control.

After a moment, he caged the beast but knew he couldn't relax. He commanded, drawing on the dominant side of his nature.

"No, Amanda. You mustn't come. Not until I give you permission." He felt her tense. He could tell from his threat of punishment that she was new to bondage play but the arousal that flushed her skin told him she'd just been waiting for the right lover. If he could stay in control long enough to give her what she needed. He reached down and thumped his cock, trying to get the thing to back off long enough for him to enjoy her.

He dragged his hand away from her pussy and patted her ass, resisting the urge to turn it pink. "Climb up, lie on your back and grab the headboard. Don't move until I tell you to."

She looked over her shoulder, meeting his gaze. Her lips trembled but she smiled, her eyes glittering with false bravado.

"Do I have to call you 'Master' as well?" The question came out husky and low. Her sex voice.

"No," he murmured, running his hand up her soft thighs, over her hips, cupping her breast. "Sir will do just fine."

She giggled—a sound more natural, her fear easing. "Sir? How Catholic-schoolgirl fantasy."

The image of Mandy in a school uniform, short skirt, tight shirt à la Britney Spears made Max's cock strain the seams of his jeans.

"Get on the bed, Amanda."

She fluttered her eyelashes at him. "Yes, sir."

He struggled between smiling as her confidence returned and punishing her for her insolence. He decided the punishment would wait for later.

He stepped back and she pushed herself, climbing onto the high mattress. She hesitated only a moment before turning onto her back and reaching up, stretching her body long as she grabbed the headboard.

The sight of her lush body displayed before him pushed the wolf to his limits. He lowered his eyes fearing they might reveal how close he was to a shift. A roar pounded inside his head and his teeth stretched long. Damn, this wasn't just the normal desires of the wolf. It was like his *were*—that third, uncontrollable personality male werewolves possessed—was trying to get free. His *were* side had never appeared before but based on his brother's description, the beast was close to the surface.

Max swallowed and considered drawing back, instinct warning him that anything that called to the *were* was dangerous. But then he looked at Mandy, stretched out, her rounded body straining. The sexual hunger that had been blatant in her eyes changed and the vague insecurity he'd seen downstairs returned.

Fuck, he was going to smack Jackson when he found him. She was a sexual, sensual woman who should never have a doubt she was the most erotic thing in the room.

"Spread your legs, baby."

The hesitancy in her gaze stabbed at his heart but he didn't let it show. He straightened and the Alpha animal in him came out.

"Spread your legs. I want to see your pretty cunt."

A shiver moved through her body and the tips of her breasts grew even tighter. Yes, perfect. Her body was taking control. The hunger and desire returned. She took a deep breath and slowly separated her knees, her feet digging into the mattress. She was fighting the urge to hide—Max could accept that. It was a vulnerable position. But he wouldn't let her conceal that sweet flesh.

"A little wider. I want to see every inch of you."

A whimper broke from her lips and she tipped her knees farther out. The blush on her cheeks painted down to her chest, giving her breasts a delicious rosy tone.

Too hot, he stripped off his shirt and dropped it on the floor. Her eyes flashed as she stared.

He stretched forward and traced his finger up the slick line of her slit. Liquid fire sank into his skin and he couldn't stop the groan. Knowing she watched, and wanting her taste to linger in his mouth, he raised his hand to his lips and licked her pussy juices from his finger.

Her fingers tightened around the slats of the headboard as she stared, her breasts rising and falling in shallow pants.

"You taste so good when you come, baby."

Chapter Five

ꟷ

Max stared down at Mandy, watching the tension pull on her muscles, her eyes locked on his lips as if she was remembering again how it felt to have his mouth on her. She struggled to hold still. The fake confidence had faded and the insecurity returned but so had the need.

She squirmed, rolling her hips upward, as if begging for his cock. Her breasts swayed as she arched her back, straining, offering herself.

The dangerous red haze left the edges of his vision and covered his mind even as his body moved. He felt himself climb onto the bed and rip open the zipper of his jeans. Not taking time to strip off the tight material, he pulled out his cock, the shaft hard and straining. It was like he was a rider in his own mind. Everything shimmered with a red tinge—not the black and white of the wolf, he was familiar with that. His heart pounded as he struggled to regain control but the *were* was too strong.

Max looked down. The thick tip of his cock was at her entrance, his fist wrapped around the hard shaft, guiding it into her cunt. Alarms screamed in his head but he couldn't stop. The noise faded as he pushed the round head into her passage. Heat surrounded him, drawing him in.

The wolf howled adding its voice to the sounds in his brain at the sight of his cock sliding into her pussy. Max snapped his teeth together to contain the violent snarl. She was tight, squeezing his dick as he barely inserted the tip in her. The urge to drive into her, plow through that silky tight flesh, pounded at the back of his skull but Max pushed it back. That bit of sanity remained. He couldn't hurt her. He gripped her hips, holding her in place. The subtle pulses of her body, arching and retreating, silently begging for his penetration were too tempting.

His mind battled for control, making it impossible to expend the energy to speak. Unable to even command her to remain still, he pushed his cock forward, sliding deeper. Lush heat poured through his skin, burning him with a powerful fire. He wanted to immerse himself in that flame, lock himself deep in the warmth until he was part of the blaze.

"Please," she begged, her voice low and breathless. She accompanied the delicate plea with a slow pump of her hips, fighting his hold, moving him deeper. As he sank another inch into her, she gasped and Max felt his teeth stretch long. A distant portion of his mind warned him to at least close his lips, to hide the change that threatened. It was the same voice that warned him not to fuck this woman but there was no way that was going to happen. He had to have her. Needed to spill his cum inside her, sink his teeth into her flesh and pour his seed down her throat. Every way that he could mark her and claim her, he would do.

A slow awareness filled his brain as he pushed his cock deeper, almost there. The heat squeezing his dick was unlike anything he'd experienced. Hotter, more connected. The reality struck her as he buried to the hilt in her pussy.

He was naked inside her. Panic and joy clashed in his brain. He couldn't come inside her but he couldn't find the strength to pull away from the sweet grip of her cunt.

Years of lectures from his father and older brother bounced around his head. If he came inside her, she would be bound to him. His heart swelled at the thought but sanity prevailed. He couldn't do that to her, not without telling her what would happen. Finding strength he didn't know he had, he inched his hips back. The wolf screamed, throwing itself against the restraints Max placed around it. The brutal noise rattled his brain but Max forced himself to retreat, dragging his cock from her passage. His determination worked on the red haze overpowering his human side driving it back until once again he maintained a tenuous control. He pulled completely out, hating the loss of her warmth.

Mandy's gasp and soft "no" only added to his pain.

"Condom," he snarled, barely able to make his lips form the word. His teeth hurt and he clamped his lips down, hoping to hide the fact that he was moments away from changing. Forcing every bit of mental power he had into his hands, he reached into his pocket and pulled out the condom he'd shoved in there, taken from Jax's stash. Not that he'd intended to fuck anyone when he'd left the house tonight but he liked to be prepared. His fingers shook as he ripped open the package. Desperate sounds rippled from Mandy's throat. The hunger in the noises grabbed his attention and he looked at her body, flushed and straining. The slick liquid glittered around her cunt, captivating him. Hours. He could spend hours with his face buried between her thighs, licking and tasting, her sweet thick cream coating his tongue.

But his cock demanded the satisfaction it had been denied all night.

He slid the thin sheath over his cock, fighting the wolf and the *were* the whole time. Damn, this didn't make sense. Yes, his wolf liked sex, even demanded it on occasion, but never had Max had to fight the animal to allow him to wear a condom. He barely managed to roll the damn thing up his dick before the wolf broke through. Max felt it, his vision turning black and white, the claws popping out of the ends of his fingers. Max ground his teeth together, holding the wolf back. The animal retreated but refused to be locked away, never quite leaving the front of his brain.

He grabbed Mandy's hips and positioned her on the tip of his cock, pausing only a heartbeat, hoping to give her some warning before he slammed into her. Her cry shattered the quiet and shocked the wolf. The animal wanted to fuck her, hard, but he wouldn't hurt her. Couldn't hurt her.

"Mandy?" Max managed to ask, his mouth and tongue more wolf than human making words a challenge.

"Don't stop," she moaned, arching her hips up, grinding her cunt onto his dick. The wolf in his head howled and Max had to fight the same noise coming from his throat. This was it. This was where he was supposed to be. This was the pussy he was supposed to fuck. *Mine.* The word pulsed through his brain, planting itself in his subconscious, digging its hooks into his soul.

Somehow it wasn't as painful as it should have been. Maybe being inside Mandy's hot tight pussy had something to do with easing any fear his possession might have caused.

She squirmed again and Max knew he couldn't remain still. This wasn't going to last long. Groaning at even the brief loss of her heat, he pulled back until only the tip of his cock was inside her. He looked down, watching his dick poised at her entrance and couldn't look away as he pushed back in, her body easing just enough to grip him, take him.

Mandy shivered as he sank into her.

"That's it, honey. God, you feel so good. So hot." He retreated again, hoping she was close. The restraint of even these two slow thrusts were driving him crazy.

"Fuck me," she whispered, her voice low and commanding.

The Dom inside him wouldn't let her get away with ordering him. Not in bed. He stopped, his cock halfway in, his thighs practically shaking with the need to thrust.

"No, Amanda." It was so easy to slip in to dominant mode with her. She responded so beautifully. Her body tightened and shifted, trying to slide him deeper but the iron grip he had on her hips wouldn't let her.

"Please…sir."

His eyes burned. And he realized he could see color again. Her pretty breasts were flushed, the tips tight and straining for relief. He reached up and circled one nipple with his fingertip. Her pussy quivered around him and she groaned.

"Very good, Amanda." He nudged a little of his cock deeper in and then retreated, holding himself back. "Is that what you want, honey? Do you want my cock?" He gave another teasing stroke.

She strained, pushing back on her shoulders, her hips fighting to move.

"Yes, sir. Please."

The wolf howled. Knowing what would soothe the beast, he drew back and thrust forward, filling her in one hard stroke. It probably would have been too much if she hadn't been so wet, so hungry for his cock. She cried out as her pussy eased to let him inside. The bite of her fingernails into his skin burned, sending spikes of pleasure into his groin.

Unable to control the need to fuck, he pulled back and sank into her again. Perfect. Her passage tightened around him, holding him as he rode her, trying to slow his thrusts but she wouldn't let him.

She planted her heels into the mattress and punched her hips up, matching his downward thrusts. The silky glide of her skin teased his hips as she squeezed him, her knees pressing in. Holding him like she couldn't bear the thought of him not inside her.

His wolf howled, furious at the thin latex layer that separated them, wanting to come inside her and fill her, mark her with his scent. Max felt his body slip from his command and his hips pounded forward, driving into her hard. Her cries ricocheted through the room and he tried to stop, tried to slow his thrusts but he couldn't, the need to feel her come around his cock, to pour himself inside her was too strong. He pressed up high, barely conscious enough to guide his thrusts against her clit.

Shivers rippled across her skin, light and hot. Max felt them as if they moved through his own body. He pumped into her again and felt her pussy tighten seconds before she screamed, her nails digging into his arms. The tiny spikes of pain made his dick even harder. He roared and felt his mind go. He drove himself into her, the desperate need to come streaking down his spine. His balls drew up and he shouted, heat ripping through his core and he came.

The red haze in his brain bloomed bright crimson as he worked his cock in her pussy, riding out his orgasm, draining every bit of cum. He sagged forward, catching himself so he didn't crush her but needing the warmth of her skin, the touch.

Satisfaction surged through his chest but it lasted only seconds before the wolf took up his howl. Max closed his eyes and concentrated, locking the cage door, strengthening the bars that held the beast. The wolf lunged at the cage he built, throwing itself against the bars.

He closed his eyes and listened to his heart beat. His climax hadn't eased any of the strain. He was hard, claws still marked the ends of his fingers and his teeth pressed against his lips. He needed distance. Needed to get away from Mandy. Long enough to calm the creatures fighting for dominance in his brain.

Max eased his cock out of her and rolled away. His feet hit the floor and he all but ran to the bathroom.

"Jackson?"

His brother's name magnified the wolf's fury and the beast growled, the noise so loud it vibrated Max's skull.

"Just let me clean up, honey." He hoped she heard him. He couldn't distinguish sounds, couldn't block out the wolf. He slammed the bathroom door shut and leaned against it, forcing air into his lungs. He looked in the mirror. He hadn't made the change but he didn't look quite human either. His irises were glowing red and the front of his jaw was pushed out to accommodate the long canines.

He got rid of the condom, pulled up his jeans and splashed water on his face as he washed his hands. He didn't understand it. He'd fucked Mandy, the wolf had gotten what it wanted. What was the problem? Guilt tried to insert itself into his brain but the wolf silenced the annoying emotion. He'd deal with the human fact of having fucked his brother's woman once he was back in control.

He took a deep breath, the scent of Mandy on his skin calming the wolf enough that Max could think. Closing his eyes for a moment, he just breathed, letting the oxygen fill his body. The return to human came slow. His teeth retracted and a quick glance in the mirror told him his eyes were back to normal color. He inhaled again. The wolf was still restless. Still pacing the mental cage. Mandy's scent helped but there was something missing.

He leaned against the counter and flipped through the scene in his brain. Revelation struck. The wolf wanted more than Mandy's scent. He wanted to smell Max—Max's seed—on her, inside her. Marking her. He'd recognized the need when he'd been fucking her but why was the wolf so determined to come inside her?

Max groaned. *This isn't good.* He needed to get out of here. Bad enough that he'd fucked his brother's fiancée, even worse if he was to mark her, claim her.

Fucking her had been unforgivable. Claiming her would be suicidal.

He would walk out, grab his shirt and get the hell out of there. It was a coward's retreat but he didn't have the courage to face her. Not now.

Once he was away from her temptation, he had to find his brother and start the long painful process of apologizing. Maybe if he apologized over the phone, by the time they met face-to-face, Jax's anger would have subsided a bit.

Or the distance could give Jax time to plan the most painful way of killing his twin brother.

Right. Shirt, escape, apologize. He shook his head and tried to imagine Mandy's reaction when he walked back into the bedroom and left. He rarely lingered after sex—even with Dani, he didn't sleep over—but bolting from the bed moments after he'd come was beyond tacky.

But never had a woman affected him like Mandy.

Nodding at himself in the mirror to give himself that extra jab of confidence, he grabbed the doorknob and cranked it. He stepped into bedroom, his eyes immediately landing on his shirt lying in a pile at the foot of the bed.

He would have made it. He liked to tell himself he would have made it out if he hadn't looked up. Hadn't seen Mandy, lying on the bed, her body partially shielded by the sheet, her arms and legs rounded and soft. He let his gaze trail up her body. Her breasts were covered. His lips pulled back in a snarl. Those pretty tits belonged to him.

He lifted his eyes to meet hers. She blinked, modesty battling with obedience for just a moment. As if she could read his mind, she pulled the sheet back. He hummed his approval. Her nipples pulled up into tight peaks, begging for his mouth.

"Very good, honey. Don't ever hide that beautiful body from me." *It's mine.*

The final words remained behind his teeth but he heard them in his head. The need to imprint himself on her drove the logic from moments before from his brain.

As if he'd lost control of his own body, he moved forward, stripping off his jeans and freeing his cock, crawling back onto the bed, matching angle to curve until they fit together. Heat radiated between them, skin on skin, fire breeding fire.

The tension, the guilt, the panic—it all evaporated as he snuggled close.

Uncertainty flitted across Mandy's face. He bent down and placed a soft kiss on her lips.

Needing to be closer still, wanting to be inside her, he slid his leg over hers, easing his thigh between hers, pressing against her pussy. The wet heat coated his skin and he groaned, his cock twitching against her skin. A low catch in her throat told him she was feeling it as well. They weren't done with each other yet. The wolf settled, signaling its approval.

She tipped her head up and kissed him, gentle, tasting. He could live forever on her kisses.

On thing for sure, they were going to need more condoms.

He bent down and nuzzled her neck. "Honey, do you have more condoms?" He slid his hand down her stomach, teasing the top of her pussy with his middle finger. She squirmed under the caress and the scent of her arousal flooded the room. "I think we're going to need them." He managed to keep his voice light, teasing.

It took a second for her eyes to focus and he could tell she was trying to process his statement.

"Uh, yes." She looked at the bedside table to her left. "In the drawer."

He brushed a kiss across her mouth and rolled over her, climbing off the mattress. Might as well check out her stash now so he'd know how many times he could have her tonight. The wolf gave him almost endless sexual hunger—almost—but he had to make sure he didn't wear Mandy out.

He reached for the drawer, hearing Mandy's gasp as his fingers settled on the knob.

"No wait—"

Too late. Max had the drawer opened. An innate wickedness spurred him on, wanting to see what she had hidden inside. *Probably a vibrator or two.* Men always assumed women were home masturbating when they were alone.

Max felt his eyes widen as the contents of the drawer entered the light.

"No, you—"

Max flashed a silencing glance at Mandy and she groaned, sinking back on the bed, her forearm draped across her eyes.

Three condom packets lay in the corner. Neatly placed and within easy reach. A pale blue cylindrical vibrator rolled toward the front of the drawer. Max smiled. The sex-toy was just like its owner. Practical, efficient. It was there to do a job and really only had one purpose.

But it was the third item that caught Max's attention. A small butt plug.

"Hmm, Mandy, this is interesting."

She groaned. Knowing exactly what caused that comment. Damn it. This was just too mortifying. No one was ever supposed to see that thing. She hadn't even used it. Thought about it. Several times. But never found the courage.

"It's not mine." The instinctive protest fell from her lips. He raised his eyebrows, laughter sparkling in his eyes. "I mean, it is," she clarified. "But I've never used it. A friend gave it to me."

"A friend?" The question came out of his mouth as a low growl and she almost smiled. He didn't like that someone else was giving her sex toys?

"A *female* friend." Her cheeks, already warm, seemed on fire now. "We were talking about sex fantasies and..."

She let her words slip away. There was no need to explain. Really.

But the dangerous glint in his eyes warned she wasn't getting away without some sort of explanation.

She tensed, preparing for a long drawn-out teasing but he once again did the opposite of what she expected. He pulled out the condoms, dropped them on the tabletop and climbed back into bed, taking his place on her right side.

She blinked and looked up at him, offering a weak smile. He was really going to let it go with that?

He settled their bodies together, sharing kisses and light caresses—enough to keep her body humming but never quite pushing her to desperate need. She floated along, stroking her hands down his chest, testing the hard muscles with his fingers.

He propped his head up on his hand so he looked down at her and smiled.

"Now," he drawled, his finger stroking a hot path down the center of her chest. "I want to hear about this fantasy that involved a butt plug."

Her cheeks instantly heated.

"It didn't."

"Hmm?"

Another long stroke. The almost casual caresses clouded her mind.

"No. It was, you know." She closed her eyes and hid her face into his shoulder. "Two guys."

He didn't answer and she thought for sure he was probably grinning to high heaven. She took a breath and lifted her gaze, finding the courage to actually look at him.

He wasn't smiling. His eyes had that strange look again, almost like they were glowing but that was a little too science fiction for her mind to accept so she decided the light had to be hitting him just right.

"Is that what you want, honey?" He ran his fingers across her jaw. "Two guys fucking you?"

She shrugged, not sure if she should deny it or admit it. The Jackson she *thought* she knew would probably look at her like she was insane. The Jackson of tonight might find the idea amusing.

Either way, she decided for the truth.

"I think about it but it would never happen."

"Why not?" The slow strokes to her skin lulled her into blurting out the honest answer.

"Can you imagine two guys wanting to fuck me?"

He moved over her, holding his body above her. The serious glint in his eyes made her cringe. His gaze locked on hers.

"Yes."

"Yes?" she said, not remembering the question.

"I can imagine two guys wanting to fuck you. I can't imagine any man not wanting to have you."

If he'd said it with any laughter, or teasing, she might have handled it better. "Oh."

That brought a half-smile to his lips. "I can imagine you taking two hard cocks. Both of us fucking you, making you scream." He bit down on her lower lip adding a touch of pain. "But tonight…you're all mine."

He covered her mouth with his own, slipping his tongue between her lips, taking her response. As he pulled back, she chased him, wanting more. Light and lust twinkled in his eyes.

He reached over and grabbed a condom off the bedside table, leaving her with a kiss as he shifted and slid the shield on.

Moments before their loving had been hot and desperate, a frantic drive to come. This was so different. He rolled over, easing between her legs and guiding his cock into her pussy. A slow push and he sank into her, the gentle penetration almost sweet. Her body eased to take him.

"You'd look beautiful," he whispered. "Two hard cocks filling you. Fucking this tight cunt and your ass, until all you could feel was sex." He leaned down and brushed his lips across her neck, up to her cheek. "You look amazing when you come. Lost in your body. So beautiful."

He held himself still, his cock buried deep inside her. His hands skimmed down her sides as he slowly pulled back and returned, sliding into her slow and gentle. He groaned as he entered her again, a little harder. "But, honey, I don't know if I could handle another guy fucking your sweet cunt, knowing how hot you are. How wet you get." He continued to fuck her as he spoke, his thrusts getting stronger. He bent down and whispered the words against her neck. "It might be too sweet to share."

Her back arched, pressing up, rubbing her nipples against his chest. His hands left the delicate caresses and gripped her ass, pulling her up hard, driving his cock deeper into her. The heavy thrust illuminated her clit even as he filled her, doubly caressing her pussy.

"Mine," he growled. She looked up at him and gasped. A foreign light poured from his eyes, the red unmistakable. Like an animal's at night. The thought evaporated as soon as it entered her mind, fading to pure sensation. He continued to whisper, the actual words lost on her but the meaning was clear—he wanted to fuck her, again and again, in every position. His voice felt like a caress, teasing her clit even has his cock slid past it each time he filled her. Delicious light touches that blended with the hard thrusts, the solid penetration inside her.

Through the fog of sensation, she watched him lick his lips and reacted with pure instinct. She closed her eyes and tipped her head back, offering her throat. The animal growls returned as he bent down scraping his teeth across her skin, almost too painful but somehow just enough. He drove into her again and the combined caresses sparked her climax, sending shivers through her clit and pussy, spreading like fire through her limbs. Her fingers dug into his shoulders and a soundless gasp filled the air.

He groaned and pushed into her one more time. Tension reverberated through his body as he held himself buried in her cunt.

Breath filled the room as they both panted, trying to recover.

He bent forward, dropping his forehead on her shoulder.

"Honey." His lips whispered across her skin. "So delicious." He licked, soothing the teeth marks he'd left. "Need more. More."

Stunned and exhausted, her body reacted. She turned her head placed her lips on his. "Yes," she whispered against his mouth.

Chapter Six

"So, how'd last night go?"

Mandy looked up, not surprised to see Tracy standing beside her. When all this had started, she'd turned to Tracy for guidance. Once Jackson had come up with the idea, and Mandy had talked fast to convince Tracy this was a good idea, she'd been quite supportive. Or as supportive as a cop who couldn't officially get involved in what really wasn't supposed to be an investigation could get. Tracy had even helped her plan last night's meeting.

Funny, Mandy mused. When she thought of last night, the meeting at the restaurant barely blipped on her radar. Her mind went straight to sex. And Jackson. *And oh, my.*

The memory washed over her. Her nipples tightened and pushed against her bra. Her pussy clenched as if reliving the long hours of having him inside her. Mandy squirmed on the hard, wooden chair, not sure if she was trying to ease the sensation or make it worse. She'd never reacted to a memory before. But it was one heck of a memory. Her body ached. Her thigh muscles were stretched and sore and she'd felt almost raw this morning but oh she wouldn't have changed a moment of it.

"It was amazing." She winced at the dreamy sound of her own voice but couldn't resist another soft sigh. Despite the minor aches and pains of too much, really good sex, her body hummed today, rejoicing that it had been so well used.

"And they bought it?"

The question jolted Mandy out of her thoughts. "Who? Sean and Brian? Sure. No problem."

"No, not just you wanting to work for them. They bought the whole act?" A strange tone lurked beneath Tracy's question.

"Yes." Mandy adjusted her purse strap over her shoulder and stood. "I don't know what you're getting at."

"Well, you said you were introducing Jackson as your fiancé, right?"

"Yes. I thought it was the best way to get them to trust him. And since neither of you would let me do this on my own…" She let the words trail off, hoping to make Tracy feel at least a little bit guilty that she didn't think Mandy could do it on her own. Tracy ignored her subtle taunt.

"And they didn't catch on that you two aren't really a couple?" Her eyebrows squished together.

Mandy drew back, more than a little offended. She wasn't the world's best actress but she'd played Lady Macbeth in her high school production. She could certainly fake a night with her fiancé.

"Did you think they would?"

Tracy shrugged. "Kind of. I mean when you see the two of you together it's kind of obvious."

"*What's* obvious?"

"That you aren't sleeping together. I mean, face it, there is no chemistry between you two."

Mandy couldn't stop the smile that spread her lips. "Oh there was chemistry." Lots of it. Like a lab explosion.

"Really?"

"Oh yeah." She couldn't keep the memories out of her voice and knew she had to be blushing.

Tracy's eyes widened and she leaned closer. The sounds of phones ringing and voices talking could cover a lot of conversations. "So, tell me more. Details, details."

Mandy laughed but didn't back up. "No details." But she just had to share. She glanced around to see if anyone was near. "Just enough to say it was amazing. *He* was amazing."

Tracy's eyes got wide. "Really? Wow. I never would have imagined that—you know, just looking at him." She shrugged. "I mean, he's gorgeous and all but a little stiff, huh?"

Parts of him. Mandy suppressed the giggle.

"There was something different about him last night—" and this morning. "Incredible." It was all she could do not to lick her lips and groan.

"Based on the twinkle in your eyes, I have to believe you. And you're sure it was Jackson right? Not some evil twin who took his place?"

Mandy laughed. "Don't be silly." Jackson's brother lived in Las Vegas. She wasn't sure he'd ever been to Alaska.

"I'll take your word for it." Tracy straightened and pulled on the bottom of her equipment vest. She slapped her hands across the pockets, making sure everything was in place, finishing with the gun on her hip. "There's your friend now." Tracy lifted her chin toward the door behind Mandy. She glanced back and saw Detective Banner heading her way.

"Not exactly that," she muttered. The corners of the detective's mouth were already pinched with irritation. He wasn't happy to see her.

"Don't let him intimidate you." Tracy's voice was low and meant for Mandy only.

She nodded, trying to borrow Tracy's confidence. She lifted her chin and pushed her shoulders back, smiling at the detective as he walked by.

"I'm getting coffee," he said. "I'll be right back."

"Great."

Tracy watched him go then shook her head. "I'd better get to work. Let's meet for lunch. I want to hear about last night."

"No details," Mandy insisted.

"I meant the dinner meeting. Your mind is all about sex isn't it?"

Mandy laughed, the tension of facing Detective Banner easing just a bit.

"Fine. Time?"

"One?"

"Scotties?" It was this hole-in-the-wall sub shop in downtown but the food was good and they usually hit the mall afterward. Mandy liked to wander downtown with Tracy in full uniform.

"I'll see you there. And yes, I expect details." She laughed and walked away moments before Detective Banner arrived at Mandy's other side.

"Good morning. How're you?"

Great. I had the best sex of my life last night.

She let the words amuse her brain but she didn't say them aloud. The detective didn't really care about her life.

"I'm good. And you?" She blinked her eyelashes innocently knowing that he didn't enjoy social niceties.

"I'm fine."

The grim set of Banner's lips warned he still didn't like the situation. He'd wanted, expected the investigation to end with her father's death. After all, he'd been all but convicted of embezzlement and fraud. But Mandy wasn't giving up. Her father was not a crook. She was going to find the money or at least find proof her father hadn't taken it.

"Come into my office."

Mandy nodded and followed the gruff detective into his office. Activity surged around her but she felt strangely comfortable. Until six months ago, she'd never been to the police station. Now she knew how to make coffee in their break room and could greet a half a dozen detectives and officers by name. Most of them were friendly but busy.

She settled into the chair across from Detective Banner.

"What can I do for you this morning?"

She'd met with the detective every week since her father's death two months ago. Mostly she'd asked questions. Now she was starting to demand answers. Or progress. Something.

"Did anything come of the papers I dropped off last week?" She'd finally gotten around to cleaning out her father's office and discovered some of her father's papers. Despite what she'd told Sean and Brian, she hadn't found a second set of books for Oyltech but it didn't hurt for them to be guessing. Wondering. Detective Banner had grudgingly agreed to have a forensic accountant look at the documents she had found. They wouldn't exonerate her father but maybe there would be doubt and that would lead to proof that he was an honest man. He never would have done what they accused him of.

"Nothing yet." She opened her mouth to protest but he held up his hand. "They are working on it. We're not a big enough department to have a full time forensic accountant on staff. He's working on it. Says there might be something there."

She did her best not too look too smug.

"Good. And I'll just keep looking from my end."

Banner's eyes squinted down. "How do you plan to do that?"

"I met with a couple of the executives from Oyltech last night and I've accepted a job with them."

Banner sat up in his chair, the springs creaking as he leaned forward. "You what?"

"I'm going to take over the accounting work that my father was doing."

"Aren't these the people you think set your father up?"

"Yes."

"So what? You're suddenly Nancy Drew, going undercover?"

"It's not exactly undercover. They know who I am." She kept her spine straight. "I'm just going to do some work for them and..." She shrugged. "Look around a bit, see what I can find."

"No."

She smiled. "Detective, you can't tell me I can't work for them. And since you no longer seem interested in investigating this, I will. And once I have the answers, I'll let you know."

She stood up, clutching her purse in both hands.

"No, no. Wait. Sit down. Let's talk about this." His voice was a little more reasonable and Mandy's knees were shaking more than she wanted to let on so sinking back into her seat was a good idea. "Now, tell me about this meeting."

An hour and a half later, she walked out of the police station and trudged to her car.

It was exhausting being grilled by a police detective. She'd been ready to confess just to get away. Detective Banner had asked her questions and re-asked them until the story was so firmly set in her mind she'd be reciting it in her sleep.

Not that she had any clear idea of what she was going to do once she actually got inside the company that accused her father of embezzling. It wasn't as if she expected to find a file that said "how to frame Charles Pengrass for embezzlement in three easy steps" but she was sure if she got a chance to go over their books—and maybe found a way to hack into their computer system—she'd find proof that her father didn't do all the things they said he did. She believed him. Now she just needed to convince the rest of the world.

She smiled. Except Jackson. He believed.

She opened her car door and plopped down into the seat. The early hum in her body had faded to a dull thud.

She tapped her fingernail on the steering wheel. She could call him. A phone call couldn't be out of line after last night.

Men could seriously not expect a woman to call after a night like that. She bit her lower lip. Would it sound desperate if she called? Did she really care?

Heck, he was probably already at the office. Jackson was never late. Maybe she could distract him with a little morning-after sex.

She groaned and willed away the sudden throb between her legs. She had a job to do. A quick glance at her clock told her it was past time she got to work. Jackson would no doubt want an update of her meeting with Detective Banner and she needed to get some work done before she met Tracy for lunch.

Agreeing to lunch had probably been a bad idea. Tracy would hound her for details and Mandy was more than a little afraid she would spill. She gripped the steering wheel and made a vow.

She wasn't sharing the amazing night with anyone.

But she was going to replay it in her mind over and over again.

It was like he'd been desperate for her, wild, almost feral. She squeezed her thighs together as her pussy reacted to her thoughts. She bit her tongue and smiled. *Wonder what Jackson is doing now?* His office was right across the hall from hers and he had a lock on the door. She could just slip inside and…

She stopped the fantasy right there. There was time for more of that later, after she'd done some work.

Even knowing she wasn't actually going to call Jackson and ask him for a midmorning quickie, she grabbed her cell phone from the glove box where she'd left it last night. He was on her speed dial. It wouldn't take much. *Do it. Be daring.* He'd seemed to like that last night, when she'd taken the initiative. Not that he'd let her lead for long but he'd let her guide their lovemaking. Actually, he'd let her beg and plead and then, finally, eventually, when she'd been a puddle of sexual desire, he'd given in.

She dropped her head back against the shoulder rest, her heart pounding at the memory of that first, hard penetration. He'd taken his time, filling her up slowly until all she could feel was him and…drat, she needed to do some work. She couldn't spend the rest of the morning daydreaming.

Do it, be daring. Grabbing onto the voice in her head like a lifeline, she flipped the phone and saw she'd missed a call while she'd been in the meeting with Banner.

A call from an unknown number.

She sighed and hit voicemail button, waited while the phone did its thing, connected, input her pass code. Impatience tightened her jaw by the time the friendly female voice said, "You have one new message. To hear your message—"

Mandy hit one and waited.

"do dinner. Call me." An unfamiliar woman's voice echoed in the background. "Oh, Mandy, sorry just listening to another message." Her mind latched onto the voice—Jackson. She started to smile but her lips didn't quite make the curve. Mandy. She'd been "honey" last night. Or Amanda when she'd been bad.

And his voice was devoid of the sexual, dominant tones of last night. That wasn't a good sign.

"Uh, anyway, listen." His tone grew serious and she could almost see him turning away from whatever was distracting him. "I wanted to call and apologize for last night. I'm really sorry. I hope I didn't screw things up completely."

Her heart dropped to her stomach and an invisible weight crushed her chest until she couldn't breathe.

Jackson continued. "There's a good explanation—or at least, it's some kind of explanation. I just, I'd rather talk to you in person. Anyway, I'm sorry about last night. I'll call you later."

She stared at the phone, willing her lungs to start working again and her heart to slow from its current on-the-verge-of-explosion pace. He was sorry? Last night had been the most incredible sexual experience in her life and Jackson was *sorry*? She didn't know whether to cry or scream.

"To save this message, press one. To delete this message, press two. To replay this message, press three." *Replay it? Are you insane?* Fury and mortification mixed in her veins and she dug her finger into the second button and listened with some satisfaction as the voicemail lady said, "Message erased."

Mandy closed her phone and smacked it on the dashboard. *Good thing I listened to my messages before I called him and offered him a little lunchtime nookie which he is obviously not interested in. At least not from me.*

I'm sorry about last night. Heck, she didn't need to save the message in her phone. She would hear it in her head all day.

* * * * *

Mandy took a sip of her coffee and sighed. It wasn't from pure pleasure—coffee was merely filler in her diet. She really didn't want to be here. When Tracy had called to confirm lunch, she'd considered crying off. It wasn't like she didn't have tons to do. But she needed to talk.

And at least here she didn't have to risk running into Jackson. He hadn't been to work all morning. Coward.

Tracy came in, her uniform a little less crisp than it had been a few hours ago. The bottoms of her pants were muddy and her boots were coated as well. She grimaced as she stamped her shoes on the rug then bypassed Mandy altogether, heading for the order counter. Moments later, a soda cup in her hand, she came to the table and plopped down.

"Long morning?" Mandy asked.

"Messy morning. Had to clear out some guys from the woods."

"At least it's not snowing."

"Yet." Tracy sipped her coffee and sat forward. "Okay, now. Spill. I need details about this wild and wicked night with the accountant."

Mandy sighed. "No details, except one." She tapped her finger on top of her phone, as if keeping the thing handy made it real. Hell, she could live with the pain. It was the embarrassment that was going to haunt her. How was she ever going to face Jackson again?

"What?" Tracy prompted. She must have seen the change in Mandy because her voice lost its teasing tone.

"He called and apologized."

"For what?"

"For sleeping with me."

Tracy's head snapped back. "What?!" Her irritation on Mandy's behalf soothed some of the pain. She took another sip of coffee.

"The most wild, incredible night of my life and he leaves a message on my voicemail saying he's sorry for last night and hopes he didn't screw things up."

The tension drained out of Tracy's body. "Oh? Is that it?"

"Is that it? The man regrets having sex with me. That's a pretty big deal to me." She huffed out her breath. "I mean, I thought he'd enjoyed himself. He acted like he had and it wasn't like it was just the one time." Lost in her own thoughts, she shook her head and stared at the paper menu taped to the wall. "Don't you think that if he wasn't enjoying himself he'd have stopped with just once?"

"Instead of how many times?"

Blinking over at Tracy, she realized she'd been speaking aloud. "Uh, four?"

"Four!" Tracy's hand jerked and her cup tipped over. With perfect reflexes, she caught it before it could fall, spilling only a few drops from the opening in the lid. After she'd placed the cup back on the table, she leaned forward. "You mean you had four orgasms? In one night?"

Mandy felt her cheeks turn red and knew she should just stop here but the intent look on Tracy's face warned she wasn't going away without an answer.

"No."

Tracy sighed and appeared relieved. "Okay. I feel a little better."

"No, four was just the number of separate times we, kind of, you know, got started." Mandy couldn't believe she was actually saying these words out loud but couldn't quite get herself to stop. "A couple of times I came twice, except that first time." She chewed on her thumbnail, mentally counting back through the night. "Unless you don't count what happened downstairs as a separate incident, then it was three times but that means three, or was it four—?"

She realized that Tracy wasn't responding. She looked across the small table. Tracy's mouth opened then shut then opened again. "Let me get this straight, you had sex with Jackson—a man I've met and who, let me tell you, doesn't come across as Mr. High Sex Drive—and you came a half a dozen times."

Mandy's blush grew deeper and she looked around to see if anyone was listening. "I wasn't actually counting at the time."

"The exact number doesn't matter. The thing is, you cannot let this man get away. At least until you're done with him."

"He called and apologized."

"Because he thinks he screwed up."

"Yes!"

"Mandy, honey, he's just going through the typical male reaction to having sex with a friend. He's worried that he's messed up your friendship by sleeping with you. He's probably thinking you're sitting here rehashing last night's events and you're regretting it, or God forbid, planning your wedding. It was a preemptive strike. Trust me, if a guy reaches for you four times in one night, he's either been in prison for ten years or he's interested in you."

It sounded so logical when Tracy said it. "Okay, but what am I supposed to do now?"

"Seduce him."

Mandy laughed. "I think we're a little past the seduction stage."

"You're never past the seduction stage. And all you have to do is show him that you want to continue the sexual relationship." Tracy's eyebrows dipped low. "You do want to, don't you?"

"Well yes."

"Good, I didn't want to have to spend my afternoon having you committed." Tracy stood up. "Let's get our food to go. We're going to hit the mall. You and I are going shopping for some wickedly sexy underwear and we'll come up with a plan."

"Right, a plan to seduce Jackson." Mandy laughed, feeling better already. Not that she actually planned to seduce Jackson but Tracy's support eased some of the pain. "Why don't we just skip the underwear and I'll just stand naked in his living room?"

Tracy clapped her hands together. "Good, good. I like the way you think. We'll refine the plan as we shop."

Tracy headed toward the door and Mandy had no choice but to follow.

It was insane of course. No way was she going to stand in Jackson's living room naked. No way.

Chapter Seven

ꙮ

Max groaned and rolled over, wishing the pounding in his head was from a hangover but recognizing the guilt thumping the inside of his skull.

He'd made love to Mandy. He'd made love to Jax's fiancée. He'd more than made love to her—he'd fucked her into the mattress. God knew how she'd found the strength to get up and go to work. He could barely move.

He'd woken up when she'd started the shower and though he considered joining her, he knew she had to be too sore to take him again. So he'd waited for her to return, fully intending to pretend being asleep until she left. But the delicious scent of her pussy and the spike of arousal when she came near had been too much and he hadn't been able to resist reaching for her again, tasting her. He smiled at the memory. He hadn't even come and it didn't bother him. The taste of her had been enough.

He licked his lips, searching for a hint of the delicious flavor.

He pushed his head back into the pillow and closed his eyes.

I'm such an asshole. Jax is going to kill me.

He'd always been a bit of a player. Admitted it, even reveled in that reputation but there were some things that were just off limits, and fucking his brother's woman had to be at the top of that list.

Damn, his mother had always warned him. Said when he fell, it would be hard. Like millions of rocks tipping off a mountain.

Max tried to soothe his noisy conscience by saying he hadn't meant it to happen. He'd planned to explain that she'd spent the evening with the wrong brother. But then she'd been there, her breasts pushing against that tight T-shirt, nipples hard and tight. And damn, somehow his lips had been on hers and after that there had been no stopping that train. He'd had to taste all of her. Her lips, her skin, the sweet liquid between her legs.

He groaned. Damn she'd tasted sweet. Like candy melting on his tongue.

He reached down and wrapped his fingers around his cock, hard and ready.

The fiery memory of sliding into her cunt, filling it and feeling it stretch swirled around his cock and he tightened his fist. Stroking the hard flesh, silently promising himself that he'd be inside her again soon.

No, fuck, he couldn't do that. In fact, he had to tell her she'd had sex with the wrong brother.

The guilt returned, nudging aside any seductive thoughts. Even his cock started to wilt.

First, he had to talk to his brother and confess. It was probably better to confess to Jax first and get his advice on how to tell Mandy. Hell, maybe *Jax* would want to tell Mandy. Maybe Jax would *have* to tell Mandy because Jax was going to kill Max when he found out.

Max could understand the reaction. He'd kill anyone who touched her or tried to touch her. Or looked at her funny.

His wolf growled his approval of Max's thoughts. Max pulled back. Strange. The wolf was an elemental creature, focused on the basics of food, sleep, safety and sex. So why was the creature echoing, hell, practically encouraging Max's weird possessive streak? Jax would probably know and he could ask him, once he found his brother.

Reluctant to leave the warmth of Mandy's bed, he rolled over and reached for his jeans. His phone had rung at some point in the night. He'd heard it but he'd been buried in Mandy's cunt and nothing could have pulled him away.

He glanced at his incoming calls and immediately recognized the number. Dani. Fuck. More guilt. Sure he and Dani were "on a break" but he wasn't sure that meant he could sleep with another woman. He hadn't even considered Dani last night.

He sagged back onto the pillow and dropped his forearm across his eyes as he hit the message button.

He waited. The voicemail connected, but silence echoed through the phone. A male voice rumbled unrecognizable words.

"Oh, Max, it's Dani." He waited for her to launch into her message but there was more quiet. Not quite silence. The phone captured the hitch of her breath. Another masculine prompt. "Uh, Max, it's Dani. Oh wait, I already said that." *What the fuck?* He sat up, holding the phone close, listening to the background sounds. "Listen, I think we should…oh God, uhm, sorry, Max, right." He stared blindly at the quilt covering his legs. He knew those sounds, recognized the breathless voice. Dani was being fucked. While she was calling him. "I think it might be better if we—"

Her voice cut off again. Whoever was fucking her was doing a damn good job of it. She had amazing amounts of focus. "What the—? Oh fuck. Yes."

His dick hardened. Not that he necessarily wanted to fuck Dani but damn, the sexual sounds coming from her would make a dead man hard.

The male voice interrupted again, low and indistinguishable.

"Oh, right, Max." Good to know he was so memorable. He smiled and shook his head. Strange that the jealousy he would have expected was missing. The fact that Dani was fucking another guy actually helped his own guilt. No need to tell her about Mandy when she was getting horizontal with another guy a week after their "break" started. "Listen, I think we should just consider this break permanent."

The air rushed out of his lungs. She'd ended it. A break was one thing but it was nice to have something to fall back on.

"It's definitely permanent." He swore he heard another groan. Damn, what the fuck was this guy doing to her? "Well, have a good night. Bye." Max pulled the phone away from his ear and stared at it. *Have a good night? Is she insane?*

He fell back onto the mattress and looked up at the ceiling. She'd broken up with him—on voicemail. That was a level of tackiness even he hadn't sunk to. *No, you just fucked your brother's woman without even thinking about the woman you were engaged to.*

He ignored his own smarmy conscience. Whatever the guy had been doing to Dani, she'd been unable to focus on a conversation that should have taken twenty seconds. Hmm, interesting.

The shrill jangle of his phone jolted him out of his thoughts. He didn't recognize the number but it was local. He rolled over as he answered. The perfume of Mandy's hair lingered on the pillow and he couldn't resist burying his face in the soft material and breathing deeply. Letting her scent fill him.

"Hello." His voice sounded rough, well used. Probably from whispering to Mandy all night. He couldn't resist telling her what he wanted to do to her, how deep he wanted to go, how good she felt on his cock. Oh fuck. His hips pumped forward, rubbing his dick against the sheets.

"Max?"

He quickly processed the masculine voice on the other end of the line.

"Hey, Gideon."

"Hey. Have you heard from Jackson?"

"No." Max paused and looked around the room. Mandy's room. Jax might have come home last night but Max hadn't been there. "He didn't call again."

"Okay. I guess...well, those guys you were meeting with last night, Jackson didn't trust them. That's why they arranged to meet at my place."

"I don't trust them either but they didn't seem surprised to see me there. I think Jax is really just out of town. He sounded okay on the phone."

"Good. That's all I was checking on." There was another long pause. "And to see what you had planned for the day?"

"Hadn't thought that far ahead."

"I have a million ideas."

Gideon's tone dropped, taking on a seductive sound that triggered Max's memory of the kiss they'd shared last night. His cock, half hard from his Mandy fantasies came back to full strength. He wrapped his fingers around the thick shaft and gave a few strokes. The wolf came awake and growled, the sound pure pleasure in Max's head. His thoughts shifted back to sex, only Mandy wasn't starring in his fantasies—they were led by a strong male body, tan skin that made Max eager to taste. He licked his lips. Mandy's flavor lingered and it blended perfectly with the memory of Gideon's kiss, that hard body against his, the first slow touch to his cock.

He groaned and pushed his head into the pillow, pressing his hips up, driving his cock through his fingers.

"Max?"

Gideon's voice pierced the fantasy just enough to let him focus.

"Sorry, stubbed my toe."

Again, Gideon laughed, as if he knew Max was lying. "Right. Anyway, plans? Today?"

"I'm open to whatever."

"Ooh, don't tempt me."

It was Max's turn to laugh. "What did you have in mind?"

"How about a hike into the Chugach Mountains?"

Max nodded. That sounded good. A chance to get out, move, be near the earth. That might soothe his wolf, calm the creature enough so he didn't flip out the way he had last night.

"Sounds good."

"Should I come get you?"

Max started to agree then froze. "Uh, wait." He flipped back the blankets and shivered as his feet hit the cold floor. He calculated how long it would take him to get home. And shower.

"Uh, give me thirty, no make it forty-five minutes."

* * * * *

Max dug through Jax's kitchen drawers to find a marker and a sheet of paper. In big block letters he wrote, "Jax, where the hell are you? Call me. Max." Just in case Jax came home. He'd said he was out of town. That could mean across the country or a fifty-five minute flight from Fairbanks. Hard to tell with Jax.

Max plopped the note on the center of the dining table as the front doorbell rang. He grabbed his coat and tugged it on. He took a long inhale as he got close to the door, taking a moment to catalogue the scents. The room smelled like Jax, naturally, but the faint scent of Gideon on the other side of the door made Max's body tighten. Even jacking off in the shower hadn't helped. Just the thought of Gideon or Mandy made Max was hard again. He'd always had a high sex drive—it was the norm in the werewolf community—but this was ridiculous.

He took another breath, this one to calm his nerves and opened the door. Gideon looked up and smiled, then he did a slow scan down Max's body. He recognized the look. He'd used it on hundreds of women—that sexual stare that said "baby let's fuck and I'll make you scream"—but he'd never been the object of it. And damn if he finally understood the power of it.

He held himself still, letting the inspection occur, hoping his dick wasn't too obvious, that his jeans managed to contain the burgeoning erection.

The smile teasing Gideon's lips and the spark in his eyes told Max that Gideon had seen he was hard. But Gideon didn't say anything. Instead he nodded toward the jacket Max had pulled on.

"Cold?"

"Yes."

"It's summer."

"It's summer but it's Alaska so it's still cold."

Gideon laughed. "It's not that bad. It's supposed to be in the mid-sixties today."

"It was over a hundred when I left Vegas."

"Yeah, your brother was like that when he first moved up here too. Got over it pretty fast."

"Good for him." He knew he sounded a little bitchy but honestly wasn't that better than grabbing the guy and humping like a dog in heat?

As he turned to lock the door, his cell phone thumped against his side. Out of habit, he pulled it out and checked it. After missing the call last night, he wasn't sure about his coverage. But at this point he wasn't sure he wanted to talk to his brother. Would Jax be able to recognize Max's guilt over the phone?

"Did he call?"

"Huh? Oh, no."

If he actually talked to his brother, he was going to have to confess what he'd done. The more he'd thought about it, the more he realized he didn't want to do that on the phone. He needed to do it face-to-face, where he could watch Jax's reaction.

What the hell do you think his reaction's going to be? Max's obnoxious conscience asked. *You fucked his fiancée. More than once.* After the second time, he'd allowed Mandy to sleep even though his wolf urged him to take her again. Courtesy said he should let her sleep or even better get the hell out of her house before he made it any worse. But being so close and the scents of their bodies mixing together…Max couldn't resist and in the middle of the night he'd woken her, fucking her slow and steady. She'd barely been awake but she'd come sweet and soft, her orgasm easing her back into sleep.

Max groaned. He didn't need a reminder of that.

"You okay?"

Yeah, except for the perpetual hard-on.

He was glad he didn't actually speak the words. Gideon might think they referred to him. Which they kind of did. The scent of the other male was intense, totally different from Mandy, spicy and warm. Strong. He leaned forward, his mind not thinking anything except getting closer to that smell, that warmth. That taste. He licked his lips anticipating the flavor.

"Max?"

He jerked and took a step back. "Sorry."

A wicked light flicked through Gideon's eyes and Max's cock twitched. Dangerous man.

"No problem. Let's go."

They got to the Ford Escape in Jax's driveway and climbed in. As Gideon pulled into the street, he asked, "How did the rest of the night go?"

Max sat up, guilt tightening all his muscles.

"What do you mean?"

"How did Mandy react when you told her?" Gideon glanced to his right.

"Uhhhhh."

"What does that sound mean?"

Gideon's stare bounced between the road and him. Max didn't know how to respond without lying.

"You didn't tell her."

It wasn't a question. Max forced his eyes forward. For some reason he didn't think he wanted to see the look on Gideon's face.

"No." *Just let it go.* Don't ask any more questions, he silently begged. Because for some reason, Max couldn't find it in himself to lie about this.

"That might be awkward later." *More than you know.* The car slowed and Gideon looked at him. "Max, what happened?" Max opened his mouth to answer but the words just wouldn't come out. "Oh fuck. You slept with Mandy."

Max winced.

"How—?"

"I don't know!" Max exploded. "I planned to tell her and then I showed up and she smelled so good."

"She smelled good?"

Gideon didn't sound like he believed it. Max smiled, thinking about the way her ass moved when she walked. "Yes. Damn good." Max lost himself in the memory. "And the next thing I know I'm on my knees with my face buried between her legs." He closed his eyes and winced. Fuck, hadn't meant to say that. "Forget I said that." Max silently begged for aliens to come and take him away for anal probes. Anything had to be better than this.

Hell, confessing to Gideon was hard. Confessing to Jax was going to be torture. Brutal, knuckle-breaking torture.

Gideon was silent for a long time, driving Max through the unfamiliar streets.

Finally, he said, "So that's why you don't seem as worried about finding Jackson. You don't want to tell him you had sex with his girlfriend."

Gideon's tone was the perfect mixture of mockery and reprimand.

"Fuck you."

"Is that an offer?" Gideon's voice changed, turning from mockery to flirtation. Max's cock twitched in response.

He swallowed and forced his lips to form what his mind knew was the right answer. "Uh, no."

Gideon chuckled, as if he knew how close Max was to "yes".

"Too bad." Gideon turned into a large open parking lot.

"What's this?" He lifted his chin toward the building. Alaska Rock Gym. "I thought we were going hiking."

"We are. I was thinking you might want to climb first." Again Gideon flashed that assessing gaze up and down Max's body. "You look a little tense. And since sex doesn't appear to be an option—oh wait, I mean *more* sex—" He winked. "How about a hard workout and then a little fresh air? Cleanse the body if not the spirit?"

Max nodded. He needed something physical. Well, something physical besides fucking. Needed to exhaust himself so he would be too tired to act on any of the crazed sensations going through his body. Because the combination of his own scent and Gideon's was making his already-hard dick hurt. He leaned back in the seat, trying to ease the constriction across his groin. The movement rubbed his jeans across his erection and he grabbed the door handle, clinging to it instead of ripping open his fly and begging Gideon to suck him off.

Max had a few gay friends and they all teased him about having a guy suck him off. Said there was nothing like it. Particularly someone who enjoyed it. He glanced at Gideon. Based on that kiss last night, Gideon knew how to use his mouth.

His mind, guided by his wolf, flipped into fantasy—Gideon on his knees, his lips wrapped around Max's cock, sucking hard.

"Max, let's go." Gideon's call yanked him from the dream his mind and his wolf conspired to create. He hesitated, giving his cock a hard thump to make the damn thing subside. The pain did its job and Max climbed out of the car and followed Gideon into the building.

He had done some climbing at Red Rock outside of Vegas but he'd never been inside a rock gym. He listened as Gideon walked him through the safety harnesses and belaying. After a quick tour, they moved to the harder climbing walls. Yeah, climbing was a good idea. A good way to expend some of the extra energy ripping through is body.

He just wasn't expecting how almost naked they would be.

Gideon grabbed the back of his shirt and pulled it up and off, revealing a strong muscular chest. Max went still, watching the tight muscles across Gideon's stomach flex and ripple, the smooth cut lines of his pecs and biceps. His wolf growled and Max licked his lips, the urge to taste some of that hard male flesh requiring a tactile satisfaction. His cock leapt and he felt the press of material against his growing erection.

Gideon's mouth quirked up in an arrogant smile. Max dragged his gaze away. *Yeah, fucking your brother's fiancée wasn't bad enough. Now you're going to fuck his best friend? Don't think so. Get it under control.* The internal pep talk seemed to help a bit as did the fast hard breath. Feeling a little more in command of his body, he stripped off his shirt and climbed into the borrowed harness. He needed to go first. Needed to make his body move.

Gideon seemed okay with that and took up his position to belay for Max. Max hooked in and felt the rope go tight. Ready to climb. Max pulled his shoulders back and reached for the first handhold, pulling himself up. The genetics of being a werewolf gave him extra strength so he made it more challenging than it had to be, barely using his legs, dragging himself to the top with just his finger strength. Gideon's voice cheered him on, the friendly sound at the bottom of the wall making him work harder. Sweat dripped from his body as he neared the finish, the strain in his shoulders and hands a good ache, something so completely not sexual. He pulled himself up toward the last handhold, reaching out to brush the bell that hung at top.

Gideon cheered and Max laughed. His dick was no longer threatening to break free of his clothes, his muscles were getting that pleasant soreness of too much use. Yeah, he might make it through the day.

He leaned back, confident that Gideon could hold him, and walked himself down the wall.

As he unhooked his harness, Gideon came over. "Great job, man."

"Thanks, ba—" Babe. Damn. He'd just about called Gideon "babe". He crushed the word and mentally slapped himself.

Gideon didn't seem to notice. "That was some serious upper body strength." The words caressed Max's skin, turning sexual in a way that made him ache. Gideon might be teasing but the effect of his words on Max's body were real enough.

"Thanks," he said, not sure he was strong enough to look at Gideon without reacting. "You ready to go up?" But he had no choice. He had to do a safety check. Max stepped close and checked Gideon's harness, the backs of his fingers brushing against the tight warm skin of his stomach. The low ripples of Gideon's muscles tempted his fingers. He licked his lips, imagining running his tongue across every groove.

Oh yeah. Gideon held still as Max worked slowly through the safety check, trying to tell his fingers to move faster but unable to get any response. It was all he could do not to stroke the tight skin. He forced his mind to focus, making sure the harness fit properly. God forbid his distraction put Gideon at risk. He tugged on the front clasp and stepped away.

"You're good."

"I know." Max's head snapped up. Gideon winked. "I'm *very* good."

Max's cock twitched. *I don't doubt it.* Those words filled his head but outwardly he rolled his eyes.

"Climb," he ordered not really sure what else to say except "I'd like to find out" and that wasn't something he was ready to admit. At least not out loud. Hell, he was having issues with hearing the words in his mind.

But all that disappeared as Gideon headed up the wall. His muscles stretched and lengthened and Max couldn't help but watch. The wolf in his head rumbled, the sound vibrating the inside of his brain. Max hummed low, liking the way the noise echoed in his head.

He watched Gideon, his eyes going to the man's ass and the thought of wrapping his hands around those tight muscles filled his head. The fantasy quickly shifting to Mandy's ass, squeezing as he pumped into her, his cock gripped by her tight pussy.

Yeah, that's it.

Gideon approached the side of the bed, his eyes glittering with lust. He leaned down and offered his mouth to Max in a long, deep kiss. Max groaned, taking Gideon's tongue. Small hot hands slid up his chest, teasing his nipples. He pulled away, fighting to draw back from the intoxicating kiss. Mandy smiled, licking her lips.

"You look good together," she whispered. Gideon grinned and leaned in, kissing Mandy. Max watched and slowly fucked his cock into her, short steady thrusts. She moaned and reached up, cupping her hand around the back of Gideon's neck, holding him in place as Max fucked her pussy and Gideon tongue-fucked her mouth.

Gideon slid his fingers over her tight nipple, just adding to the pressure. She arched up, stretching that sweet body even as she cried out, the sound muffled against Gideon's lips. Her cunt tightened around Max's cock and he fought his own orgasm. He didn't want to come, not yet. He groaned and pulled out, drawing back. Gideon met him, one more kiss before he crawled between Mandy's sleek thighs taking Max's place between her legs.

Gideon leaned forward and placed his mouth on Mandy's pussy. Max watched for a moment, captivated by the sight of Gideon's tongue slipping between her wet folds. The other male arched his back, highlight the long line of his body. The need to fuck, to be a part of the scene before him, drove him on. Max crawled up behind Gideon's strong male body, the sleek taut ass tipped up and offered to him. He eased the tip of his cock into the tight hole. Gideon tensed and lifted his head taking a breath before returning his attentions to Mandy's cunt. She moaned and her fingers bit into his skin. "Make her scream, babe, while I fuck this tight little ass."

Matching groans echoed from both his lovers as he pressed forward, heat searing his dick, making him harder as he pushed deep—

"Max, stay with me." Gideon's voice zapped the Max back to reality. He snapped his head back and looked up. Gideon hung on the wall, fingers and arms straining, the rope dangling between his legs. A sure sign that Max hadn't been paying attention.

His muscles contracted as he went up the next level. The guy was strong and lean and hot and the realty of fucking him would probably blow Max's fantasies away.

Not that he was ever going to find out.

At least if you fucked Gideon, he wouldn't be mistaking you for Jackson.

Max slapped the annoying voice in his head pulled the rope back taut. "Sorry, man." Thank God Gideon hadn't fallen while Max had taken his little trip to fantasyland. He nodded to Gideon, giving him the go-ahead to finish the climb, refusing the temptation to imagine what it would feel like to have that tight ass pressed against his hips. He'd never found other males attractive before—or not so attractive that he actually considered fucking them—but something about Gideon fascinated him. And his wolf. The horny creature practically panted in Max's ear.

He shook his head, forcing his mind to concentrate on belaying for Gideon. He shouted out encouragement as

Gideon strained in a particularly difficult section. "Come on, man. You can do it. To your left. Reach out, babe, you've got it."

The pet name slipped out but Gideon didn't seem to notice. He reached the top—his smile sparkling as he tapped the bell. Max cheered and then gripped the rope, applying pressure as Gideon rappelled down. His feet hit the ground and Max dropped the rope. He walked over as Gideon undid his harness.

"Sorry about that, man," he apologized. "I wouldn't have let you fall."

"No stress. But you phased out on me. You okay? What's going on?"

"You don't want to know."

A shrewd look filled Gideon's eyes. "I think maybe I do." He flicked his hair out of his face and stared into Max's gaze. "It's only fair, don't you think?"

Max considered the other man for a few moments. *Aw, fuck it. Why not?*

"Fine. I keep thinking about fucking."

"What guy doesn't?"

"Not like this."

The corner of Gideon's mouth pulled up.

"Fucking who?"

"Depends on the moment."

He stepped closer, the spicy scent Max had come to associate with him growing stronger, the smell of sweat just making it more enticing. He invaded the "friend" body space and moved nearer.

"Mandy?"

"Yes."

Gideon didn't physically come any closer but it was like Max could feel him reaching out. The wolf in his head went crazy, wanting free, wanting this male. It was the human who wasn't quite ready to accept it.

"What about me? Do I ever get a starring role?" Gideon asked, the teasing tone pushing Max's buttons.

"Yes." Max stared at Gideon. The faint smirk on Gideon's face helped Max make the decision about how much more to reveal. "And just to make it fun, the both of you." He bent his head down to ensure that no one could hear. "You had your face between Mandy's legs and I was behind you, fucking you hard and fast."

Gideon closed his eyes and groaned.

Good. At least someone else could try to function with a raging hard-on.

Gideon tipped his head to the side as if considering the idea. Finally he sighed. "Sounds like fun but Mandy doesn't quite seem like the type."

Max felt his mouth pull wide into a smile, remembering the butt plug and Mandy's confession of two guys.

"Don't know. She's a lot more adventurous than she appears."

"Interesting."

Max's body agreed, his dick getting hard, the exertion of his climb not quite tiring him out. That was the downside to the werewolf metabolism.

"Let's go. We're supposed to be climbing."

Gideon stared at Max for a long moment and then finally nodded.

"You realize you never should have confessed that to me."

He sighed. "Yeah. I'm pretty sure of that."

Gideon laughed and headed back to the wall. Max hooked in and reached for the low markers on the wall. He needed to work his muscles, needed to make it so his body was so exhausted that he couldn't get hard.

Right.

Chapter Eight

ꟸ

Eight hours later he was confident he'd succeeded. He was whipped. His mind as well as his body. His thoughts bouncing from one random idea to the next.

"You okay, man?"

Max nodded, grateful Gideon was with him. Gideon had kept pace the whole day, through the climbing gym then for the five-hour hike through the Chugach National Forest. It had been beautiful, the Alaska scenery stunning, but Max had pushed through it, needing to wear out his body.

Gideon was done after that but Max needed more. His werewolf metabolism gave him the extra surge of strength and he needed to burn through it. They'd stopped by Gideon's house. While Gideon had showered, Max had gone for a run, pushing his body hard, fighting the wolf every step. The animal wanted out, wanted to run on four legs instead of the inefficient two that Max had.

Either that or the wolf wanted to fuck. Gideon. Mandy. The animal wasn't picky. As long as it was one of those two. He expressed no interest in any of the hikers they'd passed. Even the gorgeous redhead with huge tits and legs that would look perfect around Max's hips. Max the human had looked. The wolf wasn't interested. Until Gideon bumped into him *then* his dick got hard.

That final run seemed to be enough. Jacking off in Gideon's shower hadn't hurt. It hadn't fixed the problem but it helped. He'd dressed in clean clothes and trudged out to Gideon's living room. Gideon gave him no chance to sit. He loaded them into the car, stopped by the grocery store to pick up food for dinner and started back to Jax's house.

Max's mind came awake for a moment as they turned down Jax's street. He looked at the bags piled in the backseat.

"What did you buy again? Because I can't cook."

"I can."

"You're cooking me dinner?" He blinked thinking his exhaustion had slowed his thoughts a bit too much.

"That was the plan." The edge of Gideon's mouth kinked up in a smile.

"Okay, but this isn't a date."

Gideon laughed. "I never thought it was. I like my men a little more awake. I'll just feed you and tuck you into bed."

And fuck if Max's cock didn't respond, coming alive when every other organ in his body barely functioned. His groan turned into a whimper and he was damn glad when his phone rang. It gave him something to think about besides Gideon. Because after two hours in the rock gym, Max knew precisely how strong and toned and powerful Gideon's body was. How good it would look bent over the end of his bed, those tight ass muscles straining as Max fucked him.

Screw trying to exhaust the thoughts of sex out of his mind—he needed to fuck. Or get the hell away from Gideon. And Mandy.

Without looking at the screen, Max flipped the phone open. "This is Max," he growled.

"And don't you sound cheery."

Max rolled his eyes and tried not to snarl. Just what he needed—a cocky son of a bitch Cat shapeshifter calling to irritate him.

"Reign, what do you want?"

"So polite. Does your mama know how you answer phone?"

"Leave my mama out of this. Now I'm busy." He said it more to piss off the Cat than anything else. "What do you want?"

Reign scoffed, the sound resonating down the phone line. "I have no idea what Dani sees in you."

"A better fuck than you'll ever be."

"In your dreams, wolf-boy."

"Listen, Cat, is there a reason you're calling me? Or did you just want to jack off to the sound of my voice?"

Reign growled and Max smiled. He'd won that round. He actually liked the Cat, except for, well, he was a Cat so you couldn't trust him. Cats were notoriously self-centered. How this one had ended up as a cop was anyone's guess.

Gideon pulled into the driveway and Max got out, his body coming alive as his mind was forced to wake up.

"Bite me."

Max smiled. He'd reduced Reign to childish comebacks. He loved that.

"And risk turning you into one of mine? Not a chance."

"Asshole."

"You know it."

Gideon reached into the backseat and grabbed the shopping bags and damn his butt looked good as his jeans slid across his skin. Two quick steps and Max could be there, his cock pressed against that slim line that split his ass cheeks, he could be buried in that space. A few swipes of his claws and Gideon could be naked, hot flesh against him. Skin on skin.

The wolf growled its approval and Max licked his lips. Gideon started to straighten and Max realized he'd been heading toward his friend, ready to complete the little fantasy his mind had created.

Jerking his gaze upward, Max retreated instead and held out a hand offering to take one. Gideon shook his head and locked the car.

"So what do you want, Reign? I have a friend here," Max said.

"I got word the bastard's back in town. There's a party tomorrow night. It's all set. Invitation only. I'll take Dani and you station yourself—"

"Can't do it."

"I know it's not your first choice but you can't walk into a Clowder." A Clowder? No way. Protective instincts roared to the front of his brain. Dani wasn't walking into a glorified Cat orgy. Not without Max in tow. It didn't matter that she was fucking some other guy. It wasn't safe. He tried to interrupt but Reign kept talking. "You'll be ripped to shreds. I'll position you close. You'll have Dani within hearing at all times. Let's meet tomorrow—"

"I'm not in town." He spoke over Reign.

"What? Where are you?"

Max tipped his head to the side and trapped the phone to his shoulder as he dug out his keys. "I'm in Alaska, visiting my brother." Or that was the intent. "Sort of. Either way, I'm not there. It can't happen. You have to wait until the next time he comes through."

There was a pause and some quiet swearing. Max liked to tease the Cat but he knew how much catching this killer meant to him and if he'd been in town, they'd be there. All over it.

Reign sighed. "I'll just take Dani myself."

"Alone?"

"No. Charlie would act as backup."

"A human? No fucking way. Dani is not going to one of your Cat orgies without someone who can actually protect her."

"I think that's her decision, don't you? She knows I'll take good care of her."

"You stay the fuck away from her." It didn't matter if they were broken up or not. He still cared about Dani, enough to want to protect her.

Gideon nudged him with his elbow and Max realized he'd forgotten what he was doing and went back to opening the door.

"Again, that's her decision," Reign drawled.

"I'll be back in town in a few days." He pushed the door open and stepped into the entryway, moving forward to give Gideon room to follow him. "You stay the hell—"

He walked into the living room. The breath left his lungs. His feet froze to the floor and he jerked to a stop.

Gideon bumped into him and grunted. Max ignored that. He ignored everything, unconsciously closing his phone and silencing Reign's voice.

His entire focus centered on the vision before him.

Mandy, standing in the middle of Jax's living room, wearing nothing but a red lace bra and panties. And four-inch heels that made her ass high and round, perfect for his hands.

All traces of exhaustion evaporated from his body and Max straightened, his cock straightened. Hell his whole body went on alert, preparing to rip the pretty bits of lace off her and bury his face between her legs. God, he could smell her arousal from here.

Her eyes were lowered, staring at the ground as if she was shy. Shy woman in fire engine red underwear that barely covered her tits. Damn, could anything be more sexual?

"Damn," Gideon whispered and Mandy must have heard the awed sound.

Her head snapped up. Her eyes widened and she squeaked. Panic flooded her eyes and her arms flopped at her sides as if she didn't know what to do, which body part to cover first. She looked around and for a second Max thought she'd make a run for it. Instead, she grabbed a tiny pillow off the couch and held it over her crotch. That left her breasts still visible. Round and firm. Max had good memories of her breasts, the tight nipples in his mouth.

An appreciative moan echoed from beside him. He glanced at Gideon.

"Stop staring at her tits," Max snarled.

"Yeah, right."

Max jabbed his elbow back, drawing another grunt from Gideon.

Mandy's blush grew brighter and spread down her neck.

"Uhm, I'm sorry. I wasn't thinking. I'll just—" She started to back away but her heel caught on the rug and she wobbled, dropping the pillow and plopping down on the couch. Her knees separated revealing the damp panel between her legs. Max felt his own knees tremble.

Mandy moaned and rolled over, curling up into a ball no doubt intending to hide her body. It only served to show her ass and rounded thighs.

Max went to the edge of the couch and knelt beside her, trying to get her to lift her face out of the couch cushion.

"Honey, it's okay."

"Go away."

"Never."

"Please?"

The tone of her plea actually gave him hope. She was embarrassed but her natural humor was coming though.

"Not happening."

She lifted her face enough to whisper. "I can't believe Gideon saw me naked."

"You're not naked." *But it would only take me a few seconds to get you that way.* This close the scent of her pussy was almost too much to resist. Only the thought of Gideon standing behind them kept him from spreading her legs and ripping her panties off with his teeth.

She lifted her head and looked at him. Her cheeks were bright red and her eyes had the sparkle of unshed tears.

"I'm sorry. I thought I'd surprise you. I didn't—"

Unable to stop himself, wanting to dispel the insecurity and embarrassment from her eyes, he leaned forward and kissed her. He didn't allow himself to deepen the kiss, contenting himself with a warm brush to her lips.

"Never apologize for taking off your clothes for me," he said with a smile and was relieved to see her smile back. "In fact, anytime you want to walk around in your underwear or even naked for that matter, I encourage it."

She laughed—that feminine kind of chuckle that said "only a man would say that."

"I should probably get dressed though." She glanced over his shoulder toward Gideon and immediately her cheeks returned to bright red. "You guys obviously had plans."

"It was nothing. Dinner."

"Still, I should..." She pushed herself upright and allowed Max to help her to her feet. "I'll be right back." Still a little unstable on the shoes, she hurried toward the stairs, obviously not realizing her miniscule panties made much of her ass visible and damn tempting.

Gideon walked forward, his gaze latched onto her backside, his tongue peeking out of his mouth.

"Stop looking at her ass." Max punched his arm. "Wait, I thought you were gay."

Gideon smiled and his eyes twinkled. "Not necessarily."

"Excuse me? You frenched me last night and tonight you're staring at Mandy's ass?"

Gideon shrugged.

"I like fucking men. I like doing women. I enjoy sex—in all its many forms and flavors." He stared in the direction that Mandy had disappeared. "And that is one interesting form. I can understand why you fucked your brother's girlfriend. Take off those ugly clothes she wears and damn, she's got an extremely fuckable body."

Max found himself nodding. Extremely fuckable. And sweet and tasty and damn, he was hard again.

"And that fantasy you mentioned earlier about you and me and Mandy…I am so into that now."

* * * * *

Mandy fought not to cry as she grabbed her clothes. She hated crying. She turned blotchy and her nose ran. And being embarrassed wouldn't kill her, right?

God, what had she been thinking? Tracy's stupid idea. Be waiting for Jackson to come home, naked, and he'd forget all about his apology. Damn, she'd never imagined he'd bring someone home with him. Her cheeks burned.

After Tracy's nagging all afternoon, Mandy had finally succumbed to the stupid, insane plan. She groaned. Naked wasn't a comfortable thing for her so she'd gone with the hot lingerie that Tracy had helped her buy. Mandy knew she could never pull off "sexy". Efficient, capable. Those were words her previous boyfriends had used to describe her. She was too practical to be sexy.

But something about the way Jackson had looked at her last night had given her the courage. He'd thought she was sexy.

She didn't know what he thought now. He hadn't minded seeing her naked but that hadn't covered his surprise. Probably from seeing her breasts squeezed and lifted. The tiny red bra made them look bigger than they already were. And the panties hadn't quite hid her not-so-flat stomach.

And God, the look on Gideon's face. How would she ever face him again? Great, this one little episode had succeeded in her not only losing a good friend, Jackson, but her favorite restaurant as well.

Getting into Jackson's house had been a simple thing. He'd given her his keys the last time he'd been heading out of town so she could run by and pick up some files. She'd just never returned it. Getting inside had been easy. Finding the courage to strip had taken a little more effort. And standing herself in the living room had taken what energy she had left. She hadn't had the strength to lift her eyes and stare seductively at the door as Tracy had instructed.

Maybe it wouldn't have taken her so long to realize that Jackson wasn't alone. And that both men were staring at her breasts and her legs.

She moaned and clutched fistfuls of hair and pulled. God, what was she going to do now? Well, first she needed to put her clothes back on. She grabbed the white blouse and navy blue skirt she'd worn to work and pulled them on, taking time to tuck in the blouse because she needed to be as in control as possible when she went back downstairs.

There was no way she could put her nylons back on but she didn't have much choice in shoes. It was the torture-test shoes Tracy had encouraged her to buy or tennis shoes. Over bare feet. Yuck. It would have to be the heels. She could barely walk in the damn things—as her lovely little flop onto the couch had proven—but she slipped her feet back into the high heels and stood up. It was amazing how high heels gave a woman confidence. Until she had to move of course.

She shoved the nylons into her purse and grimaced, her fingertips brushing the other object in her bag—the butt plug. A momentary flash of recklessness had made her grab it. Along with lube and condoms. It had seemed funny and sexy at the time. Now it just added to her mortification. She zipped the bag closed and hung the strap over her shoulder. A few deep breaths helped. She glanced in the mirror and smoothed her hair, going for cool and collected. Her heart still pounded but at least she felt a little more like herself. Now all she had to do was walk downstairs, head held high and leave.

Never to return.

She gripped her purse in her fist and forced her legs to march downstairs.

The living room was empty and for a moment she thought she might escape without being seen—it was a coward's retreat she knew but she wasn't above taking it—then Jackson appeared.

"Mandy?"

"Hi." She offered a weak wave trying to ignore the way her cheeks warmed up again. How long would it be before she could look at him and not blush? Probably never. "Again, I'm really sorry. I'll just go."

"No—"

"Well, it's all in there," Gideon announced as he walked into the room. He stopped when he saw Mandy. She braced herself for a wink or a leer or something. Instead he just smiled. "I'll let you two enjoy your evening."

"No," she protested. "You guys obviously had something planned."

Gideon shook his head. "It's no stress. There's plenty of food and—" He looked at Max and Mandy. Both stared at him—eyes wild, panic straining their muscles. Max hid it a little better but neither was ready to be alone. Together. Whatever. Just standing in the room, he could feel the tension between them.

He liked Max and after seeing Mandy tiny scraps of lace, he realized there was more to her than the staid, prissy woman she appeared to be when Jackson was around.

During the course of the day Gideon had realized that while he liked Jackson, enjoyed his company, he could fall hard for Max. The two men looked exactly alike but their personalities were vibrantly different. There were some similarities of course—they were reared by the same parents—but after the basics, they were polar opposites.

Max seemed to bring something different out of Mandy as well. Even standing there, in a frumpy blue skirt and blouse, she looked sexual—though that might have been because he knew what was hidden beneath those ugly clothes.

He'd never seen anything like lust in her eyes when she was with Jackson.

If nothing else it would be fun to watch Max and Mandy together.

Besides if he left now, Max would probably kick Mandy out or worse, tell her the truth, and the wicked side of Gideon didn't think that was a good idea.

"Can either of you cook?" He ignored Max because Max had already said he couldn't.

Mandy looked at Max before shaking her head. "Not much."

"Well, the least I can do is be your chef this evening."

Max opened his mouth like he was going to protest. Now that he'd had time to think about it he was probably going to kick them both out.

Gideon plowed over whatever Max had been ready to say. "Come on, both of you. I'll cook but I need a sous-chef."

"What?" Max asked.

Mandy rolled her eyes. "Sous-chef. They do the prep and put the plates together. Help the chef." She shook her head. "Don't you watch cooking shows?"

"No."

Gideon grabbed Mandy by the hand and pulled her toward the kitchen. "He's a plebian. *Jackson*—" He emphasized the name more to irritate Max than anything else. "Put on some tunes and let's make dinner."

Chapter Nine

ஐ

Mandy allowed herself to be dragged into the kitchen—grateful that Gideon seemed to be willing to ignore her failed attempt at seduction. She laughed as Gideon put her to work cleaning carrots. This was something she could do. She hadn't been kidding when she'd said she didn't cook much. She could do basics but based on what Gideon was doing, it was beyond her abilities.

Music flooded the kitchen. And a wave of normalcy came over her. Despite the fact that Jackson still carried himself with that tough bad-boy attitude, this was typical Jackson—smooth jazz and low blues.

He returned and Gideon put him to work. This was Gideon's realm and he ruled it well, directing each of them as he did some sort of magic with chicken and spices. The hiss and crackle of vegetables hitting hot grease filled the air.

And while Gideon cooked, he talked and laughed, teasing Jackson, almost flirting.

She'd noticed a hint of sexual tension between the two of them in the past but it was different tonight, stronger. When Gideon came over to check on Max's progress with chopping parsley, he leaned in, their shoulders touching. Max didn't shift away even though Gideon had well invaded his space. *Was it possible they were lovers?* After last night she didn't think it likely but who knew?

Both men moved around the kitchen, working together, occasionally sharing a laugh or quiet joke but she didn't sense a strong intimacy. They probably weren't lovers but something had changed in their situation. There was something definitely sexual in they way they interacted. *Or it could be that your mind is just stuck on sex,* she reminded herself.

"Man, you need to cut that a bit smaller or we'll be walking around with green stuff stuck between our teeth." Gideon looked at her and rolled his eyes.

With one look, he drew her into the sexual connection between the two of them. Her nipples hardened and her chest tightened, making it difficult to breathe. Each inhale rasped her nipples against the lacy bra. The edge of his mouth kicked, as if he knew that her body was responding, responding to a simple stare.

Heat flooded her pussy and she squeezed her knees together, trying to ease the sudden ache. Her body seemed attuned to the sexual energy flowing between the three of them. Even as she thought it, the image popped into her head of the three of them in bed, naked. She shook her head, trying to clear the fantasy but it lodged in her brain and she couldn't break free. Hot strong fingers touching her, both men sucking on her nipples, sliding into her.

She looked up, once again meeting Gideon's gaze.

Gideon's smile widened and damn it really did look like he could read her mind. Or maybe he could just read her body.

Heat blossomed in her cheeks again and she dragged her eyes away, focusing on the salad she was supposed to be making. It didn't make sense. She was a practical, smart accountant for goodness sake...she didn't inspire lust in the hearts of men. A low chuckle rumbled from Gideon but there was no mockery in it. She flashed a teasing glare at Gideon.

A soulful sax wailed in the background.

Jackson grunted. "I can't handle any more of this." At first she thought he meant the herbs he was cutting. But he handed the messy pile to Gideon and spun around, disappearing into the dining room.

Mandy pursed her lips and shared a confused look with Gideon. He shrugged.

The wailing sax went silent and moments later the opening drums to Santana's *Smooth* started and Mandy groaned.

"Oh God, I love this song." Her hips did a slow roll left and right, her body sinking into the seductive musical rhythm. The low buzz of the guitar sent a delicious tingle down her spine. She couldn't stop. Something about this song just called to her, controlling her muscles, captivating her.

"Damn, girl, that's it."

She opened her eyes and looked at Gideon. He watched from the stove, his eyes appreciating her sensuous dance. The intensity of his stare startled her and she froze.

"No, darling, keep going. You're feeling it." He swung his hips back and forth and winked. "Dance with me." He held out his hand and Mandy laughed, placing the knife on the counter and blushing as she put her fingers in his, allowing herself to be drawn to him. It took a beat or two to recapture the sound in her body. She moved with Gideon, matching his rhythm, her body reflecting the sensuous pulse. He drew her to him until their bodies almost touched, his hands sliding down, lightly fingering her hips as they moved.

She laughed and tipped her head back. She'd never danced with anyone to this song. It was the one she kept for herself, around her apartment. The sexual music and rhythm swirled through her body. He pulled her closer, trying to slip his leg between her thighs.

"Damn, this skirt has got to go." As he spoke he reached for the side zipper, his fingers dragging down the tab. The waistband sagged free even as she gasped, her mind finally catching up with the fact that he was taking off her clothes.

"What—"

"For this song, you can't wear that straitlaced, schoolmarm skirt." He placed a fast kiss on her lips. "Besides, your ass is too sweet to be hidden in ugly clothes." She stared up and blinked, standing still as he dragged the skirt down to the floor and pulled, giving her little choice but to step out of it. Her shirt hung to the tops of her thighs leaving her mostly covered. He tossed the skirt away and grabbed her around the waist, dragging her forward, his thigh sliding between her legs. It wasn't particularly sexual. He didn't rub up against her pussy, he just locked their bodies together so that everywhere she moved, she touched him.

"That's it, Mandy, feel the song."

Shock kept her frozen for just a moment but then the music and the encouragement in Gideon's eyes melted her fear and she let her resistance go. Letting Gideon lead, she allowed the rhythm to fill her and they danced, their bodies close, touching and pulling back. Yes, this was how this song should be experienced, body against body. The low ache in her pussy transformed into a throb and oh she needed something to satisfy the intoxicating need.

Max came around the corner. "There. How about—"

The sight before him locked the words in his throat. Mandy, wearing nothing but her white blouse and those high heels—where the hell had her skirt gone?—pressed against Gideon. His thigh slid between her legs. Their bodies rocked in time to the song but Max wouldn't call what they were doing dancing. Foreplay. His cock twitched, the blasted thing eager to join in.

Gideon looked up and smiled—the look sexual and arrogant and Max wasn't sure how he felt about it. But then the music changed, the chorus filling the room. Gideon stepped back, not releasing Mandy, taking her hand, and spinning her around. Her laughter sparkled through the air. Gideon guided her to a stop, her back to his front, presenting her to Max.

Passion saturated her eyes as she looked up, her body following a rhythm—set by the music and the man standing behind her, rocking his hips against her ass. She was completely captured by the music, sensual and sexual and Max needed to be a part of it. He came forward, taking the place that Gideon had occupied, his thigh between her legs. Mandy's arms slid up around his shoulders, lightly clinging to him as she moved and rocked. God, she was lust in its purest form.

He pushed closer, gripping her hips and pressing his thigh against her pussy. Heat melted his jeans as she groaned. The beat swelled inside, echoed and reinforced by Gideon and Mandy. Max began to move.

The music changed again and once again Gideon led them, drawing Mandy away, turning her, spinning her until her ass was nestled against Max's groin. Lost in the music, her hips pressed back and she rubbed against him, the thin material of her panties barely enough to stop Max from sliding into her cunt. His cock slipped into the split of her ass, close to where he wanted to be. She groaned and pressed back.

Unable to resist tasting her any longer, he leaned down and kissed her throat, laving his tongue across the tight skin. The sweet taste invaded his head, reminding him of the taste of her cunt, muted and faint, just enough to tempt him to have more.

But first he really had to fuck her.

She rocked her ass against his erection, making it harder and thicker until Max was sure he was going to come inside his jeans. He fought the pressure in his balls, even as heat covered his back. Gideon. The strong male body pressed against his, cock against *his* ass, promising, threatening, but damn, it felt good. He couldn't stop his groan, needing some release from the overwhelming seduction of the two bodies surrounding him.

As if Gideon felt free because Mandy couldn't see them, he leaned forward and scraped his teeth across the base of Max's neck, a sharp, almost painful bite. Max's gums tingled, his teeth threatening to plunge down and drive into Gideon's neck.

He took deep breath and forced the wolf back into its cage.

Concentrating on not allowing his other side to be free, he almost missed when the music change again. Except Gideon spun away, leaving Max to miss his warmth.

Bodies shifted, Mandy turned and once again she was face-to-face with Max, her legs spread, straddling his thigh, pressing against him. He groaned, needing the fiery liquid that dripped from her pussy. He clamped his hand on her ass and dragged her up until he pushed against her pussy, her clit. She raised her eyes, the gray depths dazed and blurry, as if she didn't understand what was happening to her.

"Mandy?" he asked, not wanting to frighten her.

"More." The low groan slipped from her lips as her head tipped back, hitting Gideon's chest, her hips rocked forward, pressing harder against Max's thigh.

"That's it, darling," Gideon said, his voice soft and strong, surrounding them. "Feel him."

Max watched as Gideon whispered soft kisses up the lovely length of Mandy's throat. She tipped her head to the side, giving him access. The sight of Gideon's lips on her skin swamped Max—her pleasure, wicked and pure as she moved between them, rubbing against them both.

The music had long ago faded into insignificance and the pretense of dancing disappeared. Max leaned down and captured Mandy's lips with his, driving his tongue deep into her mouth, swallowing her moan as his reward, feeling it deep in his cock. He was conscious of the fact that Gideon's hands were on Mandy's skin, beneath her shirt, close, so close to those breasts he'd enjoyed last night. Part of him braced to feel jealousy. Werewolves were notorious for their territorial nature, but instead he sensed her pleasure. And he wanted her to have more. He wanted her screaming, watching her come until her body collapsed from climaxing.

Hands worked the buttons of her blouse—and damned if he could figure out if it was him or Gideon opening them—until the laced edges of her bra appeared.

Max groaned and licked his lips. Memories of the previous night were ripe in his mind. The sweet curves, perfect for his tongue, his lips. He bent down, nuzzling the delicious mounds, licking, his wolf savoring every stroke of his tongue, the taste of her skin. His teeth stretched and the urge to bite, to penetrate that sweet flesh was almost too much.

He fought the wolf's natural desires and instead licked, sliding his tongue beneath the lace of her bra, capturing the tight nipple. Mandy's gasp taunted the wolf. The animal wanted more of those sounds, wanted her writhing beneath him. Wanted to feel her pussy opening for him.

Foreign hands reached forward and snapped the front clasp of her bra, giving him access. Silently Max thanked Gideon, his own hands too clumsy to work the delicate clasp. Max dragged down the open collar of her shirt and sucked her breast inside his mouth. Another delicate but powerful cry rang through his head and he knew he'd never be happy without that sound inside him. Needing more, wanting more for her, he sucked deeper, wanting her all in his mouth. God, he would consume her. He could—a distant bell chimed and Max snapped his head back, snarling at the interruption.

Mandy's eyes snapped open wide and the tension that raked her body warned him she was feeling much more than surprise. He stared at the floor, knowing his eyes had to be glowing with the bright red of passion, anger. Max forced himself to straighten.

"Damn—" Gideon moaned. "I guess dinner's ready."

The way he said it—flirty and a little effeminate—defused the tension in a snap.

Mandy giggled and Max allowed himself a glance toward her. She was blushing. Gideon stepped back and Max realized that Mandy had been trapped between them—not that she hadn't been enjoying the experience.

"Uh—"

Gideon placed a quick hard kiss on her throat. "You, my dear, are delicious." Then he backed away. Max noticed that Gideon's shirt was unbuttoned. Hell, his own shirt was unbuttoned. When had that happened? It didn't matter. They were standing there, the three of them, all in partial states of undress and God, if that oven timer hadn't gone off, they'd have been fucking. Max was sure of it.

Gideon shook his head. "Take the salad. And the wine—" He winked at Max. "Because I think we're going to need it. I'll bring out the rest."

It was difficult to convince his body to move but Max finally got his legs to take a step back and his cock—the most rebellious organ in his body—to leave the warm cradle of Mandy's sex. His dick rebelled at losing the heat. And moisture. Fuck, she was wet. He could smell it. Feel it. Almost taste it.

God, he wanted to taste it. Gideon's dinner couldn't compare to the compelling flavor of Mandy's pussy.

He stared down at the sweet, shy woman trying to reclasp her bra, re-button her blouse.

Damn his brother had good taste.

"Move, move." Gideon's prompt barely pierced Max's thoughts. "This isn't the kind of meal you want to eat cold. Mandy, salad. *Jax*—" Gideon's emphasis snapped him out of his ruminations. "Focus on something besides Mandy's tits—gorgeous though they are—and grab the wine." He pushed by, his hands filled with a steaming pan of something that smelled almost as good as Mandy's pussy.

Snapped out of his fog, he looked at Mandy. She shrugged, grabbed the salad and followed Gideon out into the dining room. The slight twitch of her hips warned that she was still feeling the effects of their sexual dance.

Max took a deep breath and grabbed the bottle of wine. Gideon was right, they were going to need it.

* * * * *

Max gulped down the last glass of red and knew it wasn't enough. Hell, wasn't alcohol supposed to be a depressant? Wasn't it supposed to make his cock unable to get hard? Of course, he'd started out hard. And the rest of the evening hadn't changed that situation.

Seated at the table with Mandy and Gideon both within easy reach. Fuck, it was a wonder he hadn't come already. Dinner had been delicious. The subtly seasoned meat had satisfied the wolf's physical hunger. At least one need was appeased.

Gideon had kept the meal lively, almost impersonal, except for the seductive touches as he moved around the table, serving food or wine. They'd finished the bottle of white wine and moved onto a deep seductive Cabernet. Max almost groaned as Gideon had described the full-bodied flavor.

When Gideon wasn't serving or pouring, he guided the conversation. The man was a natural-born host. Fuck if Max wasn't so turned-on, he'd have admired the talent.

Max swallowed the last of his wine, letting it settle easily on the delicious meal Gideon had created. He could do this. All he had to do was make it through the "good nights" and he could send both his temptations on their way.

And then dessert appeared. Fuck, when had Gideon had time to make dessert?

He placed a fondue pot in the middle of the table. Strawberries and bits of marshmallow surrounded the melted chocolate. Max shook his head. He wouldn't survive this.

Mandy smiled and actually clapped her hands together as Gideon set the contraption into the middle of the table.

"Oh, I love fondue." She leaned forward and inhaled. Even with her blouse re-buttoned, Max could see the rise and fall of her breasts. The red tint of her bra shone through the white fabric, teasing him to rip off the staid blouse and lick the sweet valley between her pretty tits. "That smells delicious." She bit her lip and let her eyes drift up to his. The gray depths glittered with pleasure and a sensual hunger that Max wanted transferred to him.

He gulped and glanced at Gideon. A different kind of energy flowed from him—still sexual, still hot, masculine. His gaze skimmed between Max and Mandy, the heat in his stare no less on Max than it was on Mandy.

She shook her head and Max waited, expecting her to reject the offering. That was what the women in his world did. "It all looks so good." She looked up, her eyes glowing, the need almost matching the lust he saw last night. Max grinned even as his cock got hard. It would be so easy to combine her hungers—drizzle chocolate across his dick and allow her to lick it off. Her cheeks flushed red—almost like she was imagining the same thing—and she dropped her gaze, reaching for the stick closest to her. She speared a strawberry and dipped it into the warm chocolate, swirling it around until it dripped.

An invisible band tightened around Max's chest as she raised the drenched fruit. Gideon leaned in. Max could feel the tension coming off him, knowing he watched as Mandy's tongue flicked out and caught the trail of chocolate that dripped off the strawberry. She moaned and wrapped her lips around the fruit, sucking it in.

She closed her eyes and ran her tongue across her lower lip, capturing the tiny drop of chocolate that had escaped. The scent of her pussy grew hot and Max's wolf growled.

"Oh sweet fuck," Gideon said low and hard.

Max nodded, unable to find his voice.

Mandy opened her eyes and smiled at both men—at once both purely sweet and sexual. She blinked.

"Want a taste, boys?"

Mandy heard the words come out of her mouth and could barely believe them, or the deep husky sound from her throat. She would have blushed except for the heat in their eyes. Feminine power rose up inside her, knowing she was able to entice both men. She turned and boldly met Jackson's stare.

"Yes," he growled, ignoring the fondue pot and leaning over, covering her mouth with his, driving his tongue between her lips, tasting her. She groaned as she remembered last night and the way he'd licked her pussy. He kissed her the same way now—strong, confident and sexual.

Her pussy clenched, the memory swirling through her core, making her wet and hot. Wanting more.

The wicked kiss when on and on until they both needed to breathe. He pulled back, licked his lips.

"Delicious."

"Yes." She felt her cheeks heat up realizing that Gideon was watching them. Of course, after the slutty dance in the kitchen, a little kiss couldn't be all that shocking.

She let her eyes drift toward Gideon. He swirled a marshmallow in the chocolate and offered it to her. She hesitated for just a moment.

Gideon nodded. "Take it, Mandy." His voice was low and smooth. Not as growl-y as Jackson's but seductive in its own way. "I like to watch."

She accepted the stick and slipped the dripping marshmallow into her mouth. She wasn't worried about seduction, just keeping the chocolate off the table.

Still, Jackson groaned, almost sounding like she had her lips wrapped around his cock. She glanced at him but reached out and accepted another chocolate-covered offering from Gideon. Taking her time and savoring the tastes, knowing her men watched, hungry. *Her men.* She liked the sound of that. Not that it would happen but it was a great fantasy.

And she was living it out. Taking treats offered by Gideon and sometimes Jackson, though he seemed more intent on just watching, practically drooling. He licked his lips as if he could still taste her and somehow she didn't think he was imagining the taste of her mouth.

Heat washed through her body with each bite, the delicious flush of chocolate and sex make her pussy clench and ache. She dropped her head back and allowed a soft moan to slide from her lips. She needed to be fucked. Now.

God, she couldn't believe she was even thinking in those terms.

When she opened her eyes moments later, the fondue pot along with Gideon was gone.

Jackson watched her, his eyes doing that weird red glow thing again. It was a little like a horror movie but the lust that poured from his stare killed any fear she might have.

She looked at the empty space on the table then raised her eyebrows in question to Jackson.

"Dinner's over," he said pushing back from the table and standing. "I'll get Gideon's coat."

He stalked out of the dining room. She slowly came to her feet, her body lazy, almost drunk from wine and chocolate and sex. Gideon walked in from the kitchen.

And Mandy found herself alone with him for the first time since their "dance". She couldn't believe she'd done that—or allowed any of that to be done to her—but something about the music and the men and the beat had just released every inhibition she'd had and she'd let go. Her nipples tightened at the memory. Or maybe it was because of the heat in Gideon's eyes.

"Uh, he's getting your coat."

Gideon chuckled, the sound more sensual than mocking. "That last strawberry pushed him over the edge." Gideon strolled forward. Mandy swayed, her ankles wobbling in the tall shoes. He caught her elbow, holding her upright. Her head spun, a combination of the wine and the lack of oxygen in the room, she was sure. She leaned into him, taking his support as he wrapped his other arm around her back. She tipped her head back and looked into his dark eyes.

She'd never thought of Gideon in a sexual way. He'd always been Jackson's friend. And she was pretty sure, based on Jackson's comments, that Gideon was gay. But standing there, his hips pressed against hers, she could feel the distinct bulge of a hard cock pushing into her stomach. He wasn't aggressive with it. But there was not mistaking his arousal. Was it from her? Or from Max? Or like her, was he caught up in the sex bouncing between the three of them.

Her gaze dropped to his lips, the shallow curves giving her wicked ideas of what he could do with his mouth, on her body, on Max's. The two of them both kneeling over Max, his cock trapped between their lips.

She squeezed her knees together, needing something between her thighs to counter the images flowing through her head.

Gideon tipped his head to the side.

"So, are you going to seduce your man?"

Gideon's casual question dripped sex and Mandy swallowed, feeling the sounds of his voice like little caresses in her body.

"Uh—" She'd never talked about this sort of thing with a man before. She'd rarely even discussed it with women. Particularly after an evening drenched in sex—when seduction seemed like a real possibility. Almost an imperative.

"Want some advice?" He winked. "Go naked. He's been dying to rip your clothes off all night."

Mandy blinked, not sure what to say. The picture quickly formed in her brain—her naked, kneeling, waiting for her lovers. Lover. There was just Jackson. She needed to stop thinking about Gideon and Jackson. Together. With her. What would Jackson think if he knew? They discussed it last night in theory but fantasizing about his best friend probably wouldn't go over well.

He placed two fingers under her chin and tipped her head up so she met his eyes again.

"All you have to do is crook your finger and you'll have him." The click of the closet door closing must have caught his attention and he looked up, over her shoulder. "But a little jealousy wouldn't hurt." The hand on her back tightened and he pulled her closer, pressing from her knees to chest against him. His voice dropped in the low, sexy range that just hummed through her body. "Besides, it's my turn to taste."

Before she had a chance to respond, to protest or accept, he was there, bending, his mouth on hers, his hands on her hips, adjusting their bodies so they meshed together. Mandy's overwhelmed mind took a moment to catch up with her senses and she realized she was kissing him back, really kissing him back.

She opened her mouth, silently inviting him inside, even as her mind screamed *what are you doing? Jackson is going to walk in* but then Gideon licked his tongue between her lips, a gentle stroke that tasted of him and chocolate, bound together by the rich wine they'd drunk. She shifted, moving into him, her arms coiling up around his neck. He groaned and his hands tightened, one sliding down to cup her ass, pressing her forward as he stepped closer.

The short blouse left her legs bare. He slipped his thigh between hers, nudging her legs apart. She squirmed, wanting him closer, wanting him pressed against her clit.

God, what was she doing?

Chapter Ten

ꚙ

Max stood in the doorway, Gideon's jacket hanging from his fingers. His mind flinched for a moment, trying to decide if the picture in front of him was real or another of his fantasies, sent to torment him. He watched for a moment but the image didn't disappear—Mandy locked in Gideon's arms, her red panties visible as she stretched up and wrapped her arms around his neck, opening her mouth and accepting Gideon's tongue.

Max felt his cock twitch and the wolf inside his head growled. He tensed, waiting for the animal's fury to threaten his control but there was nothing. The sound reverberated through his chest, ringing with hunger, desire, wanting.

He shook his head, trying to clear it. It didn't make any sense. He should be jealous, fuck, he should be furious. How dare Gideon kiss Mandy that way? They shifted and Gideon's thigh slipped between her legs. Gideon would feel the heat dripping from her cunt. Again he waited for the jealousy but the wolf's needs were purely sexual, driving Max to join them.

He wanted to be a part of it. Wanted to press up behind her and rub his cock against her ass, bend her over and lift that white shirt out of the way and slide his dick into her tight pussy while she sucked Gideon's cock. Or take Gideon, bend him over the kitchen table and fuck the hell out of him as a thank you for the delicious meal they'd had. His photographer's mind shaped the picture until he could see it clearly, practically feel it.

His foot took that first step forward, responding to the desires of his wolf and his own soul. Mandy cried out and her fingers tightened as she gripped Gideon's shoulders. The sight of her delicate nails biting into the pale blue shirt jolted Max. What the fuck was he thinking? Not only was he not going to fuck Mandy again he sure as hell wasn't going to encourage Gideon to have her.

She belonged to Jackson.

"What the hell are you doing?" he demanded, the anger directed toward himself but finding a convenient outlet with Gideon. Max didn't look at Mandy but he sensed her confusion.

Gideon stepped back, putting inches of space between him and Mandy. The smug bastard shrugged. "Just a kiss for the cook."

"That looked like more than a simple kiss."

"Well, she's a very tempting woman." Gideon reached down, picked up Mandy's hand and raised it to his mouth. "Darling, your presence has been more intoxicating than the wine." He kissed the back of her hand then laved his tongue across her fingertips. "Enjoy the rest of your night."

The snarl that grew in Max's throat was more for the humor in Gideon's eyes than for any true jealousy. Gideon dropped Mandy's hand and backed away.

"I'll walk you out."

Gideon smothered a smile and led the way.

"I'll be right back," Max said, glancing at Mandy. She nodded. Her chest rose and fell in long deep breaths, like she was trying to regain her control. Well, no shit. Gideon had just been munching on her like she was dessert.

He slammed the door behind him as he stalked down the steps, hurrying to catch up with Gideon.

"What the fuck was that?" he demanded, grabbing Gideon's arm and spinning him around. Gideon moved easily, turning and facing him. The teasing laughter that had persisted all day was gone. The serious glint in his eyes only made Max's irritation worse—or maybe that was from his cock twitching inside his jeans. All evening, sitting between Mandy and Gideon, he'd been in a state of constant arousal. Either way he turned his attention, his cock and his wolf found something of interest.

He pushed it aside and tried to focus on being pissed off.

"What was that?" he asked again.

"A kiss." The cool arrogant tone pushed Max's temper.

"Bullshit. That was a hellava lot more than a kiss. You had your hand on her ass. Fuck, your tongue was in her mouth."

The edge of Gideon's mouth kicked up. "Yes, it was. And quite delicious she is too." The smirk deepened. "But you know that."

"Listen—"

Gideon held up a hand and shook his head. "Don't try to convince me this is about jealousy. You stood and watched." He moved closer, encroaching on Max's space. Max refused to give an inch, refused to back up. "You watched my hand on her ass, watched me rubbing my dick against that hot space between her legs."

The words ignited the memories—and all the sensations that came with them.

"Yeah, you watched, and wanted to join in." Warmth covered Max's cock. Gideon's hand, sliding over his erection. "Wanted to slide up behind her, just like we'd been in the kitchen." His voice was so close, words spoken right in Max's ear. "Ease this hard cock between her ass cheeks and ride, nice and slow."

Max groaned. The picture Gideon presented was so clear, so right. The wolf howled, blocking out rational thought. All Max could hear was Gideon's voice, promising more. God, he couldn't take it anymore. He had to stop the words.

Max turned his head and planted his mouth on Gideon's, stopping the verbal seduction. He felt Gideon's smile against his lips but it disappeared moments later when Max drove his tongue into his mouth. Twin masculine groans rumbled between them. The sound vibrated through Max's chest and slid down to his groin. Fire and spice filled his head—delicious flavors that tempted. Without commanding his body to move, Max found his hand cupping Gideon's head, holding him in place as he learned and explored the exotic mouth beneath his.

The heat of Gideon's hand increased as he squeezed and pumped, moving up and down Max's jeans-covered cock. Unable to stop himself, he rocked his hips forward, thrusting, needing his dick inside something—a fist, a mouth, pussy, ass. At this point he wasn't sure he cared. He just needed to fuck something. Someone. Gideon.

Mandy.

Her name zapped a moment of sanity into his brain and he pulled back from the kiss. He didn't go far, couldn't make himself leave. The pulse at the base of Gideon's neck called to him and Max felt his teeth changing, preparing to penetrate, pierce his skin. Not to kill—to mark and claim.

He reined in the wolf but couldn't resist one taste. He scraped his teeth along the tight throat muscles, savoring the shudder that ran through Gideon's body. Not enough. Max laved his tongue across the tiny scratches left by his incisors, soothing, sampling. God he tasted good. And Max wanted more. Wanted to lick his way down Gideon's body, take his cock in his mouth. Yeah. *That little shudder will be nothing. He'll be screaming when his dick is sliding between my lips.*

The thoughts, desires, didn't panic him the way he thought they should. His wolf was too powerful, too strong with the need to fuck the male beside him.

Max tipped Gideon's mouth to his, sinking his tongue back into the warmth that called. He was allowed one compelling taste before it was gone.

Gideon pulled back, stepping out of the embrace, his lips shining.

Max shook his head, trying to get back in focus. The wolf's nagging growls demanded he return but the human mind crushed the noises. What had he been thinking? He'd been thinking about fucking Gideon. About sucking him off. And the idea hadn't freaked him out.

Now though, his heart started to pound and it felt like someone was standing on his chest.

"Have a good night."

Max looked up. Gideon walked away, heading to his car. Part of him thought he should call him back, part of him *wanted* to call him back but he couldn't get his voice to work. Gideon smiled as he opened his car door but sadness laced the edges of his eyes.

Gideon's car started and he pulled out into the road, with Max still watching, still wondering what would have happened if Gideon hadn't pulled back. *Bad enough you're fucking Jax's girlfriend. Don't start fucking his friends too.*

Except he wasn't fucking Jax's girlfriend. Not any more. Not again. Last night had been an aberration. He wasn't going to compound the problem by repeating it.

He was going to walk inside and tell Mandy who he was. The thought made his cock wilt.

Maybe he should wait. Stick with the plan to talk to Jax first, explain what happened, hope his brother didn't murder him and then have Jax tell Mandy.

That sounded better. He'd walk inside and tell Mandy he had an early meeting. That was a generic enough excuse to not spend the night fucking, right?

He paused at the front door, feeling like he was bearding the lion in its den. Except it wasn't the lion's den, it was Jax's and really, what did "bearding a lion" mean? The inane thoughts kept his mind busy enough that he could open the door and step inside.

For the second time tonight he stopped, two feet into the living room, his heart taking another jolt.

Mandy—naked this time, no lingerie—knelt beside the coffee table Her hands behind her back, her eyes lowered. A classic submissive's pose. Max's knees trembled. *Sweet fuck.*

The warm scent of her wet cunt filled the room. God, he'd become addicted to that smell last night and wanted more, wanted it all over his body, his mouth, down his throat.

"Mandy?" He was amazed he didn't stutter.

"I hope I please you…sir."

"You please me very well." Words fell from his mouth without conscious thought. Though that wasn't surprising because all of the blood in his body had drained into his cock. His hand moved to his fly, knowing he was close to coming in his jeans but unable to resist one light stroke, an anticipation of…what? Mandy's mouth? Her pussy? Her ass? Gideon's comments about how fuckable she was came back to him. Every part of her would know his cock. Every part.

Command returned to his body. Determination strengthened his knees. He walked forward, stopping just in front of her. He planted his feet outside her knees.

"Raise your eyes," he ordered. Tension rippled through her body. She wasn't used to following another's commands. She'd gone along with it last night but this was different. There was nothing teasing in his voice. Nothing to suggest this was less than it was—a Dominant and his submissive. He waited, thinking this might be too much for her, but then she moved, tipping her head back and looking at him.

Love and hunger surged through his body as he stared into her eyes. She submitted to his command but remained strong, allowing him control of her body.

He reached down and rubbed his thumb across her lower lip, small circles along the sensitive skin. A subtle warning that he intended to fuck her mouth. Her eyes twinkled as she opened her lips and licked the tip of his thumb.

His cock jumped in his jeans as if knowing it would receive the next caress. Max held back, not wanting to go too fast. Not wanting to rush the experience.

He stepped back and walked around her, looking at her from every angle. Gideon was right. Fuckable. Her breasts firm and round. So sensitive—as he'd learned last night. He wanted to straddle her chest and spill his cum across her skin. Mark her with his scent. The wolf growled its approval, tightening the images in his head until Max could almost feel it happening.

Strange but tonight there were no other voices in his head. No recriminations for fucking his brother's fiancée, no lingering bit of guilt.

She's mine.

The conviction of the statement didn't startle him, didn't surprise him. Almost as if he'd known the truth last night. He could only hope Jax would forgive him some day but he couldn't, *wouldn't* let Mandy go.

Her shoulders shifted as he stared at her back, continuing the slow circle around her. She rolled her shoulders again. The movement wasn't physical discomfort but insecurity. A low rumble rattled from his throat. She was sexual and delicious and he would make sure she believed that.

He walked back around to his previous position, straddling her knees. Putting his cock within easy reach of her mouth. She looked up, gulping as her gaze wandered past his erection.

He chuckled. "Don't worry, honey." He smoothed his fingers along her cheek. "You know how well it fits inside your pretty little cunt." She gasped as the explicit word. "Now you're going to see how deep you can take me into your mouth."

She didn't respond, didn't speak, but she licked her lips.

"Open my jeans and take out my cock. I want to get between those pretty lips."

Mandy shivered as he spoke, her clit tingling warning her she was close to coming—from just a few words. If she'd been alone, she'd have touched herself or gotten one of her toys out.

But she'd learned last night that he—it was still difficult to think of him as Jackson—wouldn't allow that.

Gideon had planted the idea of being naked but after she'd stripped off her clothes—for the second time tonight—she found herself remembering Jackson's voice last night. The power, the commands, and she'd put herself into this position.

Swallowing deeply, she tried to keep her heart from exploding as she pushed up on her knees and reached for the buttons keeping his jeans closed. His erection pressed against the rough denim material. She cupped her hand over the thick line, sampling it against her palm.

"You are not to tease me, Amanda. I told you to take out my cock. Don't make me punish you."

The center of her stomach seemed to drop—both with the commanding, almost parental "Amanda" and the threat of punishment. What would he do to her? And did she have enough courage to find out?

Her pussy fluttered and a wicked thought formed. She could misbehave just to see what would happen. She stared at his erection, still pressed against those tight jeans.

But not yet. First she wanted to feel his cock in her mouth—give him some of the pleasure he gave her last night.

Keeping her eyes lowered, hoping she looked sufficiently submissive when really she expected to have him on his knees in a few moments, she twisted her fingers around the first button, then moved to the next. Hmm, she understood the fascination with button flies. Every one released spread the denim wider, allowing his cock to press forward. The material of his briefs kept it from springing free and Mandy was glad. She wanted to play a bit, tease him.

She finished with the last button and spread the placket open. She leaned forward and pressed her open mouth to the hard line of his cock. Through the material, she licked, leaving a hot damp trail behind. She glanced up, wanting to see his reaction. He stared down, the line of his jaw tight, his eyes glowing with that strange red light.

Holding his gaze, she flicked her tongue out, wetting the front of his briefs.

"Honey, you're asking to get your ass spanked."

"No, sir," she whispered but couldn't resist one more lick. She slid her fingers into the waistband and tugged it down. His cock bounced up as if excited to be freed from its prison. "Poor baby." She moaned, wrapping her hand around the thick shaft and pulling it close to her mouth. She brushed a kiss along the side. "Trapped so long." A whisper of her tongue. "Needing some attention." She ran her open mouth up the full length of the shaft, stopping before she reached the head.

"Amanda." The warning in his voice was clear and only encouraged the shivers across her skin. Her nipples pulled up tight. She guided the tip of his cock to her breasts and rubbing the head across her skin. He crouched down, giving her more access. Smiling, she swirled the thick head around her nipple, spreading the drop of pre-cum into her skin. His groan drew a new rush of heat into her pussy.

"I'll try to do better, sir," she whispered, trying to hide her smile, pulling the tip to her mouth and lapping at the head. It was delicious, the sweet taste of his pre-cum so different from any other man's. Addictive. She wanted more.

She wrapped her fingers around the base of his cock and stroked, short slow pulses. His hips thrust forward once, shallow and hard. He grunted and straightened, forcing his back straight.

She looked up, letting her smile flow through her eyes. The salty taste of his skin tingled on her lips making her crave more. His eyes burned, red in the light of the living room. Wicked confidence guided her and she opened her mouth allowing his cock to fill her. She relaxed her throat and took him as deep as she could, savoring the masculine groan. Heat swelled in her chest and she moaned, letting the sound translate to his cock. He pushed forward and she sucked, drawing back, tightening her lips, wanting to feel every inch as she pulled back.

She let his cock pop out her mouth. She lapped at the head then turned her attention to the shaft, exploring, sampling inch after inch and finding those extra special places that made him growl.

His hips started move. Shallow thrusts that warned she was pushing at his control, that he wanted to fuck her mouth. The sweet pre-cum that dripped off the tip made an enticing treat and Mandy lapped it up before returning to the base of his cock. She eased her hand between his legs and cupped his balls. Tension zipped through his body and made her bolder. She squeezed, not too hard, just enough to draw a grunt from her lover. She repeated the motion, a light, gentle squeeze.

"Fuck."

The guttural curse made her smile, hunger for more made her retreat, drawing back and placing the tip against her lips.

She flicked her tongue out catching another drop of that delicious, addictive pre-cum. Feeling his gaze on her, she looked up, pausing, giving him a moment to anticipate, to crave. She opened her mouth, wide, and took him inside, pressing down, meeting the forward thrust of one of those little thrusts.

They both groaned as he hit the back of her throat. She tightened her lips and pulled back, the smooth glide of his cock caressing the inside of her mouth.

Max struggled with himself, battling his conscience. Every lesson, every lecture he'd ever had from his father, Byron, and his older brother rang through his head, like they were standing behind him screaming "What the hell are you doing?" but fuck it was almost impossible to pull back. The heat of Mandy's mouth, the sheer lust in her face as she sucked him drowned out the voices. What would be so wrong if he came in her mouth? She'd be a little turned-on for a day. That was a good thing. The little devil in his brain immediately created wicked fantasies of all the things he could do with her.

Moments before his conscience voiced its opinion. *She thinks you're Jax. She loves Jax.*

He groaned.

"Mandy, stop." He tightened his grip on her head and tried to hold her still but she kept moving, her lips sinking down and then sucking hard as she pulled back. His chest tightened like she sucked the breath out him and he felt his balls pull up, ready to come.

He swallowed and forced his lungs to expand, concentrating on keeping control—not only of his body but of Mandy as well.

"Amanda." He was pleased with his stern tone when really he wanted to whimper like a little girl. "I told you to stop."

She pulled back, releasing his cock from her mouth but rubbing her cheek against it, pressing her lips to the side. "But I want to taste you."

He shook his head, allowing his dominant nature to come to the surface.

"Disobedient girls get punished."

She moaned, rubbing her lips along his shaft. So tempting.

It would be so easy. And she wanted it so much. And really what would it hurt?

His conscience came alive with a vengeance and he found the strength to take a step back.

He almost found the strength to walk away completely. Then she looked up, her eyes filled with the lust he'd reveled in last night.

The sight silenced his conscience. He was going to fuck Mandy. Going to have her every way he could and then he was going to fight his brother for the right to keep her.

He looked around, needing a place where they could play for a while.

He didn't like using Jackson's bedroom—didn't want any memories of her and Jackson together—but it was the only bed and he had feeling when he was done fucking Mandy tonight, neither of them would be able to move. Plus the heavy crossbar along the bottom of Jax's bed was perfect for what he had in mind.

Punishment. He'd promised a punishment and based on the brightness of Mandy's eyes, he'd better follow through. And make it a good one.

Definitely the woman for him.

"You came here tonight to get fucked." It wasn't a question and he didn't give her a chance to refute it. "Did you bring any of your toys?"

Her cheeks brightened and she opened her mouth but no sound came out.

"You brought that little plug, didn't you? The one you want me to slide into your tight ass."

She gulped and nodded.

"Very good. Where is it?"

"In my purse." Her voice was soft, hesitant. Shy. "Sir."

"Very good," he said again. "I want you to go upstairs to…the master bedroom, stand at the end of bed, bend over and put your hands and elbows on the crossbar. Wait for me."

He stepped back, his cock still hard, wet from her mouth. She wobbled a bit as she stood. Max watched, making sure she was steady on her feet. She'd spent a long time on her knees and he didn't want her stumbling. That would ruin what he had planned.

She caught herself and seemed to find her balance. Keeping her chin high, she turned and walked regally toward the stairs. He stared at her back, unwilling to miss a moment staring at her ass as she moved. It was incredible. Seductive. The sexual rhythm so innate she probably didn't even know it existed. Hell, he hadn't seen it that first night, with those ugly clothes covering her sweetly rounded body. He licked his lips, thinking he liked the ugly gray suit now—no one but he would know what was hidden beneath it.

She turned the corner at the first landing and disappeared upstairs. He found the small purse and unzipped the top. Perfect. Everything he needed. Brand-new butt plug and lube. A few condoms neatly placed in the corner pocket. *Love a woman who comes prepared.*

And he was going to love her until she came again and again.

Chapter Eleven

ꟃ

Mandy made the turn around the staircase and grabbed the railing, her body a strange mixture of strength and weakness. Her knees trembled but her heart beat loud and steady. She wasn't frightened, at least not of Jackson. More than a little concerned about her own behavior. But there was no way she was going to back off now. Too many possibilities lay before her and who knew if she'd ever have this chance again. If tomorrow he woke up and regretted it again…

She pushed the thought away. Regrets were for later and she wasn't going to allow herself to think of it. Experience the night.

Not wanting to get caught lingering in the stairs, she pushed open the door to the bedroom. The one time she'd been in Jackson's house before, she'd taken a quick tour. Now she looked at it from a completely different viewpoint—a woman about to be fucked senseless. At least she hoped that was the plan.

But first she was going to be punished and that somehow involved that butt plug. Her stomach flipped over. When she'd started the day, she hadn't imagined ending it bent over the end of Jackson's bed.

Struggling to keep her breath steady, she walked into the room. He was still downstairs but she knew she didn't have much time. She looked at the big, high bed and imagined being spread out on it. She looked at the strong four posts—perfectly suited to be tied to.

Oh goodness, where is your head? You shouldn't be thinking about being tied to his bed.

No, think about bending over and having something inserted in your ass.

She moaned and the sound almost made her miss the noise of him coming up the stairs. Not wanting to be caught not following directions—at least until she knew what her "punishment" entailed, she bent over and placed her hands and elbows on the crossbar along the bottom of the bed. Cool air rushed across her skin. She closed her eyes, feeling exposed, vulnerable in this position.

She sensed rather than saw him come into the room. He didn't speak. His hand, two fingers rough with calluses she wouldn't have expected, skated up her ass. Mandy jumped.

"It's okay, Mandy. Any time you want to stop, tell me."

She nodded but didn't look up.

"Do you want to stop?"

She shook her head. "No, sir."

"Very good."

She melted under his approval.

"You're being very compliant, honey. Almost like you're trying to make me forget your punishment."

She shook her head. "No, sir."

"Because you know I won't forget."

"Yes, sir."

"That's right. Because you were a bad girl, trying to make me come in your mouth."

"Yes, sir." She shivered as she spoke the words, feeling them as little hot flicks to her clit. Unable to stop the movement, she arched her back, tipping her ass up. He ran his hand down the slit between her ass cheeks, a teasing caress that only made the ache worse.

"I know you need it, honey, but you must be punished first." He dipped his finger into her pussy, one shallow entry that only made her want more. "So wet." He thrust two fingers deep into her, shocking her with the sudden penetration.

"What's made you so wet, pretty girl?" He pulled his fingers back and pushed into her again. "Did sucking my cock make you wet? Is that why you're spilling all over my fingers?"

"Yes." God, sucking him off shouldn't have had this effect on her but somehow almost making him come had left her hungry—to be fucked and more.

"You could take me right now, couldn't you, honey? Without me even touching you, this hot cunt is ready for my cock."

"Yes," she moaned and pressed her hips, trying to ease his fingers deeper.

He yanked them away, leaving her empty.

"Yes?" he asked. The hard master's voice returned. "You must answer me properly, Amanda."

"Yes, sir."

"Yes, sir, what?" His fingers returned, not fucking her, just petting her slit, teasing her opening. God, he was so close but not where she needed him. She moaned and wiggled trying to slide him into place. "Is your cunt ready for my cock?"

"Yes, sir."

"Say it." He stepped forward, putting his groin against her ass. His jeans were closed again, covering his cock. He still managed to slide the hard bulge between her ass cheeks and press against her. "Say your cunt is ready for me."

She swallowed and bit her lip, not sure she could comply but she didn't want him to stop.

"My c-cunt is ready for you…sir."

"Not comfortable with the word, honey? Why?" He pumped against her ass. "Your cunt is so pretty, delicious." He leaned down until his mouth was at her ear. "So fuckable. But not yet." He drew his hips back, leaving her skin bare to the cool air. "You almost succeeded in distracting me from punishing you. But don't worry, I haven't forgotten.

She took a deep breath and gripped the crossbar, bracing herself. Those sweet rough fingers skimmed along the base of her spine, dipping down to tease the top of her ass, swirling random patterns across her thighs, making very nerve ending come alive with the delicate touch.

"It's time for your punishment, Amanda." She shivered at the precise tone of his voice. "But if at any point you want me to stop, really stop, say the word 'accounting'. Do you understand?"

She nodded then remembered she was supposed to answer properly. "Yes, sir."

"And if you say that word, I will stop immediately and we will go no further tonight."

"Yes, sir." She'd heard and read enough about BDSM situations to know the use of a safe word but God, she'd never pictured herself in a situation where she might need one. Still, the thought of stopping didn't even occur to her. She wanted this. Hoping she could make it through the punishment and enjoy the fucking on the other side.

But it did give her some comfort to know that if she panicked or if it hurt too much, she could call a halt.

He stepped away and Mandy focused on the brown bedspread, preparing for her punishment. She was pretty sure knew what was coming. He was going to push that butt plug into her ass and it was going to hurt and she wasn't sure—a smack splintered the air and seconds later her body acknowledge the sting on her backside. She gasped and her eyes popped open. Sure that her mouth hung open as well, she stared at the blankets six inches from her face. He was actually spanking her? Before she could even finish the question, his hand landed on her ass a second time.

This time, she yelped. Couldn't stop the sound. The initial strike wasn't painful but it lingered, burning her skin. And damn it, she hadn't been spanked since she was a child. Why did people find this erotic? His next stroke came fast and harder, landing high on her ass. She opened her mouth, ready to call a halt when he tapped her again, lighter, lower, almost to her pussy entrance.

She gasped, barely able to comprehend what was happening. It was like tiny fireworks going off in her sex.

"That's it, honey. Let yourself feel it. I want your cunt more than wet. I want you dripping your pussy juice down your thighs."

He tapped her ass again and the sensations skittered across her skin and poured into her pussy. It still hurt and God, was her ass going to be red tomorrow, but she didn't want him to stop. Not yet. Not…yet.

She lost herself in the sensations. The bright sparkles of pain followed by the seductive rush of need, wanting more. And his voice—filling her head, sliding just beneath her skin.

She heard noises and realized they were her, begging.

Please, sir. Fuck me, sir.

Her ass burned, every touch almost too much for her to bear.

And then it was gone. Heat covered her back and his hard cock pressed against her skin. Hot kisses whispered along her neck and shoulders. She tipped her head, wanting more.

"You took your punishment well, Amanda." He kissed her neck. Then she felt his teeth, hard and sharp against her throat. Fire streaked down her spine as he bit down—not breaking the skin but leaving a mark. Leaving his mark. "Your pussy is soaking wet, honey."

"Please, sir," she moaned, pushing back, trying to guide him deeper.

"So impatient." He nipped her ear and straightened, leaving her bereft and needy. God, she didn't think she could take much more. Her ass burned, her pussy throbbed. She was to the point of begging, needed to be fucked. But he seemed to have inexhaustible levels of control. She was naked, soaking wet and still he made no move to have her.

A cool, slick caress teased her ass. She gasped and pushed forward, her body instinctively trying to escape.

"No, no, honey. Let me get you ready."

But I thought my punishment was over?

His hand rubbed across her ass. "It is." And she realized she'd said the words aloud. "This won't be punishment. Pleasure. Get you ready to take my cock." As he spoke, he eased, gently, one slick finger into her ass. "That's it. Relax and let me in. It's going to feel so good when I slide in here." She tensed. There was a moment of pain but then it eased as he worked his finger in and out, not going deep, just soft shallow strokes. "My cock's much bigger. I'm going to have to fuck you slowly when I finally put my dick in you."

His words rolled through her until she could see it, feel it. She moaned and rocked her hips.

"Sh, honey, you're doing well." He removed his finger and moments later the blunt end of the plug began to follow the same path, thin but growing thicker, almost too much. "Ease back, Mandy, I won't give you too much. That's it, sweetheart. Damn, you are the sexiest thing alive." The commanding tone disappeared and seduction returned, swirling through her core like a whisper. She strained for a moment then allowed her body to relax, not fighting the foreign penetration. He pushed the plug deeper. "Oh, honey, that's it." Because she wanted to please him, wanted to hear his praise, she allowed the plug in, the thickest part causing her to whimper.

The base of the plug pressed against her skin and Jackson smoothed his hand down her ass, sliding his fingers into her slit, the loving caresses so opposite to the fact that she had something in her ass but it felt so good. The delicate sense of fullness—not too uncomfortable, but enough so she couldn't forget that it was there.

His hands ran up and down her ass, stroking, caressing, soothing. That delicious murmur of his voice whispering soft words that made her want. Made her ache. She moaned and turned her head to the side, needing something to fill her. He was there. He bent down and kissed her mouth, his tongue dipping into her mouth, seductive and compelling.

"I need to fuck you. Need to get my cock into you."

"Yes." She didn't answer with "sir". Somehow it didn't seem right. This wasn't play between Master and submissive. It was between the two of them.

She heard the rustle of a package opening and knew he was sliding the condom on. Her body moved without her direct command, arching her back, offering her pussy, spreading her legs just a little more. She needed him. Needed him hard and thick filling her.

The tip of his cock bumped against her opening, another teasing connection. Warning her but not giving her what she needed.

"Please—" Jackson. His name is Jackson. Only he didn't act like Jackson. Didn't feel like Jackson. He felt like someone totally different. Someone who made her hot and sexy in a way Jackson never had before.

"Please, what, honey? What do you need?"

"Fuck me. Please." She pushed up on tiptoes and rubbed her slit against his cock, encouraging him to slide into her.

He gripped her hips and held her in place. "Oh, Mandy, you don't learn. I decide when we fuck, when my cock comes into you." He reached between them and wiggled the butt plug, teasing her tight opening with the threat of removing it. She froze—the full sensation translating into a throb in her pussy. As if he knew, he reached forward, his fingers dipping into her slit, as if checking to see if her pussy was still wet. He tickled her clit as he brushed by and Mandy groaned. The sensations overwhelmed her and she sagged forward, wiggling her hips. She couldn't stand any more—if he didn't fuck her soon she was going to go insane.

"That's it, Amanda. You've been so good. You deserve to get fucked."

"Yes, sir, please."

He chuckled and once again she felt the head of his cock at her entrance. This time she held still, unwilling to do anything that might make him stop.

"Very good." He slipped the tip inside, nudging her opening. She gripped the bar even tighter and didn't move. It was like he was testing her. Her muscles clenched wanting to press against him, drive him inside her. He stroked his hand down her ass, cupping her hip in his palm and slowly pushed forward. She'd expected a hard pounding fuck but like all other things, he seemed to be in perfect control. He entered her with precision, like he was savoring every inch of her pussy. "So sweet," he whispered as his hips pressed against her ass. The thick girth of his cock strained her pussy. "You squeeze me perfectly, honey. How do you feel?"

"Full," she whispered.

He chuckled. "You've got that little plug in your ass." He pulled back and slowly fucked her again. "Imagine another cock back there, fucking you, filling you." The image popped into her brain and wouldn't let go. Her and Jackson…and Gideon. One man behind her, one in front, both filling her, fucking her. Gideon's mellow voice blending with Jackson's growly tones. A low whimper slipped from her throat, her pussy clenching around his cock. "You like that idea. Who were you thinking about?"

"You," she answered honestly.

"Who else?" He drove his cock into her drawing a deep throated groan from her. It was so good, almost too much but she didn't want him to stop. "Who, honey? Who do you want fucking your pussy while I slide into that tight ass."

"G-Gideon." She breathed the word and Max felt his cock twitch. Fuck, that's what he wanted. Wanted to see Gideon on top of Mandy, plowing into her. Then he wanted Gideon bent over and Max drilling his ass.

His shout filled room and he pounded his cock into Mandy. The sane portion of his brain told him to pull back, not to hurt her but she pressed back, tipping her ass up and sending him deeper. The wolf burst from his mental cage and growled, adding his strength to Max's.

"More," she moaned, her face buried in the blankets.

His body responded to her plea and he kept thrusting, driving deep in her, giving her what she asked for—more, always more.

His lips pulled back from his teeth and he stared at the sleek line of her neck and shoulder. One swipe of his incisors and she would belong to him.

"No!" he groaned, barely recognizing that he'd said the word aloud. Mandy's head came up and she glanced over her shoulder, a hint of concern in the movement. He grabbed control of his wolf, reining the beast in. "It's okay, honey. I'm trying not to come too fast. Want to enjoy you a bit longer."

The tight squeeze of her cunt, made even tighter by the tiny plug in her ass strained his control. He ground his back teeth together, fighting to cage the wolf even as he pulled his hips back and drove forward, sinking his cock into her hard and fast. She shivered around him, her body giving a quick shudder. Someone liked that. He retreated and plunged into her again, hard and deep, trying to find the same place. She groaned and bent her head forward.

"Fuck, honey, I'm not going to last much longer." Desperate to have her come before he did, he slid his hand around her waist and dipped his fingertip into the hot folds of her pussy, finding and stroking her clit. It didn't take much. Every nerve in her body had to be tingling. God knew his were. He held his finger against her clit and fucked her forward, sliding his finger along one side.

She cried out and her fingers turned white at the knuckles as she held on.

Once more he pushed forward, going deep and hard. Her pussy contracted around him, squeezing his cock and a long low cry ripped from her mouth. He shouted and punched his hips forward again, his cum pulsing from his body, filling the condom.

His wolf growled—the sound a mixture of dominance and frustration. Max immediately recognized the source of the animal's frustration—he wanted his scent on and inside Mandy. Filling her and marking her.

Mine.

The wolf rumbled in his head but Max pushed it aside. He found the fine motor skills needed to pull out and remove the condom and tie it off. He turned back to the bed. Mandy was still bent over, her ass in the air, that plug still filling her. The seductive scent of her pussy flooding the room.

She shifted and moaned. "Jackson."

The name was filled with need and hunger, pleasure and desire.

Max's chest contracted. The wolf went insane. The room turned black and white as his vision cleared and his teeth stretched.

"Mine," he growled, the sound muffled around the oversized incisors filling his mouth. The wolf filled his brain, giving him no choice but to react. He lifted Mandy from the crossbeam and spun her around. The lazy sexual glow disappeared as she stared into his eyes. The barely human part of him didn't want to frighten her but the animal needed to stake its claim.

"Mine," he said again, leaning down and scraping his teeth across her neck, hard but not breaking the skin. She moaned and tipped her head to the side, giving him the access he needed, baring her throat to him. She couldn't know what that meant, how much he wanted to drive his teeth into her. He yanked her closer, wrapping her legs around his waist as he picked her up, the hot liquid of her cunt branding his stomach.

He moved, dropping her in the center of the bed, her thighs spreading, baring her wet cunt. He growled, unable to speak, not sure there were words for what he was thinking. The wolf almost completely in control, Max felt his body moving, reacting. He caught her hips in his hands, pulling her forward, driving his tongue into her open pussy.

The faint taste of latex lingered and the wolf howled, wanting to taste Max and Mandy blended together.

He licked and sucked, letting her squirm as he removed the foreign taste, leaving just the delicious flavor of her cunt behind.

"Please," she moaned.

Max snapped his head back, staring up. The black and white vision made every other sense crisp and clear. Though he couldn't see red, he knew her cheeks were flushed. The wolf growled its satisfaction. He'd done this to her. Brought her to the edge, turned her into a sensual creature vibrating with need.

Keeping his eyes locked with hers, he leaned forward and drove his tongue back into her.

Her pretty breasts swayed as she panted, watching him tongue-fuck her sweet pussy. He hummed, savoring the flavor on his tongue, wanting more. The sound rumbled through her skin. Her thighs squeezed shut, tightening around his head, holding in place as a rush of moisture coated his lips. He lapped at the delicious liquid, taking her inside him.

"Yes." She pushed her hips up, trying to drive him deeper. "Please."

If he'd been fully in control he might have stopped, punished her for being a demanding little thing but now he needed to feel her come on his cock.

He reared back, licking his lips, capturing her pussy juices from his mouth. His body moved without direct command from his brain, reacting to the scent of her sex, the slick liquid dripping from her cunt and the sheer need to mark her as his.

He reached for another condom. His fingers trembled as he rolled it on, the wolf fighting him every step. The animal wanted more than just a fuck. The human agreed but his conscience wouldn't let him claim her, not when she thought she was fucking Jax.

Struggling against the wolf's desires and the instinct to claim his woman, Max placed the head of his cock to her opening. The intense heat gripped his cock and dragged him in. He pushed forward, slamming into her in one hard thrust. Her body arched up and she screamed, her fingers grabbing the bedspread beneath her hips. Her pussy clung to his cock as he tried to pull out, neither his cock or her pussy allowing him to retreat long before he plunged back inside.

He struggled to slow the wolf, to retake command but Mandy shifted and squirmed beneath him, wrapping her legs around his hips and pulling him into her harder, deeper.

He rubbed his lips along the nape of her neck, not really a kiss, just a touch, nuzzling and comforting as he pounded into her cunt. She reacted beautifully, arching back and offering him more. His teeth ached, the need to bite almost impossible to resist. Instead he licked and sucked, drawing up a small mark that at least would warn humans she belonged to him.

She turned her head, biting down on his shoulder. Hard. Her teeth dented the skin and his wolf went wild. The red haze returned. Max gripped her hips sliding her up and down his cock, the sweet sounds of her coming ringing in his head. Her pussy contracted around his cock, squeezing him, driving him to come. But it was her voice, soft, almost silent, whispering against his skin that pushed him over the edge.

"Please."

He pushed into her once more, her legs squeezing him, holding him as he came.

It had started so violent but a comforting peace settled over him. Still holding her, he turned his head and pressed his lips on hers, slow, sensual kisses that didn't try to seduce. Just enjoy.

He pressed back, easing her off his cock and turning her so she lay in the center of the bed. Mandy clung to him, her breasts pressed to his chest as he rolled them onto the mattress. They lay there for long moments, not talking, just touching, kissing. He had to get up here in a minute, deal with the condom and take the plug out of her ass so she didn't get sore, but for the first time in his memory, he needed to hold a woman, assure himself that she was safe, that she was close.

That she was his.

Chapter Twelve

ஐ

Mandy skipped down the stairs. Her body ached in delicious ways, her backside a little on the tender side but she couldn't stop smiling. After a night like that, she felt like singing. Jackson was upstairs getting dressed. Moving a little slow himself. Slow and easy as he fucked her in the shower. Her grin widened. A perfect way to start the day—a slow tongue-lashing to her pussy followed by a deep gentle fuck against the shower wall.

She groaned and shook her head. She needed to focus. Think about something besides sex. Her stomach rumbled. Ah, food. That would be good.

Maybe he'd want to go out to breakfast. Her expertise in cooking ran out at a bowl of cereal and since Gideon wasn't there...

Her stomach dropped away as she remembered Jackson's hot voice describing what it would be like to have both men fuck her. Her deepest darkest fantasies had included two men but now she had faces, bodies and she couldn't get the image out of her head. She squirmed. The butt plug had been tight. Just thinking about a cock sliding into her ass made her groan but didn't stop the desire. He had been slow and gentle, stretching her. Talking to her. She'd never felt so helpless and so powerful all at the same time.

The thought of taking his cock while Gideon fucked her pussy.

"Oh God." She pressed her forehead against the wall, the sudden hunger in her body making her muscles weak.

Long breaths allowed strength and energy to seep back into her muscles and she continued down the steps, holding the railing to strengthen her still trembling knees. It was a gorgeous day. The sun was shining…and she had Jackson.

Funny that she'd never recognized romantic feelings for him before. He just seemed so different, so intense compared to the accountant persona she'd known and enjoyed as a friend for almost a year now. Something about this new man drew her. *Hot sex.* She smiled. That was part of it. How could it not be? But truly, the sex was hot because of the man and the energy that surrounded him. The fact that she could get turned-on, ready to fuck turned-on just by sucking him off still amazed her.

But he hadn't wanted to come in her mouth. She rubbed her tongue across the inside of her lower lip. She'd never been much of a swallower before—always more than willing to have the man pull out—but last night, she'd wanted his cum. The pre-cum that dripped from the head had been sweet, not bitter. Sweet and addictive.

Definitely intriguing. He'd been so controlled. What would it take to make him lose that control and come down her throat? She glanced toward the staircase. They had time. And suddenly she was hungry for more than just breakfast.

The bright tinkle of her cell phone chimed from inside her purse and Mandy groaned. No. She didn't want to answer it. The only one who called her phone—besides Jackson—was Tracy…or clients. Damn it. She had to get it.

She unzipped the top, blushed at the lube and condoms stacked on top and dug to the bottom, hitting the button to answer even as she carried it to her mouth.

"This is Mandy."

"Mandy, it's Jackson."

She laughed and looked up the stairs. "What are you doing?" Wow, he sounded far away. She shook her head. Cell phones.

"I wanted to apologize in person." He paused. "Well, not in person, obviously, because we're on the phone but I wanted to at least talk to you. Not leave a voicemail."

The memory of that painful message hit her hard in the chest. Was he trying to dump her? What the hell?

"Jackson, just come downstairs and we'll talk about it." Her sexy mood evaporated. She wasn't up for playing games.

"Are you at my place? I'm in Las Vegas."

"What?" She stared at the stairway with a different intensity. It could be a joke but Jackson really wasn't the type. *You never thought he was the type of man to shove a butt plug up your ass and fuck you either.*

"Las Vegas. That's why I missed that dinner two nights ago. I'm sorry. It was a spur-of-the-moment decision to come here and visit my brother."

"Your brother?" She wasn't even sure she'd spoken aloud. Her mind retreated, processing how Jackson could be in Vegas when she'd just fucked him. Two nights in a row.

"Yeah, my brother, Max." Jackson chuckled. "But it looks like he's out of town. I've been here two days and haven't seen him." Scratches came through the line like he was covering the phone. "I'll be right there, honey. Oh damn." More scratches and the line cleared. "Uh, listen, Mandy, I'm going to be gone for a few more days." A muffled groan. "Maybe longer. We'll talk when I get back, okay?"

Numb, the shock blocking her ability to feel anything, she said, "Sure."

"Thanks, oh, yeah, I need to go."

The tone of his voice jerked her out her thoughts. It sounded sexual. Like Jackson was about to have sex and what the hell?

He groaned. "We'll talk later. I've got to go."

The connection broke and Mandy stared at the phone. Jackson was in Vegas, having sex.

Which meant he definitely hadn't been in Alaska *having sex* with her. So who? Obviously the brother. Twin brother. Fuck. Jackson had a twin. She knew that. Had known that. And that was who she'd been in bed with for two nights.

Pain bloomed in her chest, quickly changing to fury.

Footsteps jogging down the stairs snapped her head up. Her chest constricted, almost painful, nearly impossible to breathe as she stared at the man she'd fucked.

"You asshole." She threw the phone, smacking him in the chest. He caught the black box as it tumbled to the ground.

"What?" Jack—no, Max—stopped dead.

"This seemed like a fun way to spend your vacation? Come to Alaska and fuck with your brother's friends? Or just *fuck* your brother's friends."

She almost thought she saw him blanch but that would have meant he had a conscience and she didn't believe that. The pain sank into her stomach at the memories of everything they'd done, everything she'd let him do to her. Her cheeks burned. She'd let him do things she'd never allowed, never even considered with another man. And he was a stranger. Her stomach did a slow, sickening roll. She inhaled through her mouth, trying to keep from retching.

"Mandy, it wasn't like that."

"Wasn't it? Get bored and decide you need to impersonate your brother?"

"No, I meant to tell you but—"

"What? Couldn't find the time, maybe when you had your *tongue between my legs*, to say 'I'm not Jackson'. Yeah, I can see how those words would be hard to get out." She gripped her purse understanding how women shot their lovers.

She slung the bag over her shoulder and spun toward the door.

"Mandy—"

Max's hand closed around her elbow. She stopped, didn't look back, afraid that if she turned around she'd lose it.

"Take your hand off me." He must have heard the ice-cold rage because he released her. She searched her mind, looking for some suitable parting shot, some perfect exit line but her brain was blank. The emotions swirled through her skull like psychedelic lights leaving her stupid and pissed.

She yanked open the door and stalked out, storming down walkway, her car parked on the street. That should have been a sign. Jackson knew her car and wouldn't have been so surprised to see her standing in his living room. Almost naked. Fuck, don't go there. Don't—

A body filled her vision and she jerked to a stop, hands turning to fists. She might not be able to take Max down but she could make him hurt.

Only it wasn't Max in front of her. It was Gideon.

"Hey, Mandy. What's wrong?" He looked at her then at the open door behind her and winced.

The center of her stomach burned. "You knew." There was no doubt in her mind. "Perfect. I'm the only who got fucked with." She stepped around him. "And I think you're an asshole too for not saying anything."

That at least satisfied her parting shot desire. She got to her car, threw her purse in the backseat and drove off. Her eyes stung but Mandy blinked refusing to let the tears form, let alone fall. Instead she clung to the anger. She'd face the pain later when she could curl up on a ball and cry.

Bastard. Looking for an easy lay and she'd provided it.

She cranked the wheel to the right and hit the gas, driving blindly, her heart pounding in her ears, drowning out the street noise. Heat dripped down her cheeks. She didn't know what to do. The betrayal pierced her chest making it hard to breathe.

* * * * *

Max stared at the open door—she hadn't even bothered to slam it shut. Part of him screamed to go after her but for the first time in days, he ignored that voice and got a grip on himself. She hated him, didn't want to see him. At least not now. Probably not ever.

Wow, how to fuck up your life in three easy steps. First, sleep with your brother's fiancée. Second, don't tell her you're not the man she loves and sleep with her again.

He scoffed. Perfect. He'd managed to screw up his life in two steps. Such an overachiever.

Step three would probably be telling Jax and getting his throat ripped out by one very pissed off werewolf. Jax appeared to the world as controlled and reasonable. But Max knew the truth. His brother, and his wolf, had a temper that took awhile to ignite but when it let loose—everyone stood back until the sane, reasonable human regained control.

"That is one pissed off woman," Gideon announced from the doorway. Max nodded. "You told her, huh?"

"Uh, no." He held up Mandy's cell phone. "I think my brother called her."

"Ouch."

"Yeah."

"I—"

Max sighed. "I know. You told me. You told me to tell her. You were right. I should have freakin' told her. I shouldn't have even touched her in the first place but damn, she was so sexy and so sweet and fuck, aren't Christmases going to be a joy? I'll be sitting there thinking about fucking my brother's wife. If I get invited home. Once my mother finds out what happened, she's going to rip me a new one and probably kick my ass out of the house. And my dad." He covered his face with his hands. To his father—an Alpha werewolf—family, mates, pack were all that mattered. And Max had managed to fuck up all three. "Yeah, this isn't going to be pleasant so while

I agree you were right, you don't have to add to the guilt trip I'm already riding. I'll get it from plenty of other sources."

Gideon nodded and damn if there wasn't a hint of a smile on his face. Max growled. At least now he had a reason to pound Gideon into the ground. It would give him something to do for the afternoon.

"What I was going to say..." Gideon started, "is, I think you should give her a few hours to calm down and then go camp out on her doorstep and beg her to take you back."

"Right. Even if she would let me close enough to apologize, she's engaged to Jax." The thought made Max's stomach turn. Jax putting his hands on Mandy's sweet ass, holding her close while he fucked her tight, hot pussy. His fingers convulsed, lengthening and curling into fists.

"Engagements can be broken."

Gideon's calm, almost bland statement, snapped Max back to reality.

"What?"

"She can break the engagement."

"Why would she want to do that?"

"Because she loves you."

Max shook his head. "She loves Jackson. She thought I was Jackson."

Gideon shrugged. "Maybe, but listen, I've spent hours with those two, *hours,* and I've never once seen or felt the connection that you and Mandy have. God, I almost came in my jeans last night just watching the two of you together."

"That's just sex."

"It's chemistry." He held up his hands as if he thought Max would protest. "And I know you can't base a whole relationship on it, but you should see where it goes. She is a different woman when she's with you. More relaxed, sensual. Funny. They are boring when they're together. I've actually fallen asleep at the table listening to them." Gideon shrugged again. "You and Mandy fit together. Give her a little time and then go talk to her."

Max considered the idea. Maybe Gideon was right. Maybe it was more than sex. Maybe Mandy would be willing to listen to him grovel. After she'd calmed down. Though based on her anger that would take more than a few hours. He might consider approaching her sometime next year.

"Let's go to the climbing wall," Gideon suggested.

"I don't feel like it."

"Which is why you should go. You look tense and uptight. If we were sleeping together I'd say you need to get blown—"

Max's head snapped up and he saw Gideon smile. And damn if Max's cock didn't respond to the idea of a blowjob from Gideon.

"You need to work off some of your tension. If not, when you do go to see Mandy, you'll be so hyped up, you'll freak her out."

Max nodded. He was right that sex would have been Max's first choice of tension relief but since that wasn't available, what he really wanted to do was to run. In his wolf form. Unfortunately, Anchorage was populated enough that a wolf would be easily visible during daylight. The parks near the city were an option but still a risk. Gideon's suggestion was probably best.

With a sigh, Max went upstairs and changed into black pants. He and Jackson had managed to stay almost the same size despite their different lifestyles and interests. He grabbed a long-sleeved bike shirt out of his brother's closet and pulled it on.

He'd go work his body on the fake rock wall and hope it helped. Because he knew, despite the human conscience telling him it was a bad idea, he wasn't going to resist finding Mandy and begging her to give him another chance.

* * * * *

Mandy pulled into the parking lot outside the offices she shared with Jackson, the day wasted. The anger had turned to tears then faded back into fury and she'd raged. Unable to keep it to herself, she'd called Tracy. Tracy, being the good friend that she was, listened and was suitably furious on Mandy's behalf. Though she did sound a little relieved to know it wasn't *Jackson* who'd been the sex god in Mandy's bed.

Exhausted but unable to sit still, Mandy had finally left her house. Now that she knew Jackson was out of town, she realized his fish hadn't been fed for two days. She glared at the building, wondering if Jackson knew what had happened. Wouldn't that be the perfect topper to this rotten day? Was he laughing at her right now? Pitying her?

She slammed the car door shut and stalked into the building. She might be pissed at most of Jackson's relatives—including the rest of his family just for good measure—but she couldn't let his fish starve. That was just cruel.

And she still had her father's case to work on. She clung to that idea. It gave her something solid and worthwhile to focus on—besides wrapping her fingers around Max's neck and doing a slow, steady squeeze.

Asshole.

She dug to the bottom of her purse—for such a little bag, it held a lot of stuff—and found her office keys.

She glared at Jackson's door as she walked past it. Somehow being here made her feel like even more of a fool. She turned to her own office. She'd drop her stuff and go feed Jackson's fish.

She opened the door and walked in. Papers covered the desk and the top file cabinet drawer was open. What the hell—? Her overwhelmed mind couldn't process what she saw.

The door closed with a loud click and Mandy jumped. She looked up. A man stood in front of the closed door. She opened her mouth to scream.

"Quiet." The harsh command came from her right. She recognized the voice and froze. Brian Mickelson. She turned, fighting to keep her breathing calm. The sight of the knife in his fist sent her heart racing. Sean Baldino turned from the file cabinet, his eyes flashing with guilt.

Stay calm. Stay focused.

"What's going on?" Her voice quivered but she decided that was okay. They knew she wasn't a hardened criminal.

"Where are those books?"

"Books?"

"The books. You said your father kept a second set of books." He shoved the knife a little closer. "Where are they?" She blinked and tried to figure out what he was talking about. Her father didn't have a second set…then she remembered. She'd mentioned that he kept duplicate records. And he had. For most of his clients. Not Oyltech.

"I-I didn't find any. Not for Oyltech." That was the truth. She looked at Sean and crushed a scream. The smooth gloss of a pistol glinted in his fist. *Guns? We're playing with guns now?*

She swallowed trying to clear the lump from her throat.

"Uncle Sean?" She'd always hated calling him that but if she could remind him of the relationship between him and her father, it might help.

"I'm sorry, Mandy. We didn't want it to come to this but we really need those books. Where are they?"

She considered telling them again that they didn't exist but somehow she didn't think they were going to believe her. And the idea of being shot over some imaginary accounting books was too much for her to handle.

"I gave them to…" The obvious answer popped into her brain. "Jackson. My fiancé?"

Brian's eyes tightened at the edges.

Mandy shrugged, trying to maintain the "innocent and not quite understanding" look. "He's a great accountant and I wasn't sure what I was looking at, you know?" She cleared her throat.

He grabbed her arm and pulled her toward the door. "Fine. You're going to call him and have him bring us those books." His fingers tightened on her arm. "We'll make it nice and easy. You for the papers."

Chapter Thirteen

ꕥ

Max tipped head back and let the water pound on his face, closing his eyes and fighting the wolf for control. The unscented shower gel washed away the sweat and dirt but did nothing to mute the memory—Gideon's body, his scent as he'd climbed, his smile, that arrogant smirk that just made Max want to fuck him silly. Max groaned and slid his hand down his front, curling his fingers around his cock.

It was hard but then he'd gotten used to that in the past three days—a constant state of arousal. Being around Mandy and then Gideon. There was no relief. He stroked up the full length of his erection. He was close could probably make himself come with a couple of strokes but the thought didn't appeal. Not when he could have a mouth or a different hand touching him.

Or a tight ass to plow.

"Damn."

He released his cock and shook out his hair, letting the water rinse away the last of the soap. Jerking off wasn't going to help. The full moon was too close and it had been too long since Max had let his wolf run free. And having double temptation surrounding him was almost more than he could take.

Maybe he just had to face it. Push it. See if Gideon would actually be willing. If there was something behind all that teasing.

He killed the water and grabbed a towel, wrapping it around his waist. He dried off and got dressed, figuring this kind of conversation was better to have while he was fully clothed.

With a sigh, he stared at his reflection. Was he really contemplating fucking Gideon? Probably a bad idea. Based on the way he'd treated Mandy, his decision-making ability was obviously questionable at this point. Fucking Gideon would just compound the problem.

That sounded good in his head. Logical and mature. First he needed to talk to Mandy. Then once he figured out that situation, he could consider including Gideon. The right side of his mouth pulled up in a smile. Maybe Mandy would get to experience her two-lover fantasy.

He started down the stairs, glad to have that settled in his mind.

And it worked. At least until turned the corner and saw Gideon, fresh from his shower, smelling clean and crisp. Max's cock jumped inside his jeans and he stumbled forward. The compulsion to be close to the male came from deep inside him—a combination of wolf and human desires—but he didn't fight it. Didn't want to fight it.

Gideon looked up, his eyes glittering with heat. Fuck. Max reached out and wrapped his arm around Gideon's back, dragging him close, not needing to bend to match their lips together. Their mouths met, open and hot and perfect. Max groaned. Gideon's taste caressed his tongue reminding him of the night they met and he had to have more. Warmth covered his cock—Gideon moving right in, his palm covering Max's dick, cupping him, rubbing. Energy surged through his body, spinning in his veins and filling his cock.

Gideon squeezed his dick, just a light pulse that made Max moan. Fuck, what was he doing? He couldn't think with those lips on his, that tongue twirling around his, but damn he couldn't pull himself away. The flavor and texture was too addictive. The hand on his dick slid away and Max moaned, pressing his hips forward to follow the caress. Gideon's hands returned, opening his fly, wrapping long fingers around Max's bare cock.

Oh fuck.

"Yeah," Gideon replied and Max realized he's spoken aloud. Or at least moaned the words against Gideon's lips. The sighed agreement lasted only a moment before Gideon sank his tongue back into Max's mouth. Dominant instincts nagged at the corner of Max's thoughts, that he should take command of the kiss, but it felt so good, feeling Gideon's desire, Gideon's fingers on his shaft, slowly pumping.

"Gideon—" His mind went blank after that one word.

"Need this," Gideon whispered. Max didn't know if he meant Gideon needed it or realized that Max truly did. Gideon bent down and pressed a hard kiss on his neck, licking for one wicked caress before he bit down, his teeth nipping at Max's throat. His wolf came alert at the bite, loving the feel of another's aggression on his skin. He growled and pulled Gideon up, dragging him close for another hot, deep kiss.

They battled for control, teeth clashing together, neither willing to back down. His nerves gathered like vines, capturing every sensation and pulling it into his core. Gideon kept stroking, his fist firm and tight, not fast, every pull of his hand passing the entire length of Max's cock.

Gideon drew away, his eyes hot as he bent forward, biting down on Max's neck and moving lower, sinking to his knees.

Max stared down, the soft dark hair sliding through his fingers. A distant portion of his mind connected to the fact that he was stroking Gideon like a lover, not just a mindless mouth ready to suck his dick. No flutter of panic occurred. His wolf accepted it. Max accepted it. Hell, he wanted it. Wanted whatever Gideon had to offer.

Gideon released his grip on Max's cock and laved his tongue down his hipbones toward his groin. The heated lick sparked tiny triggers just beneath his skin, like someone tickling him from the inside. Gideon's cheek brushed Max's cock, the faintest scrape of stubble lighting up his skin. His cock twitched, every touch digging deep into his groin. He spread his legs and braced his knees, his body tensing. Ready to fuck. Gideon turned his head and kissed the hard shaft, rubbing his lips up the full length, tongue flicking out, tasting. Fuck.

Fingers curled around Max's cock, stroking, countering the wandering path of Gideon's lips, working the underside of the head, teasing until Max thought his mind would explode. Gideon pushed aside the tight jeans and slid his hand between Max's legs, cupping his balls, rolling them between his fingers.

Max grunted and rocked his hips forward, trying to drive his cock into Gideon's mouth. Gideon looked up, the wicked light in his eyes. He ran his tongue across the full length of his upper lip. The air left Max's chest in a rush, just the sight of that pink tongue, those lips. Nothing feminine about either but fuck, Max wanted to feel it.

As if Gideon knew he was pushing Max's control, he smiled and drew back, guiding the tip of Max's cock to his lips, lapping at the drops of pre-cum painting the head then opening his mouth wide. He pressed forward, slow, taking inch after inch until the head pressed against the back of his throat. He took a breath and relaxed his throat, letting Max ease a little deeper.

Max groaned. He ground his back teeth together, fighting the need to come, not wanting it to end too soon.

This was going to be fast. His claws popped out of the ends of his fingers and he dug them into the wall behind him, trying to hold himself still, not thrust deep into Gideon's mouth. But Gideon wouldn't let him hold back He sucked hard as he retreated and Max felt his eyes roll to the back of his head.

"Fuck!" He released the death grip on the wall and grabbed Gideon's hair, pulling what had to be a shade too hard, holding him in place as Max shoved his hips forward. He stared down, watching his dick slide in and out of Gideon's mouth. Gideon groaned and took him, took every thrust, tightening his lips as he retreated. Max's balls pulled up, his climax moments away.

He stared down. There was no way to know what would happen if he came in Gideon's mouth. Would it work the same as with a woman? Fuck he couldn't do that to Gideon without warning him.

"No, man, I can't. Wait." He pulled back, easing Gideon's mouth off his cock. The only thing harder had been resisting in Mandy's mouth. The wolf voiced its disapproval. A loud howl vibrated Max's eardrums from the inside. Damn, he needed to mark both of them, needed something to quiet his wolf. Gideon shook his head and looked up, shock flashing through his gaze. "Here." He hooked his hand below Gideon's arm and dragged him up, wrapping Gideon's fist around his cock, his hand covering Gideon's. Together they pumped the few last strokes, all it took to grab him by the balls and make him come. His hand fell away as he sagged back against the wall, his head hitting the plaster behind him with a thud. He didn't notice. His mind remained locked on his cock and the calloused hand stroking him through his orgasm, drawing every last bit of cum from his body.

He closed his eyes and licked his lips. The smell of sex and hunger filled the room, drowning his other senses.

He opened his eyes. Gideon rubbed his thumb across his lower lip, a sexual sensual reminder that Max's cock had just been there.

His cock twitched again, as if wanting to return. He leaned forward and covered Gideon's mouth with his own, tasting the blended flavors of Gideon and his own lingering traces. He growled, the wolf pacing inside his brain, wanting to complete the claiming with a hard fuck and a bite.

The dominant animal inside him demanded submission from his lover and he spun him around, putting Gideon's back to the wall, caging him with his weight.

He drew back and scraped his teeth across the strong tight muscles of Gideon's neck. The urge to bite down, penetrate and mark for every wolf to see snapped at Max's control. It was all he could do to pull back, leaving surface scratches as he bent down, ripping open Gideon's shirt, baring the hard muscular chest he'd admired at the gym. Max raked his fingernails down the smooth skin, liking the way his nails left thin lines. Yes, that skin would look delicious wearing his mark.

He slid his hand down and cupped the thick bulge between Gideon's legs. Breath caught in his throat. He'd never imagined fucking another man—at least nothing so specific as thinking how it would feel. This was different. He wanted this. The material was in his way. He wanted skin. Skin over hard flesh.

A phone ringing penetrated the edges of his lust but Max pushed it aside. He reached for the zipper to Gideon's jeans, eager to feel his cock, wanting that hard rod beneath his fingers.

Gideon's hands stopped his. "No. Get the phone."

"Ignore it," Max growled, biting Gideon's lower lip, reprimanding him for the interruption.

"It might be Mandy. Or Jackson. And you need to talk to them."

Fucking logic. Max sighed. Gideon was right and damn him for being so sane that he could still think.

Slowly uncurling his fingers from the warmth of Gideon's cock, Max stepped back, and snatched up the phone.

"This is Max," he snapped.

There was silence on the other end of the phone, then, "Max?"

Damn, his brother. But the wrong brother.

"Hey, Mikhel." His gaze darted over to Gideon, making sure he was still dressed, though why Max was worried his brother could see through a phone line he didn't know.

"I thought I dialed Jax."

"You did. I'm at his house for a few days."

"Oh. Well, uhm, is he around? I need to talk to you both."

Max rolled his eyes. Mik and their father had both left repeated messages but Max had managed to avoid the calls. He didn't know the specific reason behind the calls but he was pretty damn sure his father was going to ask him to move back again. It was a pretty constant refrain in their conversations.

Not that their father wanted them in his Pack, but he wanted his kids close.

Now that Mikhel was Alpha of his own Pack, maybe he was joining in the subtle nagging.

"No, he's out of town. Listen, Mik, uh I'm kind of in the middle of something." Wasn't that the truth? "Maybe we could—"

"No. We need to talk now."

Max covered his eyes with his hand. He'd avoided his brother so long that he'd pushed Mik into Alpha mode. And Max knew better than to ignore an Alpha wolf.

"Sure, what's up?"

"It's about the wedding."

He straightened. "What's wrong?" Damn, Mik had seemed happy since he'd hooked up with Taylor. His heart felt squeezed. He hated the thought that his brother might have lost his woman.

"Nothing. Well, I mean…listen, you remember Zach?"

"Zach? Uh yeah, Mik, he practically lived at our house growing up."

"Yeah. Okay, here it is." Max heard Mik take a deep breath but he didn't continue.

Max's heart started to pound. This wasn't like Mikhel. Whatever was going on was some heavy shit. His brother didn't hesitate, didn't dither. He was an Alpha werewolf for God's sake.

"You're starting to freak me out, Mik. What is it?"

"Sorry. You're right. Okay, here's the truth. Zach and I are mates."

"Mates?" But Mik had mated Taylor.

"Yes. We're mates. Lovers."

"What?!" The question came out as a shout that he couldn't contain. It was too much to comprehend. He glanced at Gideon. *Well, maybe not.*

"We're lovers."

"What about Taylor? The woman you're going to marry."

"She's there as well. The three of us are mated to each other. You know, a couple. Except there are three of us." He laughed but there was no humor in it. "I guess we're a trio."

Max's mind flipped over. And then again. Mikhel and Taylor…and Zach?

"Max? You there."

"Yeah. I'm here."

"Nothing to say?"

"I'm happy for you?"

Mik chuckled. "Thanks. It really is a good thing. You'll see when you get here."

"Okay." Max knew that wasn't the best answer but between screwing up with Mandy, the physical exhaustion and the fact that he'd just received the blowjob of his life, his mind was bordering on overload.

"I didn't want to tell you over the phone but I didn't want you to come to the wedding without knowing because it's going to be a three-way ceremony. I'll be marrying both Taylor and Zach." Mik's voice still held tension but the hesitancy was gone and the natural Alpha tendencies returned.

"Okay."

"Have you talked to Dad?"

"Recently? No. I've been busy." Max rubbed his fingers along the bump between his eyes. He couldn't deal with a family feud right now. "Is he freaked out about this?"

"Uh, not exactly. He's actually handled it quite well. You need to talk to Dad."

"Is something wrong?"

"No. He just wants to talk to you before you show up at the wedding."

"Okay. Sure." Like he had time for more family drama. But it didn't sound like anyone was dying or being sent to jail so he'd wait to call his father until after he'd worked out what he was going to do about Mandy.

Of course, once his father found out he'd stolen Jax's mate, he was going to get kicked out of the family anyway. If the males in his family let him live.

Max glanced at Gideon. He no longer leaned against the wall, curiosity lighting his eyes as he listened to Max's half of the conversation. *And then there's Gideon, the man you were about to blow.* Max shook his head and sighed.

"Mik, I got to go." He couldn't take any more. This was so fucked up. His life was fucked up. He's seen to that quite nicely.

"Max—"

"No. Give me a little time to process this huh? I'll talk to you later." He didn't give his brother a chance to respond. He hit the button on the phone and killed the call.

"What was that?" Gideon asked as Max dropped the phone onto the counter.

"My brother is involved in a three-way relationship. A woman and his best friend from childhood, Zach."

Gideon's eyes popped wide open.

"Holy shit."

"Yeah."

"Not Jackson, right? The other brother."

"No. Not Jackson. Mikhel." Max smiled and a bark of laughter came out. "Damn can you even imagine Jackson in a three-way?" His staid accountant brother? Not likely. Gideon raised his eyebrows and shrugged. Wow, Gideon *could* imagine Jax in a three-way. Maybe Max's imagination wasn't good enough.

No, he'd already done his fantasizing. Him, Mandy and Gideon. Both males fucking and penetrating her. Making her scream as she came.

His cock started to fill again and Max sighed. Damn, he had to get his mind off sex for at least a little while.

He looked around the room. What had he been doing before Mik's call?

His gaze stopped on Gideon's crotch. Oh right. He'd been about to blow Gideon.

"Uh—"

Gideon smiled. "No stress, man. We should—"

Feeling like a total jerk, Max moved forward. He couldn't just leave Gideon hanging like that, only the mood was kind of broken. The line of Gideon's cock grew more defined, pressing against his jeans. Max's tongue rubbed the inside line of his lips, his body anticipating the foreign sensation of having a dick in his mouth. The wolf growled its approval.

The need to have his lover beneath him overcame whatever hesitation he had about fucking a man. He wrapped his hand around Gideon's hip and pulled him forward, leaning in, meeting Gideon's mouth. He groaned as their lips met, heat and power pouring into him. Needing more, wanting more of that warmth, he pressed forward, drawing Gideon to him until their hips met, hard flesh colliding.

Gideon's moan made the wolf snarl.

The phone jangled again but Max ignored it. Nothing was pulling him away from this delicious heat. Another ring followed.

Gideon drew back, his breath harsh, his lips swollen, making Max only want to have him more.

"You'd better get it."

Max shook his head.

"Mandy."

Max sighed.

The edge of Gideon's mouth bent upward. "I'll be here when you get back."

Max's dick swelled. That arrogant stare did something to him—made him want to fuck all night until Gideon was too exhausted to smile.

"I'll get rid of them and you'd better be waiting here."

He reached for the phone even as he heard Gideon's chuckle. "Ooh, strong and dominant. I like that in a man."

The words came out teasing but Max heard the truth behind them and instantly the scene appeared in his mind…Gideon, bound, hands behind his back, naked, Max's cock between his lips. Mandy lay on the bed in the background, tied up, stretched out, the tiny butt plug filling her ass so she'd be ready for him and Gideon when they finished.

A sound tickled his hearing but didn't penetrate, the image in his head was too distracting.

"Max, the phone."

Gideon's voice yanked him from the fantasy and Max hit the button, no longer caring who was on the other end of the phone. He wanted to get back to fucking, the growling in his head too loud to think around.

"What?"

"J-Jackson?"

Mandy's voice crackled over the phone line and his wolf went on alert. The hair on the back of Max's neck went straight. She'd called and thought he was Jackson. He sure as fuck couldn't do that to her again.

"No, Mandy—"

"Jackson." Her voice was sharp and punctuated with urgency. "I need those books." *Books? What books? What the hell is going on?*

He was about to vocalize all those questions when she started again. "You know, those *papers* I gave you yesterday. I really need to…work on them." Her voice quavered, intensifying the wolf's protective instincts. Mandy grunted, like she'd bumped into a wall. "Can you bring them to me?"

Something wasn't right. She hadn't given him any papers and she knew that Jax was out of town.

"I'm kind of in the middle of something right now," he said, speaking slowly, hoping to hear some clue in Mandy's response. "How badly do you need these?"

Another hitch in her breath. "I really need them right now."

Fuck. The thugs from dinner the other night. Had to be. The world clarified around him, focusing all his attention on finding his mate, protecting her.

"Where?" The question snapped out and he had to take a moment to draw a breath. Try to sound normal, like he didn't know someone was threatening his mate. Like he wasn't planning to rip off the head of whoever dared touch his woman. "Where should I bring them? Your office?" He signaled to Gideon to get him paper and pen. Gideon seemed to pick up on Max's urgency and brought what he needed, standing and listening as Mandy rattled off the address. "Sure, honey, I'll bring them."

"Thanks, Jackson."

The deliberate way she said his name sent a shot to his heart. She was scared.

For that alone he would kill them.

If they'd harmed her—in any way—he was going to rip their lungs out while they were still using them.

Chapter Fourteen

ജ

"Max, you said yourself. These are bad guys. Thugs." Gideon chased after him, pleading his case—again. Max ignored him and kept walking. The address was a warehouse in west Anchorage. Gideon had driven him here but he'd kept trying to convince Max to call the cops, let them handle it.

"They've got Mandy," he announced. It was a challenge to speak even those simple words. His teeth were long, stretching and filling his mouth. He pressed his lips together trying to hide the wolf's presence but the animal was clawing to get out.

Worse, the other dangerous personality that hovered just off screen. The *were*. Max had never turned into his *were* form. Wasn't sure he even had one until recently. He'd always been too easygoing, too casual to get enraged enough to turn into the slavering beast the *were* was reported to be.

But that was before they'd taken Mandy. Touched Mandy.

His nose twitched and his upper lip vibrated. Red pressed at the edges of his vision. Mikhel had told him about his experience turning into the *were* form. The signs were there and God knew what would happen if that creature managed to take control. It was the ravening beast so popular in horror films.

Fuck, he had to contain this. He didn't need to change. His natural strength gave him an advantage over normal humans. And the assholes they'd met at dinner seemed less bright than normal humans.

No, he wasn't planning to change but if they'd hurt Mandy—all bets were off.

"Max, wait. At least let me call the cops." He was dialing before Max had a chance to stop him. Max didn't mind. The cops could have the leftovers.

"I'm not waiting for them," he growled. Gideon didn't flinch. He glared, rolled his eyes and spoke into the phone. Max blocked it out. He didn't care what Gideon told the cops. His eyes locked on the door, his fingers twitched, hurting on the tips where his claws poked through.

"No, I can't stop him from going in so you better get here fast." Gideon snapped his phone shut. "Let's go."

"You don't have to." It was probably best if Gideon didn't. God knew what he might see. Gideon cocked his head to the side and stared back. A kernel of tension unwound in his chest. He wasn't going in alone. Not that he couldn't handle two humans but somehow he felt better knowing Gideon would be there.

A calming influence.

Unable to stop himself, needing one more taste, he wrapped his hand around Gideon's neck and pulled him close, drawing him into a deep, hard kiss. Before he could tempt himself to take it further, he snapped his head back and looked down at the man who would become his lover. As soon as this was over.

Gideon nodded, as if agreeing to Max's mental plan.

"Let's go," Gideon said. "If we're going to go face thugs with guns, I'd rather get it over with."

Max almost smiled. Would have smiled if his teeth hadn't looked a little too wolflike at this point. Gideon was a good man. A good friend.

Max nodded and they approached the door. He paused for one heartbeat before turning the knob. It opened easily in his hand. Stupid criminals. They hadn't even locked the door? He walked into the large open, almost empty warehouse. Mickelson and Baldino. Mandy was sitting beside them, perched on a high bench, her hands tied in front of her, her mouth covered by tape. From across the room, he could see the thin tracks left by her tears but she wasn't crying now. Her fear had turned to fury. She glared at her captors like she was plotting their removal from earth. He could also see she was working the rope at her wrists, subtly wiggling and twisting her hands to get free.

A roar ripped from his throat at the damage that binding was doing to her soft skin.

The sound alerted the kidnappers to their arrival and they both jumped. Baldino raised a gun and pointed it at Max. Gideon stood at his right shoulder.

Mandy's head snapped up and her eyes widened.

"Mmmm." The muffled sound must have been her attempt at his name.

"You were supposed to come alone," Baldino protested, the words coming out a little whiny.

"Yeah, that wasn't in my instructions."

Baldino swallowed, his throat convulsing with the constricted movement. "Well, he has to go."

"But then I'd be lonely."

His sarcasm seemed to get Mickelson moving. He grabbed Mandy's arm and pulled her off the bench. She moaned as he dragged her forward, taking her almost the middle of the room before forcing her to her knees. Max started toward them. The bright glint of a blade slowed his steps.

"We aren't messing around here. That's right, asshole, stay back or I open her throat." The knifepoint rested against Mandy's neck and Max forced himself to stop. Forced his wolf to hold back.

"Are you all right?" he asked Mandy, ignoring the Mickelson completely.

Moving cautiously, she nodded once.

"Did they hurt you?"

Again she responded with a slow shake of her head.

"No, we didn't hurt her," Mickelson snarled. "But we might. Do you have the papers?"

"No."

The knife went harder against Mandy's skin. "You were supposed to bring the books."

He didn't care what he was supposed to bring but he really didn't like to see this guy touch his woman.

"Why don't you just take your hands off her and we'll all be happier."

"We need those papers," Baldino said.

Mickelson's eyes squinted down. "You better not have given them to cops."

"Cops?" He didn't need to fake his confusion.

"Yeah." Baldino's fingers adjusted on the grip of the gun. "You a cop?"

"No. I'm a photographer."

"I thought you were an accountant?" Mickelson squeezed Mandy's arm, the skin around his fingers turning white.

"Wrong brother." Max took a step closer. Flames raced up his spine, flashing over his skin until he could feel the burn invading his soul. "Really, you need to let her go."

"Get back or I'll cut her." He yanked on Mandy's arm, drawing a painful whimper from her.

Red covered his mind, ripping through his brain, a bright explosion. A howl erupted from his throat—a sound he'd never made before. The noise echoed through the room. It was the last thing he heard before the world turned black.

Mandy gasped at the sound that came from Max, reverberating through the open room. She looked at her lover—and breath locked in her throat.

His jaw punched forward and white sharp teeth burst from the gum line. Muscles ripped and bones stretched and snapped, reforming, longer and stronger. The cracking noise of his bones breaking and stretching turned her stomach, snapping and echoing through the almost silent warehouse. Another fierce roar shook the walls as his body expanded, fury erupting from the form even as his clothes shredded around the larger shape and dropped to the floor. A deadly gray cast covered his skin marred only by the white of his teeth.

When the change was finished, the creature stood over seven feet tall, the face shaped like an animal's—a wolf?—and the skin gray and covered in rough fur.

What—? She blinked and shook her head, trying to clear the image before her, but it didn't waver. Max had turned into a…a werewolf? The creature tipped its head back and let loose another haunting howl, a scream that rippled down her spine like claws.

She gulped, trying to loosen her tight throat, find the strength to inhale.

The thing—Max—lurched forward, glowing red eyes locked on Mandy. And Brian. Max's stare trained on Brian's grip, the painful hold tightening as the man faced the creature in front of him. "Max" snarled, the roar rattling the metal walls of the warehouse.

From the edge of her vision, she saw Sean fumble with the gun, his hand violently shaking as he tried to point the thing at Max.

Gideon must have seen it as well.

"Uh, gun on your left," Gideon called, pitching his voice to penetrate through whatever might be obscuring Max's reason. Max—it was easier to think of the creature by his name—whirled his head around, looking at Gideon with a mixture of rage and confusion. "Your other left," he corrected. Max tipped his head to the side then seemed to understand. He spun toward Sean, the gun vibrating in his hand.

"Shoot it!" Brian shouted.

Max snarled and jumped. The weapon went off—Mandy wasn't sure Sean had enough muscle control to intentionally pull the trigger. A bullet slashed through the air and Max screamed. He landed in front of Sean, blood dripping down his arm. He roared and swung his fist—uh, paw—and backhanded Sean, sending him flying. The thunk of his head hitting the concrete drew a satisfied grunt from the creature.

He turned, his attention once again on Mandy and Brian. Mandy glanced at Gideon. Though he seemed as surprised as she was, he appeared calm, like watching a werewolf beat up bad guys wasn't that unusual.

Low, fierce growls rumbled from Max's chest and Mandy dragged her attention back to the creature stalking toward her. The red eyes locked on the place where Brian had his hand on Mandy's neck. She could feel the fury pouring from Max and tried to shake Brian free. He really needed to let go of her.

His hand tightened, his stare a contradiction of panic and resolve. Surely he wasn't thinking to negotiate with that thing?

"Hey, Bad Guy Number Two," Gideon yelled. He waited until the other man glanced his direction. "I don't think he likes you touching her."

With a nod and a deep swallow, he pulled his hand back, dropping the knife and raising his arms as he stepped away, backing slowly for two steps before he whipped around and ran. The werewolf stalked forward, one jerking lunge before he leaped, surging through the air and landing on Brian's back. His cry rang out as Max trapped him on the ground.

Gideon ran to Mandy's side, pulling the tape off her mouth and working on the ropes that bound her arms.

"Are you okay?"

She nodded, her breath coming in rapid pants. Now was not the time to scream, "No, my lover just turned into a werewolf". Another roar shook the walls and she spun around to watch.

"Guess Max has a secret side," Gideon offered with a weak smile.

Mandy nodded, not pulling her gaze away. That was one hell of a secret.

The wolf-thing tipped his head back, its teeth open, the white tips glowing under the fluorescent lights.

"He's going to kill him," she whispered.

"That would be bad," Gideon said.

Mandy nodded. This would be hard enough to explain without an actual dead body.

Max crouched over his prey, snarling and growling. The teeth on that thing were deadly. He opened his jaw. The guy on the bottom screamed and began to sob.

"Max, stop, you don't want to kill him." The werewolf snapped his head around and growled at Gideon as if enraged that someone had interrupted his fun. "Okay, maybe you *want* to kill him but you can't."

For a moment it looked like Max was going to ignore him, but then the glowing red eyes landed on her. She tensed, feeling the full force of the creature's energy.

The body beneath him dismissed, the werewolf spun around and began its lurching strides back toward Mandy.

"It's okay," Gideon said, the words whispered through barely moving lips. "It's Max. Remember it's Max."

She nodded and tried to take a deep breath. The tight band around her chest didn't allow for much air. The gray-skinned creature walking toward her looked nothing like Max. But she'd seen the red glow in his eyes—when he'd made love to her.

The werewolf bent down, sniffing her skin, his growl growing louder as he drew near her shoulder where Mickelson had touched her. Its lips pulled back, away from the long teeth. She froze, holding herself still, afraid a sudden move would set him off. *This is Max. Max. The—her mind stuttered at the thought—man you're in love with. He won't hurt you.* The mantra seemed to help and the beating of her heart slowed to a frantic pace instead of the bust-out-of-her-chest rate it had been building toward.

She shifted her body, turning into him. The hard line of his naked cock—thick and round, almost twice the size of Max—pressed against her stomach. She swallowed. She couldn't imagine taking something like that into her body.

The werewolf opened his mouth and licked her neck, running his tongue from her shoulder up to her cheek. Another rumble vibrated his throat but this sound was familiar, more sexual than dangerous. The creature that was Max repeated the motion and she shivered, the pleasure of the rough tongue completely at odds with the terror running through her body but she couldn't help it.

One long-fingered hand reached out, the sharp claws almost delicate, scraping down the front of her shirt, pulling on the buttons and skating across her skin. She blinked and looked up at Gideon. What was she supposed to do? Take off her shirt? Flash her breasts at the ravening beast? Except he didn't seem that ravening right at the moment.

She raised her eyebrows and Gideon shrugged. The movement caught the werewolf's attention and he turned his head. He cocked his head and stared for a long moment, as if trying to place Gideon. Mandy opened her mouth ready to tell Max not to hurt him, but another of those low sexual sounds filled the room. He clamped his hand on her ass, holding her in place as he leaned over and sniffed Gideon's neck. The animal-like motion was followed by a long, slow lick across Gideon's collarbone. Gideon gave a sharp inhale and for a moment Mandy thought it was because of the creature's tongue. Then he saw Max's other hand, clawed and gentle, cupped around Gideon's cock.

She watched for a moment, her mind trying to process what she was seeing. Max and Gideon? She'd sensed a connection between them but hadn't expected this. The werewolf turned back to her, pulling her and Gideon close, almost lifting her up to nuzzle between her breasts, the rough hair around his nose scratching her skin, setting her nerves on fire. Despite—or maybe because of—the recent danger, her pussy grew wet, needing. It was insane. She'd been kidnapped, threatened and now a werewolf was making love to her. Arousal should have been impossible but she squirmed, her pussy heating, getting wet. The hard cock pressed against her seemed more sexual than dangerous. His rough wet tongue slid under her shirt, skimming the edge of her bra.

Her fingers had actually moved to the buttons of her blouse, as if she was planning to undo them, offer herself, when the sound of sirens shattered the atmosphere.

"The police."

Gideon nodded. "They can't find him like this."

"Max?" She grabbed the wolf's head and tipped it down so she met the bright red eyes. "Max, you need to come back to yourself."

"Take a deep breath," Gideon encouraged, his words directed at Max, not her.

Deep breathing exercises…with a werewolf?

"He's right, Max. Deep breath. Everything is going to be all right. We're fine."

The sirens grew closer. They didn't have much time.

"Max?" She said his name, calling to the man inside the beast. "Please, Max, come back." The wolf tipped his head and stared at her. Unable to think of what else to do, she wrapped her arms around him and squeezed, putting her head to his furry chest. "I love you, Max. Come back." She didn't know if the words were true and decided she'd figure that out later. She'd said them and they seemed to speak to the werewolf. He froze and slowly the body beneath hers changed, the cracking of muscles made her stomach roil but she didn't let go. The skin smoothed out and when she opened her eyes, it was a more normal tan, instead of the steel gray that had covered the werewolf. Her head snapped up and she looked into his eyes. They weren't glowing any longer but they weren't quite back to normal.

The warehouse door popped open and Mandy gasped. She took a step back, in time to see the claws at the ends of his fingertips disappear, flattening out into normal human nails.

"What the fuck happened here?"

Mandy looked up and felt tears prick her eyes. Relief flooded her chest. Detective Banner held his gun down and to his side, close and ready to use. His eyes scanning the room but he didn't come closer.

"It's okay, Detective."

He stalked over to where Mandy stood, Max next to her, Gideon moving protectively to Max's other side.

"What the hell happened? We get a 9-1-1 call that you're being held hostage." He looked around, the bodies of the two thugs unmoving. He glared at Gideon and Max. "They'd better not be dead."

"They aren't," Max said, his voice low and gravelly.

"I'm assuming you're Jackson. And where the hell are your clothes?"

"Uh—" Max looked up, his eyes glazed and not quite focusing.

"He fights better in the nude," Gideon offered. "It's an old martial arts tradition." A burble of laughter clogged her throat but she managed to contain it. Gideon had said it with such assurance and laughing would give the game away. And if she started to laugh, she might not stop.

Banner's lips pinched together and he sighed. "Right. Now why doesn't someone tell me what happened?"

* * * * *

Max sat behind the table sweating in Gideon's leather coat. Damn, wasn't Alaska supposed to be cold? The room was tiny but air flowed in from the ceiling. Unfortunately, it wasn't the ambient air temperature that warmed him. It was the fire inside him, the creature. His muscles tugged and pulled like the *were* was trying to return. Max didn't remember turning into the creature, barely remembered attacking the two men. His only recollection was the murderous rage flowing through the *were*.

Mickelson's hand on Mandy. Touching her beautiful skin.

The *were* had wanted to rip his throat out. Probably would have if Gideon and Mandy hadn't called him back. Distracted the beast. Baldino—the one who'd shot him—had been little more than an irritation, a mosquito that needed slapping. Fire seared his right arm where the bullet had passed, grazing the surface of his skin. He'd refused medical treatment. Hadn't wanted to explain why he was healing so fast. The cop, Banner, had tried to insist but Max had held firm.

Thank God Gideon had been there. He'd kept everything in control, smoothly explaining what had happened. The story about Max stripping so he could fight naked and unimpeded was barely believed but with Mandy, Gideon and Max all swearing to it, there was no way for the police to dispute it.

Until they separated them. Despite Gideon's protests, Banner had insisted on bringing the three of them to police headquarters. Mandy and Gideon had each been taken in separate cars. Max had been able to trace their scents in the building. They were near. He took a deep breath and tried to hold on to his human side. The muscles pulled in his throat, straining as he fought the creature. Clutching the underside of the table, he let his claws return, biting into the metal frame. The pain dragged him back.

He tapped his foot on the ground released some of the *were's* energy before taking a deep breath. The cage to hold his wolf wasn't going to work. He took a lesson from his brother who controlled his wolf through mental petting. Max closed his eyes and sent comforting thoughts to the animal pacing inside his head. He could do this. All he had to do was stick to his story and hope, pray, that Mandy and Gideon didn't tell the police about his tendency to turn furry.

Mickelson and Baldino had been questioned at the scene though they were still basically incoherent. Or at least that's what the cops thought. Mickelson kept rambling on about a monster attacking him. Baldino had looked like he was going to jump in and agree with his buddy but a quick glare from Max had made the guy reconsider.

He rolled his shoulder, trying to loosen the muscles grabbing at his neck.

The *were's* energy still surged through his body. He remembered his brother Mikhel telling him about the experience. That afterward, he'd needed his mates to ease the beast. Max didn't have that option. As much as he wanted it. Mandy was off in another room. The memory of her strength, composure lingered in his head. She'd been so strong, so determined. She'd make a fine mother to his cubs. The wolf in his head growled its approval.

And Gideon…he'd make a fine mate as well.

The edge of Max's mouth kicked up in a smile. Mik was mated with two lovers. Looked like Max was going to follow suit. Because he wasn't going to let either of them go.

If Mandy doesn't freak out that you want to fuck Gideon. Laughter locked in his throat.

You just turned into a werewolf in front of her. Fucking Gideon will seem like a minor infraction compared to that.

The door popped open and Banner walked in, the faint scent of Mandy hovering around him. Max's upper lip pulled up and he fought the urge to growl. The remnant was so weak he was almost positive that Banner hadn't touched Mandy but the thought of another male near his woman, without him…

"So, your turn."

"Where are Mandy and Gideon?"

"They're fine. I've got other investigators talking to them."

Max sat back in his chair, letting his natural arrogance through, trying to look relaxed.

"I get the big guns huh?"

Banner bent his head and Max could barely see the reluctant smile that pulled at Banner's mouth.

"So, why don't you tell me what happened tonight?"

"I got this call…"

* * * * *

"How do you think he reacted? He was upset. These assholes were threatening his girlfriend." Gideon looked up at the detective. He wasn't going to lie or change his story. At least, not until they got to the end.

"But he didn't call the police."

"No. I did."

"When?"

"When we got to the place and I realized he was planning to face these guys on his own."

"Who did you call?"

"I called 9-1-1 and told them that Mandy was being held hostage and Max was going in."

"Did you try to stop him?"

"Yeah but have you ever tried to stop a freight train?"

"He was that determined."

"He was pissed but he wasn't the one with the gun or the knife."

The detective nodded and wrote down notes. Gideon didn't know why they bothered. The whole damn thing was being taped. He considered winking at the camera but decided against it. They needed to believe his story.

"What happened when you got inside?"

"One guy had a knife at Mandy's throat. The other one had a gun..."

* * * * *

"They wanted some papers that I told them Jackson had." Mandy fingered the now empty coffee cup. She reached the top and started picking at the edge of the Styrofoam cup, tearing little pieces off and dropping them on the table.

"Max came in. He didn't have the papers, because they don't exist." She took a deep breath. "Detective Banner knows all about this."

The detective questioning her nodded but didn't say anything.

"Well, Brian Mickelson kept demanding the papers and dragging me around by my arm." She pulled back her sleeve to show the bruises. "Max kept telling him to stop and to back away. Finally, Max just seemed to have enough. He went after Brian to get the knife away from him and then Sean shot him."

"That's when Baldino shot him?"

Mandy looked down her fingers then back up to the detective. "I think so. It got a little confusing at this point."

"But you're sure Baldino shot him?"

"Yes. He's the only one who had a gun. Max pushed him down." Made him fly through the air, her mind corrected. "And then he turned to Brian. Who still had the knife."

* * * * *

"So you're telling me you just punched out someone with a gun and ran down another guy who had a knife?"

"What else was I supposed to do?" Max placed his hands on the table. They'd been in this room for thirty minutes going over the same damn things. Things Max didn't need to be reminded of. He was going to see them in his nightmares for years to come. "He had a knife to my woman's throat," he snarled at the cop. "I didn't hurt him. Much."

"Baldino's got a concussion—"

"He tripped."

"And Mickelson's saying a creature attacked him."

Max shrugged. "How the fuck am I supposed to know what's going on inside his head?" He sighed. He needed to get out of this room. Needed to get back to Mandy and Gideon. "Listen. Call Detective Alastair Reign, Las Vegas Police." He flipped open his phone. They hadn't searched him or stripped him of his phone. He read off the number and was relieved to see Banner punching it in. "I'm working with him on a case. He can vouch for me." *He'd better fucking vouch for me.* It would be just like Reign to deny knowing him just to get Max in more trouble.

Banner squinted his eyes and pouted his lips for a moment, considering if he really wanted to do this, then hit the button, sending the call. Max again took up his confident, arrogant pose.

He listened. Reign wasn't quite as obsessive about answering his phone as Max but he was pretty damn close.

His senses were tuned high from the *were's* presence so Max could hear the buzz of the phone ringing without trying to listen.

"Reign, who's this?" Aggression poured out of the greeting. Even from across the room, Max could hear it.

Banner flinched. "Uh, this is Detective David Banner with the Anchorage Police Department. Who's this?"

"Detective Alastair Reign, Las Vegas PD. What's up?"

"I'm calling about Max Haverstam. He says he's worked with you before."

"He in some kind of trouble?"

"There's been an incident. He's involved."

Max could hear the low chuckle on the other end of the line. His fist curled into a clench. He was going to deck that pussy cat one day.

"He used you as a reference."

Another laugh, then, "As much as I'd like to put his ass in a sling, he's a good guy. I'm guessing he's telling you the truth."

Banner raised his eyes and looked over at Max.

"So I can trust him?"

"Is there a hot brunette with long legs involved?"

"No."

"Then you're good. He's had my back on a couple of jobs. I'd believe him."

Banner nodded. "Thanks." There was a double click as first Reign then Banner hung up.

Max lifted his eyes, hoping he looked at least a little more innocent than he actually was.

"He seems to think you're a stand-up guy."

"I do my best."

"I'm going to check you out tomorrow, when your 'reference' isn't surrounded by club music."

"You'll get the same answer." Max was pretty sure of that. Reign might be a dick but he was honest and he wouldn't fuck Max over without a good reason and as far as he knew, he hadn't given the man a reason lately.

Banner stared at him for a long moment. Max was used to this kind of scrutiny, either from cops or boyfriends of the models he was going to photograph. Like they thought a deep stare would frighten him, or give them the ability to see into his soul. He looked back, eyes open, his self concealed.

"Fine, you can go. But I'll want to talk to you tomorrow."

Max nodded and stood, noticing that he had to look up at Banner, just a little. It was strange to find a man who Max had to stare up at.

"I'll be around." He wasn't going anywhere—not without his mates. A strange calm settled over him as he left the room. They belonged to him and he'd fight anyone, even his twin brother, to keep them.

"See that you are. I'm going to need to—"

Max walked through the open door and saw them—Mandy and Gideon, standing together. Gideon's arm around her waist, silent support as she demanded to know where Max was.

He smiled and his wolf growled. His mate was trying to protect him.

"I'm here."

They looked at him as he entered the hallway.

Ignoring whatever Banner was saying, he walked forward, his body, his *soul*, needing the contact of his lovers. He wrapped his arm around Mandy's back and pulled her near, closing the distance and sealing his mouth over hers. Her lips opened and she welcomed him, taking his tongue, sucking on it, loving it as he claimed her mouth. He drew back, biting down on her lower lip, silently vowing marks on her neck before the night was through. The wolf growled low and deep as Max turned and grabbed Gideon's head, drawing him close for a kiss. Part of him rebelled at the public display but need overcame his concern. He needed the taste, needed to feel his lovers, his mates.

He drove his tongue into Gideon's mouth and groaned at the open response, the connection as Gideon twined his tongue around Max's sucking as he pulled back. Max growled, his hand on Mandy's ass, the soft round cheek in his palm, Gideon's lips on his. They needed to go home, somewhere where they could fuck. Long and hard.

A strange restlessness erupted behind him and Max knew the cops were wondering what the hell was happening in their hallway. He lifted his head and looked at his lovers. Their lips were pink and swollen, kiss-stung. *Mine.*

Mandy lifted her head and directed her gaze around him.

"Can we go?" she asked.

"I'll need to talk to you in the morning," Banner said, his voice a little dazed. Mandy nodded. She could completely understand his confusion. Looking at her, there was no way anyone would believe she was involved with two men, particularly men like Max and Gideon. Her own head swirled with the possibilities and the firm grip on her ass wasn't helping at all. Max tugged her closer, sliding his leg against her pussy. Under the pressure of his hand, she rubbed forward, a delicious shot from her clit into her core.

"We should go," she announced. She looked at Detective Banner. "I'll call you tomorrow."

Max growled and started to turn. Mandy recognized the sound. It wasn't the sexual, I-want-to-fuck-you noise. This was the don't-fuck-with-my-woman growl he'd used facing Brian.

"Shh." Mandy grabbed Max's arm. "It's okay." She turned his face so he met her eyes, love and lust glittering back at her. Red flared in his gaze and she realized he was only partially human. That thing, the werewolf, still controlled his body. After long moments, the red faded but the hunger remained. They needed to get away from here. "We're good?"

He nodded and Mandy was pretty sure he was unable to speak.

"Let's go," Gideon said, leading them to the back parking lot of the police department. It was late, near ten o'clock but the sun was just setting, the moon rising. Almost full.

"Does the full moon make you change into that thing?" she blurted out.

Max stopped, blinked and shook his head. "No. Seeing Mickelson touch you made me change."

She gulped, telling herself that now wasn't the time to ask these questions but if she was going to go to bed with him—and based on the last five minutes in the police station there was little doubt of that—she wanted a few answers.

"Does it happen very often?"

"That was a first."

"What?"

He winced. "It's complicated." He looked at her then across the car to Gideon. "I'm a werewolf, to state the somewhat obvious. I can turn into a wolf whenever I want. I'll show you sometime. The thing tonight was a different form of the creature that only appears when it senses its mates being threatened."

He did a chin lift, indicating that Gideon should open the car door.

Mandy listened to the doors unlock and breathed. Okay, her lover was a werewolf and thought she was his mate. Wait. Mates. Plural. She glanced through the car window, seeing Gideon take the driver's seat. It made sense. The kiss at the warehouse and inside the police station. Her mind tried to freak out but she was too tired.

They climbed into the car, none of them speaking. Questions swirled around in her head—how long had he been a werewolf? Did he get bitten? Did Jackson know? Her breath locked in her chest. Was Jackson one too?

She stared forward, unable to make any of the questions audible. Instead they just slammed around inside her head, making her dizzy.

"Where am I going?" Gideon asked, turning the engine on. Max didn't respond. Gideon raised his eyebrows and turned to her.

"Jackson's house," she answered, thrilled she could at least speak. Gideon pulled out into the late evening traffic. Mandy shifted in her seat, trying to see Max without looking like she was looking. *A werewolf. He's a werewolf.*

She took a deep breath and released it slowly, letting her shoulders relax just a bit. It helped some but there was way too much tension in her body for deep breathing to cure.

Sex. That would be perfect energy release. A soft chuckle teased her throat but she clamped down on the sound, afraid it would turn into hysterical laughter if she let any of it free. True, sex would ease her tension but could she even imagine making love to Max after tonight? She turned her head and looked out the window, the reflections of light splashing off the window and reminding her of the red glitter in Max's eyes. When he'd turned into that thing, that werewolf, he'd wanted her. She could still feel the press of his cock against her stomach, the slow lick of his tongue across her neck. Her nipples tightened remembering the caress and the heat in her pussy returned.

A low growl rumbled from the backseat and she sat up. It wasn't possible, couldn't be possible that he could sense the changes in her body. She glanced down between the seats. Max's bare foot—his boots destroyed when the creature appeared—tapped lightly on the floor, a jittery motion she didn't expect from Max. He was too calm, too in control.

Gideon focused on the road, his fingers tight on the steering wheel. The tension was getting to him too.

He guided the car through the streets, taking only a few minutes to reach Jackson's house in South Anchorage. He pulled into the driveway and waited.

For a moment, none of them moved, then Max reached for his door. "We should probably talk."

It was more of a command than a suggestion. Max climbed out. She looked over at Gideon. He turned his head and met her gaze. Neither spoke. Finally he shrugged and opened his door.

Taking a deep breath, she did the same, following both men up the walkway into Jackson's house.

Max walked into the living room and did a slow circle around the coffee table as if he couldn't decide where to sit. Or if to sit. He scanned the room, his nostrils flaring a bit, the animal lurking beneath his human veneer. He scraped his hand through his hair, the leather coat he wore opening as he moved, revealing the hard planes of his stomach, the ripped muscles of his chest.

His hard cock.

She stood next to Gideon, watching Max pace the floor. Strange how she could see the animal in him now.

He looked up, meeting their stares boldly. "I'll be right back."

With that announcement he ran up the stairs, taking them two at a time, leaving them alone.

Silence settled on the room and she was afraid to break it, afraid of what she might say, questions she might ask. For a moment, Mandy considered running for the door but the pragmatic side of her personality wouldn't let her. She'd seen her lover turn into a werewolf. She wanted some answers before she had her nervous breakdown.

Max trotted down the stairs and tossed three condoms and a tube of lubricant on the coffee table. They hit with a thud and echoed a challenge to the room. He looked up, his eyes ringing with defiance.

"So, here's the truth and I hope you'll keep it just between the three of us. I'm a werewolf. I come from a large family of werewolves."

"Jackson too?"

Max nodded, the corners of his mouth turning down. "We turn furry. We're super strong and we pick mates. For life." He rattled off the facts like he was describing a plan of attack. "Normally this is one person. I'm just guessing but for some reason, it seems my wolf has chosen two. You two."

The announcement hung between them until Gideon spoke.

"The wolf has chosen us." He folded his arms on his chest, his stance almost as aggressive as Max's. "What about you?"

A hint of smile curled Max's mouth. "Trust me. If I didn't find you attractive, want to fuck the hell out of you, the wolf's preferences wouldn't make a difference." He came forward, the animalistic grace balancing out the glowing red eyes. "I don't know what the future is going to be like. I don't know if the three of us will manage to make it work or even if you'll want to try." He stared into Gideon's eyes then looked down at her. "And I know you have questions but I'll tell you now," the red blazed in his eyes, "if you stay here, we won't be talking. We'll be fucking."

Chapter Fifteen

ꙮ

She felt her eyes widen and heat rushed between her legs. His lips twitched and he trailed that wild gaze down her body, stopping at her pussy. She struggled not to move, to squirm under that intense stare.

She swallowed to get the lump out of her throat. "Are you sure that's a good idea? I mean with everything that happened and…" She didn't know what else to say. How was she supposed to reply when her lover practically challenged them with sex, daring them to fuck him?

"Then you need to leave," he said bluntly, placing himself in front of her. "We'll talk tomorrow or later. But right now, all I can think about is sliding between your legs and fucking you until you scream." Liquid rushed between her legs and she shook her head, trying to draw the focus of her body upward. But layer upon layer of stress and tension—from being kidnapped to seeing her lover turn into a werewolf—piled on her and she couldn't force her mind to think beyond fucking. Max's voice dropped as he leaned forward. "I'm not sure I could carry on a conversation."

"You seem pretty calm to me," Gideon drawled, the tension building in his body, matching the battle lines she saw in Max's muscles. His upper lip twitched and for a moment it looked like he would growl at Gideon.

"He has a point," she interjected. "You look like you're doing fine."

"Really?" He opened his eyes and stared at her. There was no mistaking the weird red glow in his eyes. This wasn't something that could be explained away. He opened his mouth, just a bit and revealed bright white teeth, long sharp incisors too big for a human mouth.

She pressed her fingers to her lips, trying to contain the gasp. She was only moderately successful.

"I'm keeping a handle on the *were*, that thing I turned into," he explained. "Barely. We either fuck or you two have to leave. Because if you stay here I'm not sure I can stop it from having you. Hard and long." She swallowed, trying to find her voice but every harsh word, meant to frighten her, was like a tongue on her clit, making her ache. "Until you can barely breathe, until you feel me everywhere, inside and out. That's what's going to happen if you stay here." He circled around, whispering, speaking the words against her ear. "Are you ready for that?"

The words vibrated through her head sending delicious shivers across her skin. She opened her mouth just a little to allow more oxygen into her body. It did nothing to cool the heated little pulses in her pussy. Squeezing her knees together just made it worse.

Another low growl erupted from his throat and she shivered. The sound was pure sex, wicked and delicious. His arm wrapped around her back and he yanked her close, plastering her body against his, chest to knees, his leg moving between hers, pressing against the V between her thighs. A sweet shock fluttered from her clit and she pushed forward wanting more. Max groaned and bent down, capturing her mouth, licking his tongue inside for a fast taste before driving deep and commanding her response.

Mandy moaned into his mouth, her body coming alive—every bit of tension and stress rippled to her nerve endings, making her skin tingle. Heat covered her ass, Max's hand pulling her closer, pulsing her hips until she was rocking against his thigh, her nipples aching as she pressed against his chest. God, she needed more. Needed him inside her.

He snapped his head back and stared down at her. He could feel the heat in his eyes and knew they were glowing red. A part of him wanted to turn away, didn't want to frighten Mandy any more than she already was but the other side of him wouldn't allow him to hide. She needed to see what she was getting.

She swallowed and took a shallow breath. She didn't look frightened. She looked aroused, hungry. His cock strained against his fly and his teeth ached. The *were* clamored to get free, wanting its mates. He glanced at Gideon. He'd taken a step away, closer to the door, he was ready to run. Bad idea. Max was in full predator mode. He growled a warning and Gideon looked up, his eyes flashing with anger.

Max licked his lips, tasting the energy on the air. Mandy's arousal, Gideon's anger. The edges of his vision turned red but this time he didn't fight it. The were's senses were strong, powerful, flooding Max's brain with scent and taste and touch. Hmm, touch.

"Now's the time to decide. Stay and fuck. Or go."

The air disappeared from the room, sucked out by his challenge.

Mandy blinked and her stare bounced between him and Gideon.

"If you stay here, you'll both end up getting fucked."

"Don't I have any say in that?" Gideon asked. He lifted his chin and glared, daring Max to say no.

Which Max did.

"Not really," he said.

Gideon's eyes tightened down and he stalked across the room, four steps to end up in front of Max.

They stood nose to nose, male aggression vibrating between them making Max's already hard cock throb. The *were* rose up inside Max again, sensing the challenge from its mate, feeling the need to prove its strength. "What? You think I'm just going to bend over and take it."

The human side of him was just arrogant enough to smirk. "Yes."

"Asshole," Gideon said.

"Stop it. Both of you." Mandy's voice held strong as she gave the command snapping Max's attention back to her. She came close, almost putting herself between them. Tears glittered at the edges of her eyes but her chin was set, determined. "This isn't helping."

Delicious scents wafted from their bodies—arousal, fear, anger—and blended into a perfect passion, filling his head.

Unable to stop himself, he bent and captured Mandy's lips, swallowing her gasp and any chance that she might have a logical answer to his desire. She hesitated for a moment but then the heat returned and she moaned into his mouth, wrapping her tongue around his, her hunger almost as strong as his. Fuck yeah. He pulled back just enough to bite down on her lower lip, not too hard, letting her feel his teeth, warning her of his true nature. There was still a chance, a small chance, that if she pulled back now, he'd be able to contain the *were*, let her go. Except she sighed and chased his lips, stealing another kiss.

The presence of his other mate teased the beast. Max felt like a rider in his own mind. He knew the creature was in control, could feel the emotions—harsh almost violent need—surging through his body. Max looked at Gideon. He watched, his eyes focused on Max's mouth. Again, Max let his teeth show, just enough to warn his lover. Holding Mandy to him, unwilling to let her go, he wrapped his hand around Gideon's back and pulled him close. The male moved into the embrace, opening his lips as Max turned his head to meet him. Heat and strength flowed through the kiss, the spicy flavor of Gideon's mouth, subtle but distinctive. It blended perfectly with the sweet taste of Mandy's mouth and the seductive flavor of her pussy.

He growled but the sound turned to a groan as he thought of having them both. Needing the male's submission, he sank his tongue into Gideon's mouth, the struggle for dominance brief before Gideon retreated, accepting Max's penetration. He thrust into Gideon's mouth, mimicking the fucking he'd be giving his ass soon.

Vision almost completely red, Max pulled back and turned to the sweet female beside him, her perfume flooding his brain. She was wet, probably drenching her panties, that sweet pussy juice slipping down her thighs. He took her mouth again, loving the blend of flavors on his tongue. Gideon pushed his hips forward, rubbing his cock against Max's thigh, heat streaking from his leg to his dick, hard and fast.

"Fuck," he whispered as he turned back, sealing his mouth to Gideon's, needing to have them both. A heavy moan rumbled in Gideon's throat as he sucked on Max's tongue. Something in the sound triggered a moment of restraint and Max lifted his head, looking down. Mandy's lips whispered down Gideon's throat, her pink tongue slipping out and flicking across the slick skin.

Max pressed forward, needing to taste them together. He slipped his tongue up, sliding along Gideon's neck, stroking Mandy's tongue before she could retreat.

"Fuck you taste good together." He wasn't sure he'd spoken the words aloud until they both turned to him, lips meshing together, a three-way kiss that scrambled his brain. The wolf in his head howled and Max grabbed his lovers, needing their bodies against his, their presence comforting and arousing at the same time. He wasn't sure who pulled away first but no one was going far—Max took Mandy's mouth and Gideon kissed her neck, both males turning their attention on her. Her nails bit into Max's arm, holding him in place.

"Naked." He could barely make his lips form the word, his teeth were aching, stretching, ready to sink into their flesh. The sweet smell of Mandy's cunt drugged him and he couldn't think beyond tasting her, fucking her. "Now."

He reached out, his tips of his fingers spiking out into claws. He grabbed the front of Mandy's blouse and pulled, listening to the buttons pop and scatter across the hard wood floor. She gasped but didn't retreat. Instead, she blinked and looked at him, her eyes filled with hunger.

He looked down, her pretty breasts straining the lace of her bra, the dusty pink of her nipples barely visible through the white material. For a moment, he expected a tirade, some protest. Instead her lips bent upward into a purely sexual smile. The shyness of the past two nights was gone and a wicked seductress took her place. Mandy stepped back and skimmed her hands up her sides, the perfectly manicured nails whispering across her skin. She stared at him, a wild, wicked woman, as she reached between her breasts and undid the front clasp of her bra. The sides split open, dragging across her nipples as she peeled back the edges.

"Damn." Gideon's whisper echoed the sentiment in his own brain. Mandy's gaze flashed over at Gideon. A moment of insecurity flickered through her eyes but whatever she saw in his stare made it disappear.

She bit her lower lip—the action more seductive than fearful—and arched up, pushing away the blouse and bra, leaving her breasts bare. Max couldn't hold back any longer. He dropped to his knees, inhaling the sweet scent of her cunt, loving her heat, knowing she was wet for him. The beast inside him snarled, wanting her pussy now, but Max held back. Soon he would be inside her but now he needed to taste.

Mandy held herself still. The change in Max was subtle as the creature returned. He didn't turn into a slavering beast but she could tell he was no longer the lover from the two previous nights. Not only the red in his eyes but the strength in his hands, holding her almost too tight. He licked the low curve of her stomach, swirled his tongue around her bellybutton. The delicious caress sent tiny shock waves through her body, settling in her core. Max brushed away her hands, laving his tongue across her breast, sucking lightly on the nipple.

Gideon eased back as he watched Max kneeling before her. Questions echoed in his eyes and she could practically hear his mind racing. She shook her head, warning him not to leave. She needed him. She didn't understand it but she needed his presence. He was the only other person to see the werewolf and she needed that support right now.

Add to the fact that she was fascinated by the idea of watching the two men, their bodies moving together as they fucked…she wasn't letting him go. Not yet. Finding a boldness she didn't know she had, she reached out and grabbed the front of his shirt, dragging him toward her, pulling him into a kiss. Their lips met, tentative at first but the hunger reverberating through their bodies wouldn't be denied for long. Max bit down, an almost painful nibble to her breast. She gasped and opened her mouth, needing the contact. Gideon turned his head and pushed his tongue between her lips.

Max lifted his head and watched, low sexy rumbles filling the room. The heavy whoosh of Gideon's coat hitting the ground pulled them apart for just a moment. The pale light in the living room etched lines on Max's cheeks, highlighted by the glow in his eyes. She looked past the bright eyes to the naked form—muscles tight and strained as if he waged an internal battle with the beast. Knowing what she would find, she leaned back and looked down. His cock stood hard and strong away from his body, long and thick. Mandy slapped her hand on her stomach, practically feeling him inside her already.

His upper lip hitched up in a snarl and he put his hands on their hips and pushed, sending them backward. Mandy landed in the center of the couch. Gideon tripped and caught himself before he fell on top of her.

"Damn it, Max," he groused.

"More." Max issued the command as he crawled up her body. He draped himself over her, pressing his erection into the vee of her thighs. A little bit of the man she'd fucked the last two nights had returned. He stared down at her as he rocked his cock against her clit, those wicked pulses that sent lovely shocks into her core. "Beautiful," he whispered. He cocked his head to the side. "Isn't she beautiful, Gideon? The way she wants it so much, the way she needs to be fucked?"

"Beautiful," Gideon agreed. Mandy swallowed and looked up the other man. The man who would be her lover when this was over. If she was willing to let it go that far. The enormity of what she was about to do hit her all at once.

"It's okay, Mandy," Gideon said as if he could read her thoughts. Sense her panic more likely. "Nothing will happen that you don't want." His assurance helped a bit but in truth…she wanted it all.

Vaguely aware that Max was watching their interaction, she ran her fingers up Gideon's arm, lightly hooking her hand around his neck. She didn't drag him down but she nudged him that direction, guiding him back to her lips, offering her mouth to him. A soft groan slipped between them as he met her, a sweet, sexy kiss that lingered. She slid her fingers into his hair and held him in place, losing herself in the kisses.

Max grunted, a sound immersed in satisfaction. As if he couldn't stand to be left out, he pressed up on his knees, moving into their kiss. He licked his tongue between their mouths as if wanting the taste of both of them. They turned, changing the kiss into a wicked three-way connection of lips and tongues. The flavors and textures filled her head until she couldn't think, couldn't do anything but taste, experience. Hands skated across her skin, cupping her breasts, teasing her nipples. Max drew back from the kiss, leaving Gideon's hot mouth on hers.

He pulled back, just enough to meet her gaze. "Are you okay with this?" he asked, his eyes bright with concern and lust.

She nodded. It was insane but she wanted this. Wanted her fantasy to come true. "You?"

His lips bent upward in a wicked smile. "Oh hell yeah." She smiled back, her lips open, her tongue peeking out. He leaned down and covered her mouth with his, easing his tongue between lips. She wrapped one arm around his shoulder, clinging to him, drowning in sensation. Max kissed the valley between her breasts and moved lower, harsh biting kisses marking her breasts, her stomach, the soft curve of her hip. Little flashes of delicious pain sank into her pussy and she squirmed, needing more.

She moaned into Gideon's mouth, arching up. An almost painful pinch to her nipple made her cry out. Gideon hummed encouragement and bent down capturing the peak of her breast in his mouth, swirling the tip of his tongue around the tight nipple.

Soft murmurs, unrecognizable words painted her skin as Max moved down her body. Even knowing what to expect, she wasn't prepared for the heat. Hot breath washed across her thighs as he dipped his fingers between her legs and spread her pussy lips. Gideon's dark hair teased her breasts as he laved her skin with kisses. Her nerves sang with need.

A heartbeat later Max's tongue trailed up the full length of her slit, gathering her moisture, tasting. She groaned and rolled her hips, trying to find a deeper, harder touch. She felt rather than saw his smile, a mere bending of his lips before he flicked the tip of his tongue across her clit. The tiny caress sent matching shivers up her spine.

"Beautiful." Gideon's compliment heated her nipple and she realized he was watching Max, stroking his hand down to join Max's oral caresses. He slid his hand between her legs, following the slick path of Max's mouth, dipping his finger into her opening, spearing her pussy with one fast penetration.

Max snarled, the sound reminiscent of the creature she'd watched him become tonight. Gideon just chuckled.

"Possessive asshole," he drawled giving Mandy a wink. Max's head jerked up. He looked confused for a moment then shook his head as if clearing his mind. His gaze dropped to her pussy, the thin tip of his tongue peeking out from between his lips, lapping at the slick liquid that glittered at the edge of his mouth.

Max reached behind him and grabbed one of the condoms off the coffee table. Heat billowed from his stare as he rolled the latex sheath up his cock.

The process should have been practical but the blatant way he did it, a warning that she should be prepared to be fucked drenched her cunt.

He rose up and put the tip of his cock to her pussy entrance. He didn't wait for permission and she wouldn't have refused. In one fast stroke, he drove his cock into her, the hard entrance sparking her orgasm. Her soft cry triggered a low snarl from Max. His fingers tightened on her hips and he plunged into her again, drawing more shivers through her pussy.

"Sweet fuck." Gideon's voice hummed with reverence. "Want to see that again."

Max's hands tightened on her hips and he pulled back, drilling his cock into her, the movement strangely mechanical. He raised his head and Mandy gasped. His teeth glistened in the light, looking far too large for his mouth. He looked more animal than human.

"Max?"

The sound of his name seemed to snap him back and he flinched. Staring down at where their bodies met. His fingers gripped then released her and she felt him start to pull back.

"No."

"Don't want to hurt you."

She skimmed her hand up his arm, drawing his attention back to her.

"You aren't hurting me but..." She bit her lower lip and glanced at Gideon, looking for some support, encouragement. He gave a shallow shrug. "I just want to make sure it's really you."

Max nodded, the frightening tension sliding from his body. He met her gaze and she saw the man return. He seemed to brace himself, his hands sliding up her thighs, holding her in place as he pushed his hips forward, sliding his cock deep and hard into her but now the control returned, the lust real. It was Max inside her.

He continued the slow, deep fuck, watching her eyes, as if he wanted to prove he was in command of himself. He pumped his cock in and out, tipping her hips so every penetration and retreat stroked her clit. Mandy gripped Gideon's hand, using his strength to hold her in place as Max fucked her.

The red glow returned to his eyes but it wasn't the dangerous distant heat. This was pure animal hunger.

"Please." She rocked her hips up, trying to move him faster. Her plea seemed to reach him and he pushed in, the tightly wound control wavering. "Yes, more." She wanted him on the edge, lost in her body. His thrusts lost their steady rhythm, going for hard and deep. Mandy wrapped her legs around his back and pulled, sending him deeper each time he filled her. Her sensitized clit tingled warning she was close. He entered her again, just enough, a whispered brush to release the sweet tension chained in her body.

She tipped her head back and groaned, letting the energy zip through her core, stretching hot trails out to her limbs.

"Max!"

His name screamed from her pretty lips as she came sent him over the edge and he plunged into her one final time, feeling her pussy contract along his cock, delicate little squeezes that drew out every bit of pleasure.

"Damn."

Gideon's whispered declaration drew Max's attention. The other man watched, his hand covering his own erection, rubbing the hard flesh beneath his jeans.

Max eased back, slipping his cock from inside Mandy, his eyes latched onto Gideon's hand working his dick.

"Stop." The natural dominance of his wolf flowed through the command and Gideon froze. He looked up, meeting Max's stare with a mixture of defiance and lust. "Not yet."

Max removed the condom, tied it off, and threw it away. He looked at his lovers. He was naked, Mandy wore her skirt. Only Gideon was still dressed.

That wouldn't last long.

But he wasn't done with them yet.

"Upstairs."

Mandy's eyes fluttered open. She looked up at him, dazed, a little confused.

"Hmm?"

"Let's go upstairs, honey. Get you stretched out on the bed so I can have you properly."

She stood up, wobbling a bit. Gideon and Max both reached to steady her.

She laughed. "If that wasn't properly, I don't know what is." Her blouse gone, her skirt crumpled, she brushed her hair away from her face and walked toward the stairs. She glanced over her shoulder hesitating for just a moment then continuing on, leaving Max alone with Gideon.

The two men stood and faced each other. Gideon for all his bravado wasn't quite sure about all this. Max could understand. He'd had few days to at least consider the idea and he had the wolf driving him forward.

Gideon's gaze turned to the stairs and Mandy's departing figure. He didn't make any move to head toward the stairs.

"Now you," Max said. Gideon looked at him and Max couldn't help but smile. "And don't think for a moment that I'm not going to have you as well," he warned.

"Properly?" Gideon leaned forward, challenging Max's stare.

"Yeah. Bent over, my cock, your ass." He stepped closer, leaning in to place a kiss on the soft skin where neck and shoulder meet. He covered Gideon's cock with his hand, squeezing, rubbing. The hard shaft pulsed in his palm. "Don't worry, babe, I'll make sure you get to come."

Gideon turned his head and opened his mouth, an offer Max couldn't refuse. The spicy flavor of Gideon's lips clouded Max's mind for a heartbeat, making his cock bounce up. A tiny gasp reverberated from the stairs. Mandy watched, her eyes wide, her mouth open. The delicious sway of her breasts as she breathed deep drew his attention.

"Upstairs, Amanda." She blinked but didn't look away. "Amanda." This time he added enough warning to his voice to remind her of the punishment she'd receive if she didn't obey him. Her cheeks flushed red and she turned, walking up the stairs and around the corner.

"Going to help me fuck her?" Max asked, rubbing his hand across Gideon's ass. He nodded, his eyes never leaving the space Mandy had vacated moments before. "Yeah, both of us. Her pussy and her ass."

Gideon snapped back to reality. "What?"

"That's what she wants."

"Damn."

"Yeah." He patted Gideon's backside. "But first, I'm going to fuck your tight little ass into next week."

Tension zipped through Gideon's muscles and for a moment Max thought he might balk. He waited, watching the man his wolf had claimed, loving the play of pale light across his skin.

"Get upstairs, Gideon."

So sweet. Just like Mandy, Gideon hesitated, a shade too long. Enough for Max to vow punishment. Oh yeah.

Chapter Sixteen

ꟗ

He followed Gideon upstairs, his eyes locking on the tight ass. Strange, he'd never considered himself an ass man before, now it was all he could think about.

Maybe it was the thought that in a few moments he was going to be buried in that ass, making Gideon his lover in truth.

They entered the bed and saw Mandy curled up on the bed, naked, her fingers clutching the sheets.

"You okay, honey?" Gideon asked.

She nodded, her gaze bouncing up to them and then back down at the deep brown sheet.

"Are you guys going to..." Her voice trailed away for a moment then she seemed to find her courage. "Uh, fuck?"

Max stood beside Gideon. "Would that upset you?" He'd warned her downstairs, warned her that he was going to fuck Gideon. He didn't know what he'd do if she said yes. He needed to claim Gideon. Even if he couldn't bite him, he needed to have his cock inside the other male.

She shook her head then looked up, her eyes meeting his in a hungry stare.

"Can I watch?"

The corner of his mouth pulled up in a smile. "Honey, you can help."

He nudged Gideon forward, pushing him onto the mattress. Gideon climbed up following Max's direction, until he was above Mandy, his knees straddling hers. She rolled onto her back, thighs pressed close together but there was no question about her interest. A shy smile filled her eyes as she bit her lower lip, one tug of her teeth and she pushed up, placing her mouth against Gideon's. Max took a step back, watching, his mind clear now of the *were*. The wolf lingered, calm and sated. Comforted by the presence of its lovers.

Gideon hesitated for just a moment then turned his head, opening his mouth and taking Mandy's in a deep kiss.

A strange contentment filled his chest as he watched them, Gideon's dark hair striking against Mandy's pale skin. The hums and murmurs as they kissed, their bodies shifting, moving to better feel the other.

Max ran his hand down Gideon's backside, slipping around the front and undoing the button and zipper of his jeans. He tugged the material out of the way and curled his fingers around Gideon's cock. Both men jumped, their groans harmonized in the air. Max realized this was the first time he'd actually touched Gideon's naked cock. He'd felt it through material, but never bare and soft.

He ran his hand up the full, long length, captivated by the foreign sensations of another man's dick in his hand. Strange, the sensation didn't freak him out. His fingers tightened and he pumped the shaft, watching Gideon's muscles work pushing his dick through Max's fist. He bent forward and placed a kiss on Gideon's back, leaving with a scrape of his teeth.

"Naked."

Gideon lifted his head, his lips wet and swollen from Mandy's mouth. "Huh?"

"Get naked."

As if irritated that he'd been interrupted, Gideon reached behind him and pulled the shirt off over his head, tossing it in the far corner. Then wiggled and pushed his jeans and briefs the rest of the way off.

"Happy?" he asked, the question a mixture of annoyance and teasing.

"Getting there," Max drawled in response.

Gideon smiled but turned back to Mandy, stretching out, body to body, her legs twining with his. The soft curve of her thigh curled around his hip, holding him in place as she rubbed her pussy against his knee. The seductive scent of her arousal flooded the room and Max waited for a spark of jealousy. This was more than a few kisses. This was naked body-to-body rubbing, almost fucking.

He listened to the wolf but the animal didn't rise up in anger. The only thing that irritated him was Max wasn't involved.

Max reached out and grabbed Gideon by the hips, pulling him back toward the edge of the bed. He'd grabbed the lube he'd taken downstairs—a dramatic gesture but effective—and opened it, dripping it onto his fingers as Gideon pushed up on hands and knees, his tight little hole displayed. Max slipped one finger up and pressed forward, sliding into Gideon's ass for the first time, slow and steady, the squeeze holding him inside as he pushed in. Gideon grunted and the muscles gripping Max's finger relaxed just a fraction.

Mandy sat up, moving closer, rubbing her mouth against Gideon's. He turned his head and met her as Max pushed a second finger inside, feeling the tight squeeze ease just enough for him to enter. That was enough for now. He held his fingers inside him not moving until Gideon squirmed, signaling that he wanted more.

Max began a slow fuck with his hand.

He watched his lovers, the hot open mouthed kisses, Mandy's pale hands on Gideon's tan skin, stroking and soothing, distracting as Max worked his fingers in and out of Gideon's ass. Gideon rocked with him, moving with the shallow penetrations, making it hard for him to go slow.

"Max, fuck, do it."

Hands shaking just a little, he grabbed another condom and rolled the sheath up his cock, slathering on the lube. He didn't want to hurt Gideon. Or have any reason to stop.

"You ready?" A strange calm came over him. He'd been craving this—not just for the penetration but the power, the claiming. He placed his cock to Gideon's tight opening and waited.

"Yes." The moaned response was low and tight.

Max looked up, finding Mandy's wide eyes. She stared, the fast rise and fall of her chest giving a delightful shimmy to her breasts. She wasn't panicked or freaked out—she was turned-on.

Heat surrounded his cock as he pushed forward, pressing through the natural resistance. He sank a little deeper and Gideon's muscle clamped down. Max froze.

"I don't want to hurt you, babe" he said, pulling back.

Gideon's head snapped back and he stared over his shoulder, eyes flashing. "Don't you dare fucking stop." He rolled his hips, pressing his ass back. "Fuck me." Strong muscles shifted beneath his tan skin. Max growled, the need to feel that ass against him was too strong. He replaced the tip of his slick cock against Gideon's hole and started again.

He stared down, watching as his dick disappeared inside Gideon. The urge to drive hard was tempered by the fear of hurting Gideon. Max kept his movements slow listening to the soft sounds slipping from Gideon's throat.

Skin across the sheets grabbed his attention and he looked up. Mandy rolled over, her legs spreading as she watched. Her lips opened, her chest rising and falling in long breaths, her eyes locked on their bodies. Her hips rolled with him as he pressed forward, as if she was the one taking his cock.

"Touch yourself, baby." His command seemed to jolt her and she looked up.

"What?" Innocent blinking eyes looked at him for a moment.

"Touch yourself. Fuck that pretty cunt with your fingers." Gideon moaned beneath him. He checked and Gideon's eyes were focused on the same sweet sight—Mandy's spread legs, her fingers slowly tripping toward her pussy. Max reached around and grabbed Gideon's cock, squeezing even as he pushed a little deeper, still giving Gideon time to adjust to his penetration. "We want to watch you, don't we, man?" He bent down and trailed a kiss across Gideon's spine. "We'll watch her finger-fuck herself while I take this tight ass, yeah?"

"Yeah."

Needing another shiver from the man beneath him, Max scraped his teeth across the bare skin. Gideon's hips pressed back, pushing Max's cock deeper. "Yeah, watch her fingers slide in and out and think about when we're going to fuck her. You and me. That slick little pussy and tight ass."

Gideon's body tightened beneath him and he pushed more cock inside him, a little harder, deeper. Almost there. Mandy froze and looked up—the wild stare in her eyes wasn't from fear.

"Don't worry, honey. You'll love it." Max licked his lips. "We'll fill you up and make you scream."

"Oh yeah," Gideon breathed.

"Now, let me see those fingers slide into that pretty pussy I'm going to fuck."

Mandy's tongue peeked out from between her lips as she finally slid her hand between her legs. She stroked through the wet folds, the juices from her cunt glittering in the bright light of the bedroom.

"That's it, honey. Now, fingers. In your cunt." He felt his teeth stretch as she followed his command, pushing her index and middle finger into her pussy.

Gideon's groan echoed Max's. He gripped Gideon's hips, holding him in place as he drove that last two inches into his ass, his groin pressed up against the strong muscles. The *were* in his head loved to see his lovers, one bent before him, the other spread out, fingers dipping into her pussy.

Pain shot through his fingertips as his claws popped out, biting into Gideon's skin. Part of Max's mind struggled to regain control but the other heard the low moan from his lover, feeling the tiny painful bites of his claws. Max pulled his hips back, holding Gideon in place as he retreated then slowly pushed back in, savoring the tight grip of Gideon's ass.

Mandy panted as she fucked her pussy with her fingers.

Max couldn't decide which he wanted to watch more—the tight hard body stretched under him or the pretty pink cunt before him.

He tipped his hips down, driving a little harder into Gideon. A shiver ran through the taut body beneath him. "There?" Max managed to ask as he pulled back, the need to fuck making his thrusts harder. Gideon nodded and Max searched to find that spot again.

Mandy's fingers sped up, timed to match Max's thrusts. Red flushed her chest and her breasts bounced as she rolled her hips up, meeting her fingers.

The sight was almost more than he could take.

"Fuck." Gideon's curse was low, soft. Max tracked his gaze and followed it right back to Mandy's cunt.

"We're going to have her," he whispered, pumping into Gideon's ass. "We're going to take her."

"Yes." The sound was almost a growl. Almost a werewolf's response. Max tipped his head back, resisting the urge to howl. His mates were perfect, made for him. His eyes stayed on Mandy's pussy and the pale glide of her fingers between the wet lips. He couldn't stop the steady thrusts in Gideon's ass. He held Gideon in place to take him, fighting the urge to pound into the sensitive ass that grabbed his dick so deep. Gideon's breath sped up and Max knew he was close, needed him there. He pumped his hand up and down Gideon's shaft, driving his hips forward with each penetration. "Want to feel you come."

Their grunt-groan combination filled the room. Mandy looked up, her eyes glittering as she watched them. Her lips opened and the tip of her tongue touched the inside edge of her mouth, her eyes locked on Gideon's cock thrusting through Max's hand.

"Oh fuck, she wants to taste you. You see that?"

"Yes." Gideon pushed back, driving Max deeper. The word finished with a hiss and Max's cock hit that one place inside him. He cocked his hips and angled them to strike the same point, wanting to drive Gideon crazy. He got another grunt and push. The world zeroed in on his cock fucking Gideon's ass, finding that spot over and over until Gideon was begging, pleading to come.

"That's it, man. Take it." Max tightened his grip around the cock in his palm and drove his hips forward. Gideon tipped his head back, baring his throat—a temptation almost too much for Max to resist—and cried out. The scent of Gideon's cum filled the air as he poured across Max's fingers. Subtle contractions worked through Gideon's ass gripping Max's cock, sending him deep one more time as he came. The wolf howled in his brain, wanting to spill inside his lover but the human sensibilities prevailed.

Gideon dropped onto the bed, his cheek flat against the sheets. Max leaned forward and licked his neck, loving the taste, the scent of sex fogging his brain. Gideon turned his head, his mouth open and Max couldn't resist the invitation, not when his dick was buried in the guy's sweet ass.

"Delicious," he murmured as he drew back.

His cock barely softened as he withdrew, pulling out slowly, stripping off the condom and wiping away the lingering lube from his thighs. Gideon wasn't moving much faster as he pushed himself to standing, swaying a bit as he straightened. Max caught him and turned him around pulling their hips together.

"You okay?"

Gideon nodded. "Just had the strength fucked out of my legs."

Gideon was the first to pull back, his eyes a little wild. Max couldn't let him go without one more taste. He bent down and scraped his teeth across Gideon's shoulder, knowing he would be putting his mark there soon. Gideon grunted as Max sucked on his skin, pulling up a mark. It wasn't as permanent as the werewolf bite but it would do for now, showed his claim on that smooth skin.

Mandy curled up on the mattress and watched the beauty of their male bodies, the hot kisses, strong and powerful. Max's mouth on Gideon's neck. Gideon closed his eyes and pushed his hips forward, pumping his cock into Max's touch. The pleasure and pain visible on his face made her ache. She plunged her fingers into her pussy, the need to come almost desperate. But she couldn't seem to find the touch. A low whimper escaped her mouth. Both men turned and looked. The red flared in Max's eyes as he stared at her hand.

He licked his lips and slid away from Gideon, crawling onto the bed, looking more cat than wolf. Her laughter startled her as he grabbed her leg and pulled, dragging her away from the headboard and into the middle of the bed. When she expected him to flip her onto her back and fuck her, he did the opposite. Guiding her, he rolled her to her side and snuggled up behind her, putting her in the curve of his body. She sighed, relaxing into the warmth that covered her back.

He reached down between her legs and pulled her hand away. The light glittered on the pussy juices coating her fingers. He carried her hand to his mouth and sucked her index and middle finger into his mouth, his tongue lapping, sliding across her skin. "Delicious." He hummed and trailed his tongue up her finger. "Love the taste of your cunt."

She shivered, the sight of his tongue on her, the wicked words, the subtle caresses too much for her body to contain.

Movement at the corner of her eye drew her attention. Gideon turned off the bathroom light and stood near the door, naked, his cock semihard. He wasn't as thick as Max but he was long. Max sucked on the tip of her finger, moving it between his lips like he was sucking a cock. The tickling caress felt so good on her finger, she couldn't imagine how it must feel on his cock.

The sensuous atmosphere made her bold. She let her gaze trail down Gideon's body, lingering on his cock, watch the long shaft fill and get hard.

"That's it," Max said, pushing her finger into his mouth again. "He's hard just looking at you, imagining your mouth on his dick." He kissed the tip of her finger. "Is that what you want, honey? His cock in your mouth. Sliding between your perfect lips."

As he described it, the desire built in her core. That's what she wanted. Sucking off Max had been incredible, powerful. She wanted to do the same to Gideon.

"Do you want to taste him, honey?" Max asked, giving her finger another kiss. She licked her lips and nodded, staring at the hardening cock before her. "Come here, man. Let her suck that pretty cock."

Gideon's eyes widened and he stumbled forward. He seemed to be under the same spell she was—sex dazed and lust crazed. He climbed onto the mattress and bent down greeting her with a kiss. His kiss was different from Max's, less commanding, more subtle, still seductive. Max bit down on her shoulder, not enough to hurt but just enough to draw her attention.

Her lips felt swollen as Gideon knelt beside her stretching his arms forward to grab the headboard, pushing his cock toward her. She slid her hands up his hips, cupping the tight curve of his ass in her palms as she guided him down to her mouth. Murmurs of encouragement tumbled from Max's lips, urging them both on. Knowing that he watched, that he wanted her to suck Gideon's cock sent a flurry of need and power through her pussy. Every inch a seductress, she lapped her tongue at the rounded head, smiling at the groan from Gideon. She looked up. His eyes were locked on her mouth, watching as she licked and kissed.

With Max holding her body, she couldn't move much to reach more flesh, so she attended to the first few inches of cock. Gideon adjusted his hips, giving her more, sliding his shaft deeper into her mouth. She swished her tongue along the underside of his cock, loving the hot sensation on her tongue.

"Fuck, that looks sweet." Max moaned the words against her shoulder, turning her just a little until her ass was pressed into his groin. The position was a little awkward with Gideon kneeling over her and Max cuddled up behind he but she didn't care. Every part of her body felt alive and touched.

Hot kisses covered her shoulders as he slid his hand between her thighs, lifting the top one and draping it over his knee, opening her legs. A cool rush of air washed over her skin make the need even stronger. He tickled her clit, circling one fingertip around the sensitive point before sliding past, between her pussy lips. She squirmed, needing more, her body on the verge of coming. A whimper sounded from the back of her throat.

Max chuckled and if she hadn't been busy, her lips wrapped around Gideon's cock, her pussy aching to be filled, she might have glared at him.

"It's okay, honey, we're going to take care of you." Max pushed two fingers into her opening, her pussy contracting around the firm thrust. Groaning, desperate for air, she pulled back and breathed, too many sensations overwhelming her body.

"Let me see you suck him, baby. Take that big dick in your mouth."

The sexual words just made her want it more. She opened her mouth and accepted the head of Gideon's cock between her lips. He pushed forward, sending his shaft deep into her mouth, bumping up against the back of her throat. She choked a bit and he pulled back.

"Sorry, Mandy. I'm a little…"

She drew back, his cock glistening with her saliva. "I'm fine." She lapped her tongue across the head. "Let me taste you."

His head dropped back and he groaned, holding still as she sucked the tip. He didn't move, let her work his cock.

Max dropped his head and put his lips to Mandy's ear.

"Beautiful. You look so sexy with his cock in your mouth. Oh fuck, honey, that's hot, Suck him hard." She moaned around the flesh in her mouth and followed Max's command, sucking as she pulled back. Gideon's fingers grabbed the back of her head, holding her in place as his hips rocked forward, fucking her mouth. She groaned, rubbing her tongue across the head of his cock, trying to keep up with his thrusts.

"Stop, Gideon," Max commanded, reaching up to slow his hips. Gideon's jaw clenched, the muscles rippling in protest as he eased his cock from between her lips. She could see the snarl that wanted to be released. She leaned forward—because she wasn't done with Gideon's cock and because she didn't want Max to think he was in complete control—and licked her tongue across the head of Gideon's cock, catching a drop of pre-cum on her tongue. Both men groaned and power surged through her body. No, she wasn't done with sucking this cock yet.

Max drew away. She heard the crinkle of a condom wrapper and glanced over her shoulder, just long enough to see Max roll the sheath up his cock. She licked her lips. Oh yeah. She was going to get fucked but she wasn't done with Gideon just yet. She turned her head and reached for him.

Before she could open her mouth to take him back inside, Max pulled her away, flipped her onto her back and spread her legs. She had time to get one deep breath before he lifted her hips and drove his cock into her pussy. The heavy deep penetration rippled through her core, teasing her clit, sparking a climax that shocked her system. Her body tensed, bracing for the surge as he thrust into her again, drawing out a delicious aftershock.

Max held her hips still, holding her with one hand and spreading his knees wide on the mattress. He looked down, his eyes watching as he lifted her on and off his cock, working his shaft inside her.

"So pretty," he murmured. She shivered at the words caressing her skin, her body vibrating from the climax but aching for more. Something. She wanted something. He ran his finger across her lower lip. "Your mouth is swollen from sucking his dick. Your pretty cunt wet and hungry, begging to be fucked. Don't worry, honey. You'll have all the cock you need, want tonight." His hands slid down her back, cupping her ass and lifting her higher, sinking his cock deeper. She shivered and closed her eyes, trying to capture the sensations, keep them from exploding too fast, too hard. His fingers slid between her ass cheeks, one long digit teasing her opening. She gasped and opened her eyes, staring up at Max. The hungry animal was gone. And a playful commanding Max was in its place. He pressed his finger into her opening, not deep, just a promise. The memory of the plug in her ass last night shimmered through her brain. She pressed back, urging his finger a little deeper.

"That's what you want, isn't it?" He rocked his hips, a shallow thrust that nudged her clit. He put his mouth to hers. "Both of us fucking you."

He kissed her, catching her moan as he teased her with his cock and his finger. When he finally released her mouth, he asked the question again. "Is that what you want?"

"Yes!" she cried out, arching her back, trying to move between his cock and his hand, needing to be filled. Max lifted his head and looked to Gideon, waiting for the other man's nod.

Max wrapped his hand around her back and rolled, keeping his cock inside her. She gripped his shoulders and held on, opening her eyes to find herself straddling Max, her knees digging into the mattress.

"Damn, Mandy. I need to have you in this position more often." As he spoke, he reached up and cupped her breasts, lightly pinching her nipples. Even the delicate touch was enough to make her whimper, make her need.

"Please, Max." She rocked her hips back and up, driving Max's cock into her, hard and deep. More. She needed more. Max's hands held her hips, locking her to him. "No, Max, I need—" She squirmed, fighting his hold, needing him to fuck her.

"Hold on. We need Gideon to slick up your tight little ass." Max slid one finger down her split. "Get this tight hole ready to take him."

Panting, fighting the need to come and the desire to hold out for more, she planted her hands on Max's shoulders and dug her nails into his skin. He grunted at the tiny bite, his hips pumping up, thumping against her clit.

He grabbed her ass cheeks and eased them apart. She leaned forward, feeling exposed as one cool slick finger touched her opening. Fighting the instinct to tense up, she stared at Max, watching his eyes, the lust in them giving her strength to relax as Gideon slowly pushed one finger in, easing into her.

"This is what you want, isn't it, Mandy?" Gideon asked, his voice low, intimate. "To be fucked by both of us."

She nodded, unable to speak, fighting the urge to move. He slowly fucked her ass with that one digit, giving her a chance to get used to the sensation. Max's cock was so hard inside her, buried deep, the slow penetrations to her ass making her squirm. She shifted, pushing back against Gideon's hand. She needed more.

He seemed to hear her unspoken plea. He pulled back and added a second finger, repeating the process of slowly stretching her until she was filled with three fingers.

"That okay, Mandy?"

She whimpered and pressed down, taking him deeper, her pussy contracting around Max's cock. Max groaned and his fingers bit into her hips.

"Oh fuck, man, you got to get inside her now."

The fingers slipped away and Max pushed up, taking her mouth in a deep kiss that shook her to her soul. She moaned, thrusting down on Max's erection, vaguely aware that Gideon was pulling out another condom, slicking up his cock, preparing to enter her.

Max fingered her opening, just teasing touches until Gideon replaced those fingers with the slick head of his cock. He held still, just nudging against her, warning her. She knew he was giving her time to change her mind.

Drugged by the lust surging through her veins, Mandy arched her back, offering her ass to Gideon. The pressure returned as he slowly pushed in, the penetration steady, relentless. She tensed, her body moving on instinct.

"It's okay, Mandy, just let him in." Max's voice swirled through her head and she nodded, telling him she heard even if she couldn't make her voice work. She took a deep breath and consciously relaxed. The steady pressure returned, burning just a little, his cock wider than the three fingers he'd used.

Gideon's breath washed the back of her neck. She was surrounded and filled by these men. Her men. The heavy penetration ended, Gideon's groin pressed against her ass.

"Okay?"

She nodded. "Full."

"Yeah, you're full of us."

They held still. She didn't know if they were waiting for a sign from her but she wasn't ready to move, not just yet. Warmth surrounded her, comforting caresses from Max and Gideon, whispered hot kisses that made her skin tingle. The burning in her ass eased and the need returned. She wiggled, the sudden compulsion to move, to feel them both fucking her was too much to resist.

"Please." She could only manage to speak the single word.

"That's it, honey. We're going to have you now." Vaguely she heard Max instruct Gideon, telling him to go slow. She felt the cock slide out of her ass, sending hot shivers up her spine. He pushed back in, the burn easing, her body stretching to take him. He filled her even as Max retreated, pulling back, his cock skimming her clit as he tilted her hips. A hitch in her breath made both men freeze.

"Don't stop," she groaned. "More."

A low growl, familiar and exciting, bounced off the walls. Max rocked into her pussy, brushing the tight bundle of nerve endings along the way. Gideon pulled out, matching Max's slow entrance.

They worked together—penetration and retreat, keeping her filled, her body buzzing with sensation. Feminine power flooded her core as they moved inside her. She was their center. Nothing existed for them except her, fucking her. She opened her body to them, giving them what they needed. The slow, steady fuck built, delicious and sexual. They whispered, telling her how hot she was, how sexy she was, their voices blending into one until she couldn't distinguish which lover spoke or whose hands touched her.

Her body moved, or was moved, controlled by Max and Gideon, and the hunger burning inside her. Her fingernails dug into the hard muscles of Max's shoulders, holding on as they fucked her, filled her over and over, sliding slowly across her clit, moving in and out of her ass. There was no way to tell where she ended and they began.

Every nerve glittered, pulsing until she knew she was close.

"Max?" His name a question that she couldn't speak.

"Come on, honey. Come for us. Let us feel it." He sounded desperate, needy. Hands held her still as Gideon drove into her ass, a little harder, a little deeper. She cried out, the thrust pushing her down on Max's cock.

Her pussy shimmered with one orgasm followed by another. The sweet vibrations fanned out in waves from her cunt, flowing into her limbs, draining her of every bit of strength.

Masculine groans followed, Max then Gideon, their bodies straining as they came.

Gideon slumped down on her, crushing her into Max but she was too weak to protest.

She knew she would feel it tomorrow—too much stress on her ravaged body—but for now she floated, letting her lovers slip from her body, clean up and cuddle her. Safe.

She rested her head on Max's shoulder, not sleeping, drifting, letting her mind and body meld until thoughts disappeared and the scent and taste of her lovers consumed her.

* * * * *

Max closed his eyes, letting his body rest. The sun was up but that didn't mean anything. It was midsummer in Alaska. Hell, the sun was always up. Gideon and Mandy were obviously used to sleeping in the light. For Max, his body wouldn't calm enough to let him go.

The *were's* presence had disappeared, sometime during the long night of fucking the beast had released his hold on Max, letting the wolf return, allowing the human mind to retain control. He looked at the pale bruises on Mandy's hips, the puffy look of Gideon's lips. Part of him knew he should regret the rough treatment to his lovers but last night hadn't been a night of gentle lovemaking. They'd been fucking and all three of them had wanted it hard, deep and long.

He stroked the backs of his fingers across Mandy's stomach, teasing the top of her pussy with just a touch. She squirmed and a faint groan rolled from her throat but she didn't wake up. Max wasn't actually trying to wake her but he couldn't resist touching. He stretched his hand across her body and ran his fingers along Gideon's hip, the hard bare flesh perfectly molded to his hand.

He smiled. Gideon's ass would look perfect beneath his hand as well. He could just see it. Gideon and Mandy, both being punished, their asses pink from his touch, both begging to be fucked. He gave a gentle squeeze to Gideon's hip and received a disgruntled grunt as he shifted away.

Max smiled and considered waking his lovers but they needed the sleep. He could go downstairs, coffee sounded good, but he wasn't ready to leave Mandy or Gideon. He just wanted someone to talk to.

As if the universe had heard his request, the first strains of *Who Can It Be Now?* rang, muted and almost beneath human hearing. He rolled over and slid silently off the bed, grabbing his cell phone off the dresser. He punched the answer button even as he walked toward the bathroom, keeping his voice low.

"This is Max."

"Hey."

"Jax? Man, where are you?" Relief flooded his chest and tension he hadn't realized he was still carrying rushed from his body. The events from yesterday had pushed his brother from his thoughts but hearing his voice eased not only the human but the wolf inside him. "Are you okay?"

Jax chuckled. "I'm fine. I hear you're in Alaska. And you got arrested? What the hell are you doing?"

"I didn't get arrested. I was helping the police." That was close enough to the truth, at least until Max could tell Jax face-to-face what had happened. "And where the hell are you? I fly all the way up here and you're MIA."

Again Jax laughed. "Yeah. Guess where?"

"Where?"

"Vegas."

"What?"

"Came to see you."

Max shook his head and stared in the mirror. They were definitely twins. Same thoughts. They laughed for a moment then the silence settled between them.

"What's going on? What have you been doing in Vegas without your little brother to take care of you?" He expected a laugh but there was silence. "Jax?"

"I'm here." The tone of Jax's voice shifted, turning serious and dark. "Stuff's been going on. I'm okay. I was with Reign last night, that's how I found out you were in Alaska."

Max rested his hip against the bathroom counter and tried to picture it. Jackson and Reign together. Not in a sexual way, of course, but still, he couldn't imagine the two of them had anything in common.

"What were you doing with Reign?"

"It's a long story. And something we should talk about later. You know, face-to-face."

Max nodded even though his brother couldn't see him. "I hear that. When are you coming home?"

"Uh...don't know yet. I could hang around for a few days, wait for you here."

He stared at the closed bathroom door. Mandy and Gideon on the other side. The bond between them was too new. Not completed. He'd fucked them but he hadn't marked them, hadn't come inside them. He'd conquered the werewolf's natural urges to claim his mates. He wanted Mandy and Gideon to understand what it meant to be a werewolf's mate. They needed to understand because there was no going back.

His own thoughts made him smile. He'd always been the reckless brother, pushing the limits and taking what he wanted. His father always swore Max would end up bonded to some blonde bimbo with big tits because he couldn't control himself.

Won't he be shocked as hell when I show up with two lovers? Mom won't. She'd always said when he fell in love, he was going to fall hard and fast. And he had. Now he just had to make sure his mates were willing.

He licked his lips, remembering the taste of Mandy and Gideon. It had been hard, fucking hard, not to sink his teeth into their skin. He'd fought the *were* and won. When Mandy and Gideon awoke, they needed to talk.

"Max?"

Jackson's prompt shook him from his thoughts. "Uh yeah. I'm actually going to stay in Anchorage for a few days." He chuckled and there was no need to fake the sound. "I'm not sure the cops want me leaving town just yet."

"What did you do?"

"Nothing. Much." He rolled his eyes under his lids. Jax *so* wouldn't understand. "It's another face-to-face conversation we have to have."

"Well, don't think you're getting away from telling me *everything*," Jax warned.

He thought about last night. He'd shared other sexual tales with Jax. Explicit details, usually late-night wine-and-gin-fueled conversations. But somehow he didn't think he was going to share details about last night. That was too intimate. Personal.

A link that connected him to his twin broke and Max felt the pain in his chest.

"Max?"

This time the call came from the bedroom. Mandy's voice sinking into his heart, filling the strange space created between him and Jax.

"Listen, I've got to go."

"Yeah, that's good." Jax sounded distracted. "We'll talk later."

"Yeah, later."

Max tapped the screen to end the call and opened the door. Mandy stood at the end of the bed, leaning against the bedpost as if she was too tired to stand on her own. Her hair was rumpled and her lips slightly swollen.

"Who was on the phone?"

"Jax."

There was no glimmer of guilt, no hesitation. She nodded and licked her lips, her eyes drooping closed.

"You weren't actually engaged to him were you?" Max asked.

She shook her head and dragged one hand through her hair. "Part of the plan." She blinked and looked up at him. "Why am I up?"

He smiled. "Because you got cold when I got out of bed?" he suggested.

"Yes. Don't like sleeping without you."

"You won't have to, honey." He scooped her up in his arms and carried her the three steps back to bed, placing her in the center. Practically asleep already, she moaned and rolled over, draping her arm around Gideon's chest and dropping her head on his shoulder.

Max stood and watched, his heart swelling at the sight. They looked beautiful together. Delicious. It wasn't going to be easy. He didn't even want to believe that it would but he wasn't going to let either of them go. They'd have to find a way to make it work.

"Cold," Mandy muttered, wiggling her ass. He stretched out on the bed, cuddling up behind Mandy, reaching his arm across to include Gideon. As if all three bodies strained when one was missing, a subtle profound calm settled between them. He buried his face in Mandy's hair and closed his eyes, feeling sleep pull at him.

He was content, his wolf was happy. And he was going to make sure neither of his mates slept without him again.

Epilogue

ꟗ

Max zipped his bag and tossed it on the couch. He still had four hours before his flight took off. Plenty of time to imprint himself on his lovers one more time. He hated the thought of leaving them, even for a few days, but he had to get back to Vegas.

He had a photo shoot that he couldn't put off. And he needed to start tidying up his life there.

They hadn't made any decisions about where the three of them would live but it made more sense for him to move to Alaska. His job was portable.

They'd spent the past week getting to know each other better. He'd explained about being a werewolf and being a werewolf's mate. He hadn't physically claimed either of them yet but they all knew it was coming. He didn't mind taking it slow.

He smiled. Jax was going to be impressed by his restraint. He felt almost noble giving Mandy and Gideon a chance to get used to the idea before he sank his teeth into their skin and marked them forever. His gum line ached just thinking about it.

The upside of this trip to Vegas was he'd get to see Jax. They'd talked over the phone but it wasn't the same as seeing his brother. The tension he'd heard in Jax's voice—the instigation for this trip—had disappeared but a new strain had appeared and seemed to grow every time they spoke. Jax was hiding something and whatever it was, it made him feel guilty. Didn't matter. Max wasn't letting his brother escape this time without a full confession.

And Max needed to see Dani. Before he could settle in with his new lovers, he had to see her, make a clean break. Sure she'd broken up with him, but he needed to face her, say goodbye and good luck. Because he did wish her the best. No jealousy or even strong emotions lingered around his thoughts for her. She'd found someone else. Good for her. He truly hoped she was happy.

Things were going smoothly in Anchorage. It looked like Mandy's father would be cleared of the embezzlement charges. Facing a charge of kidnapping, Baldino and Mickelson were spilling their guts about their company. Turns out they were doing more than embezzling—bribing state legislators and attempting to bribe a judge. Mandy's dad had been an easy fall guy. Someone to distract the feds while they cleaned up their mess.

Max glanced at his watch. Time to find his lovers.

He went to the kitchen. Gideon was cooking. Again. Mandy was "helping"...which really meant she was sitting at the counter acting as the official taster. He stood in the doorway and watched for a moment. They looked good together. The past few days had given them a chance to get to know each other as well and they'd be spending the next few days alone together. A strange surge of jealousy invaded his chest but he brushed it aside. The three of them were bound together. There was no need for him to be jealous. The relationship was new but growing and he had no doubt they would make it.

He leaned his shoulder against the doorframe.

"Will whatever you're making be good heated up?"

Mandy spun around on the high stool, her eyes lighting up when she saw him. That jealousy he'd ignored disappeared completely. His lovers would miss him and be waiting for him when he returned.

"Are you planning to cool things off?" She leaned back on the counter, the movement pulling up the oversized shirt she wore, revealing those delicious thighs. He was stunned by the change in her in just a week. She'd become more comfortable in her sexuality and confident in her sex appeal. Maybe it was because he and Gideon had spent every available moment getting her naked and showing her just how much they appreciated the sight of her body.

She reached between her breasts and undid the next button on the shirt giving him a better look at her deep cleavage. Her fingers dipped into the space, teasing his eyes, tempting.

He shook his head. "Cool is not what I was going for."

Gideon grinned over his shoulder. He looked at Mandy and winked. He pulled the pan off the stove and slipped it in the oven. Slamming the door shut, he spun around and leaned against the counter.

"We have an hour," Gideon announced.

"An hour?"

"Dinner will be done in an hour."

Mandy sat up, looking efficient, in a debauched sort of way. "We'll have time to eat and get you to the airport two hours before your flight."

Two hours? He didn't need to sit in the airport for two hours. Not when he could be fucking.

He shook his head. "It's going to take more than an hour for what I have in mind."

Mandy's eyes got wide and her knees snapped together. He turned and drilled her with a stare, letting all his hunger, lust and love flow through that look. She took a deep breath and eased her legs apart, hiking the shirt up to her hips, revealing her wet pussy.

"Very good, Amanda." Red painted her cheeks and Max fought the desire to smile. He liked that she was getting comfortable with her body but still blushed at the thought of fucking him.

He turned his attention to Gideon. He stood by the counter, looking amused and arrogant. Max was going to fix that when he returned from Vegas. He hadn't yet had a chance to spank Gideon's ass but there was time enough.

"How long before your dinner is ruined?" See him trying to be the considerate lover.

Gideon turned down the heat on the oven then strolled by Max, rubbing shoulders as he passed. "Ninety minutes. Think that's enough time, stud?" He said it with a smirk that made Max's palm itch to tap Gideon's ass.

Mandy blinked up at Max her eyes still wide.

Max shook his head and grinned.

In the end, it was closer to three hours. Dinner was a total loss but no one minded. Max had to catch a cab because neither Gideon nor Mandy was coherent enough to drive.

He sat in the backseat of the taxi and smiled. That was the perfect way to leave his lovers—exhausted, sweaty, barely able to move.

The perfect memory to hold him until he returned.

Also by Tielle St. Clare

&

eBooks:

After the Ceremony
By Daylight Come
Christmas Elf
Close Quarters
Collective Memory
Ellora's Cavemen: Dreams of the Oasis III *(anthology)*
Ellora's Cavemen: Jewels of the Nile IV *(anthology)*
Ellora's Cavemen: Legendary Tails II *(anthology)*
Ellora's Cavemen: Tales from the Temple II *(anthology)*
Fairy Dust
First Moon Rise
Just One Night
Kissing Stone
Marvin and the Three Bears
Matching Signs
Shadow of the Dragon 1: Dragon's Kiss
Shadow of the Dragon 2: Dragon's Fire
Shadow of the Dragon 3: Dragon's Rise
Shadow of the Dragon 4: Dragon's Prey
Simon's Bliss
Taking Shape
Through Shattered Light
Wolf's Heritage: After the Ceremony
Wolf's Heritage 1: New Year's Kiss

Wolf's Heritage 2: Summer's Caress
Wolf's Heritage 3: Maxwell's Fall
Wolf's Heritage 4: Jackson's Rise
Wolf's Heritage 5: Shadow's Embrace

Print Books:

Christmas Elf
Ellora's Cavemen: Dreams of the Oasis III *(anthology)*
Ellora's Cavemen: Jewels of the Nile IV *(anthology)*
Ellora's Cavemen: Legendary Tails II *(anthology)*
Ellora's Cavemen: Tales from the Temple II *(anthology)*
Enter the Dragon *(anthology)*
Feral Fascination *(anthology)*
Irish Enchantment *(anthology)*
New Year's Kiss
Shadow of the Dragon 1: Dragon's Kiss
Shadow of the Dragon 2: Dragon's Fire
Shadow of the Dragon 3: Dragon's Rise
Shadow of the Dragon 4: Dragon's Prey
Through Shattered Light
Transformations *(anthology)*

About the Author

ꙮ

Tielle (pronounced "teal") St. Clare has had life-long love of romance novels. She began reading romances in the 7th grade when she discovered Victoria Holt novels and began writing romances at the age of 16 (during Trigonometry, if the truth be told). During her senior year in high school, the class dressed up as what they would be in twenty years—Tielle dressed as a romance writer. When not writing romances, Tielle has worked in public relations and video production for the past 20 years. She moved to Alaska when she was seven years old in 1972 when her father was transferred with the military. Tielle believes romances should be hot and sexy with a great story and fun characters.

ꙮ

The author welcomes comments from readers. You can find her website and email address on her author bio page at www.ellorascave.com.

Tell Us What You Think

We appreciate hearing reader opinions about our books. You can email us at Comments@EllorasCave.com.

Why an electronic book?

We live in the Information Age—an exciting time in the history of human civilization, in which technology rules supreme and continues to progress in leaps and bounds every minute of every day. For a multitude of reasons, more and more avid literary fans are opting to purchase e-books instead of paper books. The question from those not yet initiated into the world of electronic reading is simply: *Why?*

1. ***Price.*** An electronic title at Ellora's Cave Publishing runs anywhere from 40% to 75% less than the cover price of the exact same title in paperback format. Why? Basic mathematics and cost. It is less expensive to publish an e-book (no paper and printing, no warehousing and shipping) than it is to publish a paperback, so the savings are passed along to the consumer.
2. ***Space.*** Running out of room in your house for your books? That is one worry you will never have with electronic books. For a low one-time cost, you can purchase a handheld device specifically designed for e-reading. Many e-readers have large, convenient screens for viewing. Better yet, hundreds of titles can be stored within your new library—on a single microchip. There are a variety of e-readers from different manufacturers. You can also read e-books on your PC or laptop computer. (Please note that Ellora's Cave does not endorse any specific brands.

You can check our website at www.ellorascave.com for information we make available to new consumers.)

3. ***Mobility.*** Because your new e-library consists of only a microchip within a small, easily transportable e-reader, your entire cache of books can be taken with you wherever you go.
4. ***Personal Viewing Preferences.*** Are the words you are currently reading too small? Too large? Too... ANNOYING? Paperback books cannot be modified according to personal preferences, but e-books can.
5. ***Instant Gratification.*** Is it the middle of the night and all the bookstores near you are closed? Are you tired of waiting days, sometimes weeks, for bookstores to ship the novels you bought? Ellora's Cave Publishing sells instantaneous downloads twenty-four hours a day, seven days a week, every day of the year. Our webstore is never closed. Our e-book delivery system is 100% automated, meaning your order is filled as soon as you pay for it.

Those are a few of the top reasons why electronic books are replacing paperbacks for many avid readers.

As always, Ellora's Cave welcomes your questions and comments. We invite you to email us at Comments@ellorascave.com or write to us directly at Ellora's Cave Publishing Inc., 1056 Home Avenue, Akron, OH 44310-3502.

Discover for yourself why readers can't get enough of the multiple award-winning publisher Ellora's Cave.

Whether you prefer e-books or paperbacks, be sure to visit EC on the web at www.ellorascave.com for an erotic reading experience that will leave you breathless.